Courteous, courageous and commanding—
these heroes lay it all on the line for the
people they love in more than fifty stories about
loyalty, bravery and romance.
Don't miss a single one!

REBECCA WINTERS

STRANGERS WHEN WE MEET

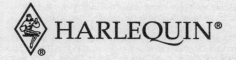

TORONTO • NEW YORK • LONDON
AMSTERDAM • PARIS • SYDNEY • HAMBURG
STOCKHOLM • ATHENS • TOKYO • MILAN • MADRID
PRAGUE • WARSAW • BUDAPEST • AUCKLAND

Recycling programs
for this product may
not exist in your area.

ISBN-13: 978-0-373-36278-3

STRANGERS WHEN WE MEET

REBECCA WINTERS

whose family of four children has now swelled to include five beautiful grandchildren, lives in Salt Lake City, Utah, in the land of the Rocky Mountains. With canyons and high alpine meadows full of wildflowers, she never runs out of places to explore. They, plus her favorite vacation spots in Europe, often end up as backgrounds for her romance novels, because writing is her passion, along with her family and church. Rebecca loves to hear from readers. If you wish to e-mail her, please visit her Web site at www.cleanromances.com.

My sincerest thanks to First Lieutenant Edwin V. Rawley of the army air force for sharing some of his war experiences and helping me get inside the mind and heart of a soldier who lost limbs in combat, yet is still serving God and country by helping others adjust to similar losses. He's what being a hero is all about!

Credit also goes to Jerry D. Braza, Ph.D., and Kathleen Braza, M.A., who most graciously consented to let me use some of the valuable information in their book, *Coping with War and its Aftermath,* copyright © 1991. Though out of print now, it can probably be found through your local library. I obtained other information by phoning Kathleen Braza, Bereavement Consultant at Healing Resources (1-800-473-HEAL).

A special thanks to Ronald L. Webb, C.P.O. of Shield's Orthotic Prosthetic Services in Salt Lake City, Utah, who gave his valuable time to help me understand in a small way the adjustments a vet or any other person who has lost a limb must make.

To all veterans and their families this book is lovingly dedicated.

CHAPTER ONE

"ZACH?"

"Rosie? Good morning, sweetheart." The huskiness in his tone told her he hadn't been awake long. It was barely seven.

"Good morning."

Dear God. Help me.

"I've been dreaming about us. Our cruise didn't last nearly long enough. The only thing that keeps me going is the knowledge that you're going to be my wife in June. I wish you were here right now," he murmured. "Why don't you come over for a little while before you have to leave for work? I want to *show* you how much I love you."

She wouldn't be going to the university today; in fact, she'd already called Chow Ping, one of the graduate students, to cover her classes.

"Rosie? Why aren't you saying anything?"

A shudder passed through her body. She wished she could tell him everything he wanted to hear. But the last urgent message, one of many left on her answering machine by her in-laws, had turned her world upside down for the second time in her life. They'd called again from a hotel in Ogden, Utah—not five minutes after she and Cody had walked in the door from their trip with Zach.

"Zach…we have to t-talk!" She swallowed hard. "I'm just glad I caught you before you left for work."

"Sweetheart? Something's really wrong. What is it?" She could feel his concern. There wasn't a more understanding man than Zachery Wilde. But when she told him…

"Rosie?" he prodded. "Don't go all quiet on me."

"I-it's about Nick."

"What about him?"

Zach's voice had dropped to a lower register. Nick had been the ghost between them far too long for Zach's liking. Rosie was terrified of what this news was going to do to him, but she couldn't put it off any longer.

"H-he didn't die in the war, Zach."

As soon as she'd said those words, the silence on the other end was so eloquent with shock, Rosie didn't know if she could bear it.

When she'd been given that news, she'd gone into shock herself, unable to tell her in-laws what had happened on the cruise—that she'd accepted Zachery Wilde's proposal and would be marrying him at the end of the spring quarter, hopefully with their blessing.

She hadn't been counting on it of course, because Nick's parents were still in mourning over their only son's death. She was well aware that they would have trouble allowing Zach into their grandson's life on a permanent basis, let alone accepting him as her husband.

But with one phone call, everything had changed,

and her world no longer made sense. After six and a half hours of soul-searching agony, it still didn't. She was in love with Zach, but she'd never stopped loving Nick.

The joy she'd experienced on hearing he wasn't dead, after all, that he'd be home in a few hours, was indescribable. Everything had taken on the properties of a fantastic dream.

When her normally sober Cody heard the news, he ran around the house making whooping noises, leaping in the air at odd moments—behavior so uncharacteristic she barely recognized him—while she'd been in a sort of stupor.

Not until she could function well enough to carry her suitcases into the bedroom did thoughts of Zach intrude on her consciousness. Then she was overwhelmed by guilt. *Consumed* by it.

Zach was in love with her. And she adored him. She couldn't wait to become his wife.

But Nick was alive! Her beloved husband who'd been missing in action and was presumed dead. The husband she hadn't seen for seven years.

Zach's sharp intake of breath sounded like ripping silk. "So what are you saying? Is he a POW?"

"He *was*." Rosie couldn't keep the tremor out of her voice. She couldn't stand the thought of what Nick had been forced to live through.

"Was?"

"He's been released, a-and is on his way home."

"You mean to Germany?"

"No. I—I mean he was in Germany for debriefing,

but that's over. The air force is flying him into Hill Air Force Base this morning."

Another ghastly silence. "I'm coming over."

"No, Zach!" She panicked. "You can't!"

"*Rosie*—"

The anguish in his voice devastated her.

"There's no time, Zach. His plane is landing at nine-thirty this morning. As it is, Cody and I are going to have to rush to make it. His parents drove up there yesterday. They're meeting us at the base."

God forgive her for putting off this phone call until the last minute, but she didn't know any other way to do it. She dreaded the idea of causing Zach any more pain when he'd waited two years for her to agree to marry him.

"I don't believe this is happening. I just put my ring on your finger ten days ago. *Rosie*..." he cried in agony.

She reeled, clutching the headboard of her bed for support. *The bed she'd shared with Nick for seven years.* In eight weeks she'd be sharing Zach's bed. Now Nick was coming home....

"Will you be wearing it when you see him?" She knew it was anger that had made Zach lash out, anger and pain.

This was only the beginning.

"Zach—" her voice shook as tears gushed down her cheeks "—you know how much I love you. You *know* it."

"Mom?" Cody hollered. "Hurry up! What if Dad's plane gets in early? I want to see him come in!"

"I'll be right there," she called.

Cody was in shock, too. Euphoric shock. The kind only a thirteen-year-old boy could experience. A boy who'd just learned that his hero father, the man whose memory he'd always idolized to the exclusion of every other male, including Zach—especially Zach—was alive.

To Cody, everything was so simple. His dad was coming home to be his dad again. Cody had huge plans for them, plans that toppled the foundation Zach had been carefully laying to reach some sort of understanding with her son.

One phone call had wiped out two years of work. Already Zach was a memory. No one could compete with Cody's flesh-and-blood father, who was coming home to stay. What more could one ask of life? End of story.

A groan escaped her throat. "I—I've put your ring in my jewelry box."

"And where are Nick's rings?"

She closed her eyes in fresh pain. "The same place."

"For how long?" he demanded, his voice fierce with hurt.

Dear God. That was a question she couldn't answer.

He muttered a few bitter curses, sounding as out of control as she felt. "I had no right to ask that of you. No right at all. But I'm warning you, Rosie. I haven't spent the last two years loving you, only to give up now. Remember *that,* even if you can't remember *me* after today!"

"*Zach!* I'm in love with you, darling. I swear I'll call you before the day's out. *I swear it!*"

"Don't make promises you can't keep."

"Have you so little faith in me?" she cried.

"Mom?" Cody opened the door of her bedroom and poked his head in. "Hurry up!"

She nodded, signaling that he should close it again and leave her some privacy. He frowned his impatience before the door clicked shut. He knew she was on the phone with Zach.

"*Lord,* Rosie. This has nothing to do with faith and everything to do with the kind of marriage you and Nick once had. So let's not pretend."

She flinched from his bitterness. "I—I'm not pretending."

"Oh, hell, Rosie—"

"I have to go," she whispered.

"I know, and I'm being an insensitive bastard." She could hear the tears in his voice. "But I also know that the next time I see you, things'll be different. You won't be the same Rosie who finally made every damn dream of mine come true."

"I haven't been the same Rosie since I got that phone call," she admitted in a dull voice. "To be honest, I don't know who I am, Zach. Right now there's only one reality—I'm terrified."

"You don't know the half of it, sweetheart."

The line went dead.

"I'VE GOT A PIT in my stomach bigger than Kennecott," R. T. Ellis muttered, his fingers clawing the armrest.

Nick Armstrong gazed dispassionately at the bandaged stump below his left wrist, then flexed his right hand, as if reminding himself it was still there, He leaned across the man who was closer than a brother to look out the window of their C-141 transport plane.

They were passing over the huge Kennecott open-pit copper mine, reputed to be the largest in the world. Nick surmised that heavy air traffic or high winds must have caused the pilot to swing this far south before turning around to make the rare southerly approach to the base.

held prisoner in a godforsaken desert, they were returning to one.

He sat back and closed his eyes. "I know the feeling."

The plane engines droned on, filling the eerie silence that had been building the nearer they came to their destination. Both he and R.T. had survived captivity at various locations inside Iraq, but they'd never known the names of places or the coordinates. The Iraqi soldiers had moved them by truck a total of fifteen times, and each time they'd been blindfolded.

Both Nick and R.T. had agreed that when they got out, they didn't want their family reunions to happen in Germany. They just wanted to be debriefed, receive any medical attention at Fitzsimmons Army Hospital in Colorado, then fly home without losing any more precious time.

There was to be no press coverage, no news leak that

would result in their pictures being plastered all over the *Salt Lake Tribune* or *Deseret News*. No gruesome details to recount of an experience they preferred to forget. All they wanted was their privacy and the right to carry on with their lives.

The powers-that-be in Germany didn't like the idea, not with the politicians breathing down their necks. But

R.T. and Nick had discussed every conceivable problem they might face after being gone this long and presumed dead. All POWs did. The worst fear among the married ones was the very real possibility that their wives had moved on and remarried. The prisoners with children had the additional worry that some other guy was raising their family.

Nick's thoughts fastened on Rosie, who'd never been out of his heart for a moment. Theirs was the kind of love destined to last a lifetime and beyond. They'd talked about everything before he'd left with his unit, everything that could happen—except the chance that he might be taken prisoner, a subject Rosie refused to even contemplate.

But it didn't matter, because he knew she'd wait for him, till the end of time if necessary. That knowledge had been the only thing to keep him sane during his long incarceration.

But nothing—not hope or even faith—could have

prepared Nick or R.T. for the hell of not being able to talk to their wives yet. Rosie had a new phone number and address, listed under R. Armstrong, which came as a jolt. All he got was a U.S. West answering-machine voice telling him to leave a message, which he didn't feel ready to do. He preferred his first contact with Rosie to be in person.

R.T. couldn't even find his old phone number. The operator had insisted there was no listing for a Cynthia Ellis or anything close.

He'd been raised by an aunt before his marriage to Cynthia. She was the only relative of his still living in Salt Lake. But when he called her, he'd been forced to leave a message, asking her to get in touch with his wife to inform her that he was alive and on his way home.

As Nick watched R.T. retch into a bag, he realized that the trauma of not knowing anything had finally caught up with him. The thrill of coming home had been swallowed up in the anxiety of being this close to loved ones without having made that first vital contact.

Neither of them spoke aloud what they were thinking—that his bride of a year had remarried. Nick grimaced; R.T. had lost his breakfast after leaving Denver and still couldn't keep anything down.

Not until Nick had undergone an emotional reunion over the phone with his parents did the tight band around his own chest relax a little. His overjoyed mom and dad not only reassured him that they were in good health, thank God, but they answered his single most important question.

Rosie hadn't remarried. She was doing a wonderful job of raising Nick's look-alike son, who was thirteen now and already approaching five foot ten. Nick's mother forgot her tears long enough to add laughingly that it wouldn't be much longer before Cody rivaled his father's six foot two.

Nick couldn't talk after that. Nothing else mattered. The details of their lives he'd catch up on later.

Rosie was still waiting for him. She'd never given up hope.

If there was a black cloud on the horizon, it hung over R.T., who had no idea what future awaited him. It wasn't fair, Nick thought, not when R.T. had just been released from the depths of hell, only to be thrust down all over again if it turned out he'd lost his wife because of a damn war over oil.

"She isn't going to be there, Nick."

They'd been through too much to lie to each other.

"Maybe, maybe not. If that's the case, plan on coming home with me."

AS SOON AS HE'D YANKED on a pullover, Zach phoned his secretary at home, but she'd already left for work. When he called his office, he got the answering machine.

He waited for the beep. "Barb? I'm back from the Caribbean, but I won't be in until tomorrow. Reschedule all my apppointments for another day."

Within minutes he'd locked up his condo, located at the base of the foothills, and sped off on his racing bike toward the mountains. Mid-April meant spring in the valley and snow on the peaks, but he gave no thought to his sur-roundings as he headed up Little Cottonwood Canyon.

Strong winds buffeted him during the steep climb to the ten-thousand-foot summit. When he got up there, he hoped he'd pass out from overexertion and find forget-fulness, if only for a few minutes.

Until two years ago, he'd always lived in California. But after losing his fiancée two years before that to a rare form of brain cancer, he'd needed an outlet for his restlessness. Biking had always been one of his favorite sports, and now it became a necessity of life.

In the beginning, the pain of his loss had been so acute he'd deliberately pushed himself to the extreme, with the result that for a few hours each day, the physical agony camouflaged his heartache. As time went by, he found a certain satisfaction in seeing how hard he could drive himself. He began entering national bike races and eventually traveled to Europe to race. Two summers ago, he'd ended up in Park City, Utah, not far from Salt Lake. Having turned pro, he'd attended a special racing camp to train for the Tour de France.

Utah was where he'd met Rosie Armstrong. She'd been out cycling with her son and his friend. They were in the middle of a private mountain road when Zach came upon them at full speed. He'd almost crashed into them on his bike. Once apologies were made on both sides, he realized he wanted to get to know her better. From that moment on, his world had started to right itself.

Though he continued to compete in cycling races

both in Europe and America, he never did enter the Tour de France. Everything he'd wanted was right here in Utah, where he intended to put down roots—where there was the promise of love, marriage and a ready-made family.

Virtually overnight he'd relocated, expanding his family's lucrative outdoor-sign business to Salt Lake City. Wilde Outdoors was a successful enterprise he'd helped his father and brothers build throughout high school and college.

It had taken two years to make Rosie see *him,* instead of Nick. Finally, on that cruise, she'd turned the tables and reached out to him, telling him she loved him, begging him to ask her one more time to marry him.

That was what he'd been waiting for.

He'd pulled out the diamond ring he'd purchased three months after meeting her—a promise to himself that one day he'd win her love and be allowed to put it on her finger—then slid it home with an overwhelming sense of fulfillment and joy.

All that was shattered by her phone call an hour ago.

He didn't die in the war, Zach. The gut-wrenching premonition that the pain he was experiencing now might never go away, might become worse than anything he'd ever known before, tore through him like a jagged shard.

Visions of his beautiful golden-haired Rosie running into the arms of the man who'd loved her since high school almost destroyed him.

Zach pedaled harder against the wind.

It was God's truth that Nick Armstrong had more right than anyone to return to the land of the living and reclaim the wife and child who'd probably been the only reason he hadn't committed suicide in prison.

But it was also God's truth that when her husband had been reported missing in action and presumed dead, Zach and Rosie had been given every right to meet and fall in love, to enjoy a full rich life with Cody.

When his first love had been cruelly taken from him, there had, at least, been a sense of closure, because her death was final, irrevocable.

But there could be no closure if he lost Rosie. Knowing she was living in the same city he was, yet knowing he couldn't see her. Knowing that the woman he loved was affording her husband the pleasure of her company, her sweetness and humor, her intelligence, her sunny smile.

Tonight she'd be sleeping under the same roof with Nick….

Could she forget what she and Zach had shared over the past two years? On the cruise?

Would she turn to Nick tonight and give him the comfort of the beautiful body her husband must have been craving for seven hellish years? The body Zach had yet to possess?

Even if she wasn't physically or emotionally ready to sleep with Nick again, the real possibility that she might make love to him out of the love she'd always felt for him, out of her compassion for all he'd suffered, ripped Zack apart. Agonizing pictures filled his mind, blotting out any awareness of his surroundings.

It took the blare of a car horn on the narrow stretch of curving road to alert him to the drop-off not two feet from his bike tires. The more he thought about it, the more he welcomed the idea of a nine-thousand-foot plunge to certain oblivion.

The only thing holding him back was the sure knowledge that she'd fallen deeply in love with him, Zach. So deeply, in fact, that he could never doubt theirs was the forever kind of love. Rosie was with him, heart and soul. He had faith in their love. It wasn't going to go away just because Nick had come home. Love didn't work like that.

No matter how much she still loved her husband, the man had been gone seven years. Tremendous changes had taken place in her, and undoubtedly in him. She was a different person now, in love with a different man—and it wasn't Nick!

That was Zach's edge.

By all that was holy, he intended to keep that edge until Rosie walked down the aisle with him. Unfortunately Cody would fight him every step of the way.

Cody was Nick's edge.

Cody had never liked Zach. He'd made it plain from day one. Rosie had insisted that, given time, Cody would come around and get over his initial resentment of Zach's intrusion into their private world.

To Zach's chagrin, however, that resentment had grown into dislike—the major reason he hadn't brought up the subject of marriage a year earlier. They'd taken Cody on the cruise, hoping to forge a bond that included the three of them. But when they'd told her son they were planning to get married, Zach saw the hurt in Cody's eyes. Worse, Zach felt the boy's silent brooding anger and realized they had a serious problem on their hands.

Rosie reasoned that Nick's parents, who had a lot of influence over their grandson, had fueled some of his negative response by not accepting Nick's death.

Zach had been encouraged and relieved when he heard Rosie admit that her son could benefit from some counseling. She'd announced that, in spite of Cody's problem, she intended to marry Zach. As soon as they got back from their cruise, she would make an appointment for Cody to see a specialist and get the help he needed.

But with one phone call, everything had changed.

The boy's father's unexpected return from the dead precluded any such appointment. All Cody's problems began and ended there.

That bitter irony brought a sardonic twist to Zach's windburned lips.

He took the next dangerous curve at full speed, surprised and ashamed of his own jealousy over a man who'd been gone seven years in the service of his country. A man who continued to inspire unqualified love and devotion in the hearts of those he'd left behind.

Surprised, because such a destructive emotion was unworthy of him.

Ashamed, because he planned to fight a valiant, honorable, innocent man for Rosie's love—and win!

"GRANDMA! GRANDPA!"

Before Rosie could turn off the ignition and get out

of their compact car, Cody had jumped from the passenger seat to greet Nick's parents. Rosie locked the door and started toward them. The wind seemed stronger than ever, molding her slim silk coat-dress to her body.

Cody was so excited his hostility over her engagement to Zach might never have been. The fear that he would bring up the subject before she'd had a chance to tell her in-laws in private was momentarily abated.

"Dad's alive! He's coming home!" His voice cracked; it was changing and came out half an octave lower than it used to. "I can't believe it!" he shouted. His cries of joy mingled with theirs as he ran into their outstretched arms, the tears streaming down his happy face.

I can't believe it, either. I can't. Something must be wrong with me. Nick's supposed to be arriving in a few minutes. I'm afraid it isn't true, that none of this is real....

"Rosie?" Janet rushed up to her and gave her a welcoming hug. "It's a good thing you got back from the cruise when you did. After all he's suffered, can you imagine how Nicky would feel if his own wife wasn't here to welcome him home?"

No. She couldn't.

There was more than a hint of accusation in her mother-in-law's tone. Though she'd practiced restraint by not voicing her opinion about that cruise with Zach, her disapproval had been simmering beneath the surface.

"This has all happened so fast George and I are still in a state of shock."

"So am I," Rosie whispered. But shock didn't begin to cover it.

"Do you think that's his plane, Grandpa?" This from Cody as they proceeded toward the hangar. All four of them turned to the north to watch the plane's approach.

Rosie's heart leapt into her throat. Could Nick really be on that plane coming in at such a sharp angle?

George had his camera ready, then lowered it. "Nope. That's a C-130. Your dad's coming in on a C-141. Come on. Let's keep going."

"Are you sure this is the right place?"

"I'm sure." His grandpa chuckled before throwing an affectionate arm around Cody's shoulders. "This is the Base Ops terminal, where all the transports come in."

"But there aren't very many people around here. Maybe we got the wrong time."

"Maybe your dad's the only one flying in. After all, he's a war hero, and that makes him a VIP," he added with great pride. "When the Days of '47 comes around in July, he'll have to ride in the parade, and I know he'll want you right there with him."

"Cool."

While they watched the sky, Rosie half listened to Cody's excited chatter followed by his grandparents' patient responses.

They were wonderful people. The two of them had been making the five-hour drive from their home in St. George to Salt Lake City every other weekend since

Nick had left for the Middle East. When they weren't in town, they phoned Cody several times a week to stay in close touch. They'd always doted on their grandson, but when Nick was missing in action and presumed killed during the Desert Shield phase of the war, Cody had become their raison d'être.

Rosie had never known her own parents, who'd died in a car-bus collision soon after she was born. The grandparents on her mother's side had stepped in to raise her. Not long after she'd married Nick, they'd died within a year of each other. Yet she considered herself a fortunate woman to be loved by Nick's parents.

She owed George and Janet Armstrong everything for making her feel an integral part of their family, for loving Cody like their own. Without their support during that black period when Nick was first reported missing after an enemy attack near the Saudi border town of Khafji, she had no idea how she and Cody would have survived the ordeal.

Because they'd been so close to her over the years, it never occurred to her that they might be upset when Zach unexpectedly came into her life.

Throughout the first six months of their tenuous relationship, Rosie had kept it very low-key. He was either working at his business or off winning bicycle races. When he was in town, she urged him to date other women, since she had no plans to remarry and didn't want to lead him on.

Rosie explained all this to Janet and George when they began asking questions about Zach. To her surprise, they admitted they were hurt that she would even consider dating. Not until then did Rosie realize that Nick's parents still held out hope he was alive. Their reaction made her feel guilty, because she was more physically and emotionally attracted to Zach than she was willing to acknowledge. But like her in-laws, she'd never been completely able to accept Nick's death. The conflict between those emotions tortured her.

She had decided to put Zach off, but she'd underestimated his determination to have a relationship with her. He demanded to know why she was avoiding him. When she finally told him the truth, he pointed out that even if Nick had been taken prisoner, all of them had been released and accounted for years earlier. The Gulf War wasn't like Vietnam.

His argument made sense, and she recognized that she couldn't go on living in limbo. It wasn't fair to her *or* Cody. It definitely wasn't fair to Zach, who'd confessed he'd fallen in love with her and was willing to wait as long as it took to get a commitment from her.

Since Rosie couldn't deny the strong feelings between them, they dated each other exclusively when he was in town, despite the senior Armstrongs' reservations.

But in doing this, she not only incurred her in-laws' displeasure, she brought out an ugly side of Cody she hadn't known existed. All because they could sense the growing bond between her and Za—

"There's a plane, Grandpa!"

"Where?"

"Right there." Cody pointed toward the southern sky.

George shook his head. "Wrong direction."

"You don't think it's Dad's?" The disappointment in his voice spoke volumes.

"I don't know. We'll just have to wait and see."

Rosie stared at the four-engine transport, which had started its descent. The ground crew was scrambling in preparation for its arrival.

For a moment it felt like déjà vu. Only, the last time she'd seen that type of aircraft, her eyes had been swollen shut from crying, and the plane had been headed into the blue, carrying away the husband she adored.

Suddenly she was twenty-four years old. The excruciating pain of that moment exploded inside her all over again.

She gasped for breath as pure revelation flowed through her.

Nick was on that plane.

Its wheels came down. In another minute it touched ground and taxied along the runway before making a U-turn toward them.

"Do you think it's Dad?"

"George?" Janet cried, her excitement almost tangible.

"It's your father's plane." Rosie's voice shook with conviction. "Come on, Cody." Galvanized into action, she grabbed her son's hand, and they began running against the wind. George and Janet weren't far behind.

As the plane pulled to a stop and the engines were cut, the ground crew stood ready to help lower the steps to the ground.

A couple of dark-haired airmen started down. Adrenaline had Rosie almost jumping out of her skin.

"Mom?"

She knew what Cody was asking and shook her head. Her gaze fastened compulsively on the door opening.

A painfully thin man with reddish-brown hair and gaunt cheeks, possibly mid- to late twenties, appeared at the threshold carrying a duffel bag. He was wearing the pine green full-dress army uniform and garrison cap.

Rosie watched him watching them before he took his first step down the stairs. The look of disappointment on his face haunted her.

"Where's Dad?"

"There he is!" both grandparents shouted at the same time.

Rosie's breath caught as a lean pale man emerged slowly from the interior, half a head taller than the soldier preceding him down the steps. He wore the same green uniform, but was carrying his cap along with a duffel bag in his right hand. His black hair was cut in a buzz.

She'd already made her first mistake. She was looking for her dashing, twenty-five-year-old husband, who'd worn his hair a little long. Who'd always been tanned and fit. The man who'd been her entire world from the first second she'd laid eyes on him.

The soldier she was staring at now bore a superficial resemblance to that husband. But this man was obviously older—thirty-two—and thinner. It was like looking at a drawing of someone as the artist might have imagined that person appearing over the passage of time and altered by circumstance.

Seven years had gone by. *Seven!* The realization clutched at her heart.

"Nicky!"

"Son! Over here!"

Nick waved.

"Oh, George—" Janet broke down "—he's lost so much weight!"

"None of that, honey. Give him a couple months of Rosie's home-cooked meals and he'll put it all back on. Except for that, he looks great," George muttered gruffly.

"Dad!"

Cody broke free of Rosie's hand and sprinted toward his father. In the next instant, they were embracing. Cody's initial tears eventually were replaced by joyous barks of laughter as they began inspecting each other. Already that strong father-son bond established during the first six years of Cody's life was back in full effect.

How strange to see the two of them together, yet how...*right* they looked. Cody had inherited his father's build and coloring. Even certain mannerisms were the same.

Still, Rosie checked her steps. Like a faulty imprint on a coin, Nick's image appeared blurry, while Cody's stood out in stark relief, dear and familiar.

Just then Nick raised his head, and a pair of black-lashed, flame-blue eyes no length of time could ever change sought hers over Cody's shoulder. The secret smile he'd always reserved for her alone shone from his face.

His remembered smile conjured up a myriad of emotions from their frozen prison, and now they nearly overwhelmed her.

"Nick..." she cried, reaching blindly for him.

He met her halfway, clutching her to him so hard she could feel his ribs through his uniform—graphic evidence of the inhumane treatment he'd received in captivity.

His body quaked. "If you hadn't been here waiting for me, I would have died before my feet touched the tarmac."

That solemn pronouncement of truth shook her to the core. *If she and Zach had extended their trip one more day—*

"Rosie..." His deep voice broke. On a low moan, his mouth closed over hers.

How many times had she known her husband's possessive kiss? How many times had she been swept away by his passion, brought to tears by his tenderness? Who could count all the ways his mouth had brought her infinite pleasure, the times he'd made her feel immortal, no matter the hour, mood or situation?

Yet this kiss was different from the others.

His soul was searching for hers, seeking to ascertain that it still belonged to him, that there were no secrets, no shadows.

Not completely satisfied, he deepened their kiss. When Nick went in pursuit, his instincts never failed him.

Her body, that tangible conduit to the soul, started to tremble.

His body went perfectly still before he relinquished

her mouth. In his eyes she glimpsed unspeakable pain, and had to look away.

He knows, her heart groaned.

CHAPTER TWO

"NICKY—WHAT HAPPENED to your hand?"

The undisguised horror in Janet's voice, coupled with a muffled cry from George, filled Rosie with unnamed dread.

She eased herself far enough away from Nick's chest to see his hands. He glanced down. Out of the others' hearing, he said, "It appears we've both mislaid our wedding rings."

Staggering guilt and pain knifed through her body before she saw what the others had seen—there was a bandage where his left hand had been. In the next instant, graphic pictures of combat scenarios flashed through her mind.

She started to weave.

Don't scream out loud, Rosie.

Through narrowed eyes, Nick registered her horrified reaction before she felt him shut her out and turn to Cody.

"As I told my boy—" he tousled the dark hair with his right hand "—I've gotten along just fine without my other hand, but I'll check out the latest hardware to see about making some improvements."

The mocking tone, perfectly gauged to alleviate their

son's fears, devastated her. In desperation Rosie put an arm around Cody's shoulders, as much out of a need for his physical support as the desire to reassure her son. He was fighting a losing battle to hold back the tears; obviously, fresh shock over his father's loss had begun to settle in.

Her in-laws fared no better. George was ashen-faced and Janet had broken down sobbing. All Rosie and Cody could do was stand by helplessly and watch the reunion between Nick and his parents, two of the most devoted generous people in the world. People who'd steadfastly refused to believe their only son was dead.

Her heart underwent another convulsion. She couldn't get over the cruel irony that after seven years of unutterable suffering to both body and soul, *Nick* had to be the one comforting all of them.

In that regard, he hadn't changed. Her husband had always been a take-charge kind of man, watching out for everyone else, never worrying about his own needs.

Early in their relationship, she'd come to cherish that unselfishness in him; she'd considered herself blessed to be his wife.

She still did, didn't she?

He hadn't died. He was alive. His flesh-and-blood body was here, just two feet away. His spirit animated his body.

Then why did it seem as if they were standing on opposite sides of a transparent glass wall, able to see each other but unable to break through and make contact?

"There's someone I want you to meet."

Nick had gently disengaged himself from his

mother's clinging arms to beckon the thin soldier Rosie had seen leaving the plane first. He'd been standing a good distance away. She hadn't even realized he was still waiting at the airfield.

"R.T.? Come here and let me introduce you."

R.T.? Rosie vaguely remembered the name from Nick's early days in the army reserve, the seemingly safe route he'd chosen to help pay for his undergraduate schooling.

The other man shook his head. "I don't want to intrude, Sergeant."

Rosie saw Nick's jaw harden. "You're not intruding, and the days of calling me Sergeant are over. We're civilians now," he asserted in an authoritative voice. "Everybody, say hello to R. T. Ellis. He was named Rutherford Topham for his grandfather, but nobody knows that except me." Nick grinned.

"He lost an eye when our truck hit a land mine, but that didn't stop R.T. We managed to walk a good fifty miles and give an Iraqi patrol fits before they picked us up and moved us to an underground bunker. The rest is…history."

R.T. gave a solemn nod to everyone. "The sarge lost his hand in the same explosion. Since the Iraqis don't give medical care to prisoners, we were lucky the blast burned us, because it cauterized our wounds so there wasn't any infection. The doctors in Denver cleaned us up with a little surgery before sending us home."

Nick nodded. "Our superiors at the base told us there'd been word that a few isolated soldiers had been taken prisoner for negotiation purposes in case Saddam Hussein wanted to start another war later on down the road. Our incarceration just lasted a little longer than we'd expected," Nick joked. "You could say we've adopted each other. Since his wife and aunt don't know he's back yet, I've invited him to stay with us." As he spoke, Nick's eyes focused on Rosie. The message was clear and unmistakable.

Whatever's wrong between us, for the love of God, don't let me down in this.

She started shaking and couldn't stop. The fact that R.T.'s wife—let alone other members of his family— hadn't shown up could mean anything. But Rosie couldn't help fearing the worst; she sensed the same was true for Nick.

Galvanized into action, she threw her arms around R.T. and hugged his stiff form. "Welcome home, soldier. Thank heaven you and Nick had each other." She kissed his wooden lips in salute.

"Thank heaven is right," he whispered. His body suddenly relaxed and he hugged her back. "As far as I'm concerned, your husband walks on water. He thinks you do, too, but I guess you already know that."

"I do." She couldn't dislodge the boulder in her throat. "Apparently he feels that way about you, too."

Following her lead, Nick's parents took turns hugging the soldier, showering him with genuine affection because he and Nick had helped each other stay alive. That made him family, and it was good enough for them.

R.T. shook hands with Cody and put his garrison cap

on him, easing any awkwardness there might have been. "You and your dad are spitting images of each other, you know that?"

"Yeah." Cody's smile wreathed his whole face as he stared at his father with open worship. He'd attached himself to Nick's side once more; Rosie guessed he'd stay there for the duration.

"Why aren't you boys wearing your Purple Hearts?" George wanted to know.

A trace of a smile curved R.T.'s lips. "We're no heroes. We should've looked where we were going."

"You can say that again," Nick added with a rueful grin.

George shook his graying head, which had been as dark as Nick's and Cody's, his eyes suspiciously bright. "That's a matter of opinion, R.T."

"Do you have a Purple Heart, Dad?" Cody asked.

"We both do. It's given to all soldiers wounded in the line of duty. When we get home, you can go through our stuff all you like. How about that?"

"Awesome. I'm going to take everything to school and show my friends."

"By the way, where is home?"

Again his gaze shot straight to Rosie, his eyes asking more of her than his words. No doubt he'd tried to reach her at their old apartment in the Sugar House area and found it no longer existed....

Telling Nick about the changes in their lives was like teaching a child about the world. But it was an infinitely more difficult task because Nick wasn't a child eager to explore his new world for the first time. He was a thirty-two-year-old man whose memories were being tainted, one by one.

She couldn't bear to add to his pain, but she knew it was inevitable. None of them had been given a choice, another brutal side effect of war.

"With money from a couple of excellent investments you made as a stockbroker, plus your monthly government stipend, I was able to get into a house up by the Hogle Zoo," she explained. "It's in a neighborhood with a lot of boys Cody's age."

Nick blinked, his keen mind assessing every piece of information. "That means Clayton Junior High and East High. Was their football any good last year?"

This from a former all-state linebacker for Skyline High, one of East High's arch rivals. Nick's old year-books showing his football feats sat in Cody's room and were pored over on a regular basis.

"Yeah, they had a great season. They've rebuilt East so it won't collapse if there's an earthquake. You should see the brand-new football field. Lights, bleachers, everything—" Cody rattled on.

"He's the first-string center for the Eastside junior team over at Sunnyside," George interjected with grand-fatherly pride.

"Center, huh? That's one tough position. I'm proud of you. We'll have to rustle up a game."

"How about this afternoon? I'll call the team as soon as they get home from school!"

"Cody!" Rosie and Janet cried at the same time. His

naïveté at such a fragile precarious moment in their lives stunned them both, but Nick paid no attention.

"You took the words right out of my mouth. There's nothing I want more than to meet your football buddies."

Suddenly Cody gave his father a fierce hug. "I love you, Dad. I'm so glad you're back. Don't ever go away again."

Nick put a consoling arm around his son, allowing him to shed tears of sheer happiness.

No matter how much Rosie had heard or read about a boy needing his father, no matter how well she thought she'd understood the importance of a male role model, it didn't hit home until now.

No wonder Zach hadn't been able to get anyplace with Cody.

While she stood marveling at the indestructible bond between father and son, she caught sight of the private look Nick flashed R.T. In that brief glance, she read *need*. Obviously they'd grown so close in prison they were in the habit of turning to each other for emotional support.

Like the harbinger of bad news, Nick's silent exchange with R.T. seemed to warn her there was more grief on the way.

To think there was a time when Nick had shared everything with *her*.

Nick answered his son. "We're not going anywhere, Cody. Are we, R.T.?"

R.T. picked up his hat, which had been blown to the ground by the wind. "Hey, Cody?"

The boy lifted his head.

"You know the song, 'Oh, Give Me a Home'?"

"Yeah?" He wiped his eyes with the back of his arm.

"Well, your dad and I kind of rewrote it. His part goes like this—'Oh, give me a home, where my Cody can roam/where the Jazz and the Trappers do play/where the wife I adore, feeds me barbecue galore/and the sky isn't cloudy all day.'"

At that point Nick had joined in, his voice as off-key as R.T.'s "'Home, home to the West/where the parents I love still reside/Among mountains so high, that's the place where I'll die/my beloved close by my side.'"

While the words drove another shaft through Rosie's heart, George cleared his throat and clapped. "Change the name of our city baseball team from the Trappers to the Buzz, and you've got it."

"The *Buzz?*"

"The team got sold, so they gave it a new name, Dad. You know—'cause we're the Beehive State! 'Cause the Pioneers brought bees here." All of this was said on one breath.

Both men smiled.

Janet made a nervous gesture with her hands. "I think it's time we left for Salt Lake. What would you like to do first, son? Are you hungry? Shall we stop for breakfast on the way?"

Rosie nursed another hurt when she detected the invisible line of signals running between Nick and R.T.

"I think we'd like to go straight home. Did you all drive up in one car?"

"No." Rosie shook her head. "Cody and I met your mom and dad here."

Nick eyed his parents. "If you'll let R.T. ride with you, I'll drive my family home."

"But you haven't driven for so long! And you don't have—"

"Good plan," George interrupted his wife, who hadn't recovered from seeing her son minus a hand. In this circumstance, however, she'd voiced one of Rosie's concerns, yet had been overruled.

She and Janet shared a legitimate fear. George probably felt it, too. Nick didn't really need both hands to drive an automatic. But he hadn't been behind the wheel of a car for seven years, and the freeway was more crowded than ever. After such a long confinement, she wondered if his nerves could take the stress.

In the past, Nick had always done the driving when they'd gone anywhere together. For the last seven years, Rosie had been getting herself around without his help, but…he was back home now.

Before he'd left for the Middle East, Rosie had never given a thought to such things as who would drive. That had never been important one way or the other, not when their marriage had been based on a solid partnership.

It wasn't important now. Yet all she seemed capable of comprehending were the changes, the differences…

"Come on, R.T." George fought valiantly to maintain a semblance of calm. "As soon as we're on our way, I want to hear *your* version of that song."

"It's lousy, sir."

"Let us decide that." George grabbed R.T.'s duffel bag, and the three of them began walking toward the parking lot.

Cody, strong and tall for his age, paced his stride to match Nick's, determined to carry his dad's bag to the car without help. Judging by the struggle, it had to be heavy.

Their son was trying hard to prove he'd become a man in Nick's absence. It was a wise father who knew better than to interfere. Rosie could only stare at Nick in wonder for knowing exactly how to handle Cody's feelings.

Needing to do something before the feelings inside her exploded, she hurried ahead of them to unlock the doors of her Nissan with the automatic device, then open the trunk with her key.

"Rosie?" Nick prompted. He was standing right behind her once Cody had tossed the bag inside.

Her head jerked around. Their eyes met. In those blue depths she saw anger, bewilderment, disillusionment. She saw pain. Oh, yes. Excruciating pain.

They stared at each other almost as if they were adversaries locked in a strange room, reluctant to begin engagement because they didn't know the rules. Every question of his, every comment of hers, seemed to turn into a weapon capable of inflicting more pain, more confusion.

I'm not your adversary, Nick. I love you. I've always loved you.

"Do you want to give me the keys?"

"O-of course."

He put out his left arm to reach for them, but at the last second, put out his right.

Was it an unconscious gesture on his part, or was this his idea of forcing her to face what had happened to him and deal with it?

Either way, she couldn't stand the sight of his bad arm. Not because of its physical reality. She was grateful the explosion hadn't taken the whole limb.

The loss of his hand could never rob Nick of his appeal. If he'd come home with no arms or legs, he would still be that handsome man, exuding a powerful masculinity undiminished by the cut of his hair, his weight loss, his pallor or the severing of one of his extremities.

If anything, the years had brought him new stature, a new wisdom and maturity, all of which she was discovering made him attractive in ways she'd never been obliged to consider.

No. She hated his bad arm because of the horror it must represent to Nick.

How could he ever rid his mind of the blackness of those years when he had to live with such a reminder for the rest of his life?

He'd been in combat and been taken as a prisoner of war. He would suffer post-traumatic stress disorder until the day he died. So would R.T., she mused heavily. It was every soldier's nightmare, every wife's.

Now it was hers.

Rosie needed someone to talk to. Ironically her first

instinct was to turn to Zach, which was out of the question. Yet he'd been her rock for so long....

Darling Zach. The pain he had to be in...

But all their pain combined would never match Nick's. Only someone like Linda Beams, head of the family support group for the Ninety-sixth Regional Support Command at Fort Douglas, would be able to help Rosie understand what her husband was going through. Linda had been there for Rosie when the news had come that Nick was missing in action.

Rosie needed her right now.

NICK LOVED the feel of the steering wheel in his hand. He loved the sensation of speed, and the power that came from being in control of his life again. To be able to go where he wanted, when he wanted, was something he'd never take for granted again.

"The car's a little beauty, Rosie." A gleaming white exterior of classic style and clean rounded lines, with an interior that, thanks to the sunroof, felt airy and unconfined. After being forced to live in darkness for so many years, he craved the light. "I like it. I like it a lot."

The choice of car was a reflection on Rosie herself. That thought put him in mind of the golden-haired, eighteen-year-old girl he'd made his wife fourteen years ago. Her lilting smile and extraordinary leaf green eyes had worked their magic straight into his heart.

Where was that girl who'd sworn she'd wait for him till the end of time?

The composed elegant woman occupying the front

passenger seat, gleaming hair caught in a large tortoise-shell clip at the back of her head, was a far cry from his loving, passionate young wife. The day he'd left, Rosie had clung to him at the base airport, refusing to let him get on that plane because they both knew it might be a year before they held each other again.

As it was, they'd made love all night long, not willing to waste a second of the precious time left to them, never dreaming it would have to last seven years.

There'd be no night like that tonight. Perhaps never again.

He'd known that much when he'd kissed her, trying to get something from her she couldn't give. Her mouth had always been like a spring of fresh water to him, but when he went to drink, he discovered that the source had stopped giving freely. He'd only caught a trickle.

After glimpsing his injured arm, she'd attempted to cover up her repulsion, but it didn't work. When her initial horror had fled, he saw only a sorrowing pity in her eyes, the one emotion he couldn't tolerate from her. Not his Rosie.

But she isn't your Rosie. Not anymore.

Who was the man? How much did he mean to her?

She's taken off your rings, Armstrong. That's how much the guy means to her.

How many times has he held you? Touched you?

How long have you been going to bed with him, Rosie?

A cold sweat broke out on Nick's body. He knew he was going to be sick like R.T., so he took the Bountiful turnoff, searching frantically for the nearest gas station.

After pulling to a stop alongside a set of pumps, he got quickly out of the car. "I'll be right back."

He barely made it to the rest room in time to empty his stomach. While his hand still clutched the wall to support his weakened body, Cody walked in and shut the door.

"Dad? Mom was worried about you and sent me to see if you're okay. How come you're sick? Do you have one of those Gulf War diseases they talk about on Channel One?"

Before the war, if he'd been sick she would have followed him to find out for herself that he was all right.

As soon as the sickness passed, Nick rinsed out his mouth, then turned to Cody, anxious to take away the panic.

His hand went to Cody's left shoulder. "What's Channel One?"

"It's a news channel we have to watch at school. They've had all these stories about vets from Desert Storm who have unexplained diseases. Even their wives and kids are getting them. Do you have one?" The tears trickled down his cheeks.

Nick sucked in his breath. "Have you ever thrown up just before a football game?" His son nodded.

"Well, getting bumped around in that transport over the Rockies and then being reunited with my family after seven years kind of made me feel the same way I used to feel before a game against the Highland Rams."

"Honest?" Cody's eyes were hopeful.

"I wouldn't lie to you, son. The fact that R.T. and I

were held in semi-isolation below ground throughout our imprisonment probably protected us from a lot of things, including disease. Our unit had hardly arrived before R.T. and I went out hunting for land mines and were captured."

At those words, relief broke out on Cody's face.

"There's nothing wrong with either of us that a weight gain of forty pounds won't fix. I dreamed about double-thick chocolate marshmallow malts the whole time I was captured, figured you and I would make a stop at Snelgrove's our nightly ritual for a while. In fact, I'm craving one right now. What kind do you like?"

"Chocolate-chip cookie dough."

"Are you putting me on?"

"No. Honest."

"I've loved chocolate-chip cookie dough since I was a little kid. You're my son, all right."

Cody grinned. "What about R.T.?"

"He likes butterscotch. We'll pick one up for him, too."

"He doesn't look very good, Dad."

"That's because he hasn't been able to get in touch with his family yet. We'll let him hang around with us until he can find out what happened to his wife and aunt."

"Does he have kids?"

"No. But after six and a half years of hearing me talk about how terrific you are, he can't wait to have a Cody of his own."

"Dad…"

Pleased to see the light back in his son's blue-green

eyes, Nick decided it was time to prepare him for certain new realities. "You'll probably hear me and R.T. talking in our sleep," he began. "We might even scream and act strange. Don't let it scare you and don't be afraid to ask us questions. It won't last forever. But it'll happen for a while because our minds will be working overtime, remembering things we don't want to remember. We're going to hate certain things now."

"Like what?"

"Oh, going into the basement, being in a dark room, being enclosed in a crowded place where we can't get out."

"Will it bother you to be at a stadium?"

He could see where this conversation was headed and ruffled Cody's hair. "No. That's different. That's outdoors in the fresh air and sunshine. Being confined so many years has taught me a lot of things about myself.

"I know I don't want to work behind a desk as a stockbroker anymore. If I had my way, I'd buy some property up in the mountains near Heber and do a little farming. Keep some horses. Grow a garden."

"Hey—they're selling property up there right now! A whole bunch of my friends' dads have already built places near the Jordanelle Dam. They boat in summer and ice-fish in winter."

Ignited by Cody's enthusiasm, Nick's heart started to pick up speed. "The Jordanelle Dam?"

"Yeah. They've built this dam and made a huge lake— it's just before you get to Heber. It's fantastic. I've already been waterskiing there. Could we do that?"

Cody's eyes were shining like stars at the mere possibility.

"Well, I don't see why we couldn't check into it. Of course, your mom's going to have something to say about it."

Now would be a perfect opportunity to ask Cody about the man in Rosie's life, but he couldn't do that. It had to come from Rosie.

Cody hadn't said a word. Neither had Nick's parents. Either everyone was keeping quiet to protect Nick from being hurt or none of them knew how deeply Rosie was involved with the other man. But that didn't seem possible, not when she wasn't wearing Nick's rings.

No. The family was guarding the big secret. In any event, it didn't matter. Nick would confront his wife before the day was over.

"Mom won't mind. She could drive to the university every day. Everyone commutes."

Nick blinked. "Is she still in school?"

"No. She's a teacher on the faculty."

Stunned by the news, Nick opened the rest-room door and headed for the counter to buy some gum. She'd once talked about getting her elementary-teaching certificate....

He offered Cody a piece before they went out to the car. "What does she teach?"

"Chemistry. She got her doctorate last year." Nick heard the love and pride in his voice. "Mom has her own office. Her students call her Dr. Armstrong. Isn't that neat?"

Chemistry? Dr. Armstrong? Nick remembered what

a whiz she was at chemistry and physics in high school. All the kids used to ask her for help. Certainly, teaching at the university would pay fairly well and promise her a challenging career.

Was that where she'd met the new man in her life? Was he a professor, too?

As Nick got back in the driver's seat, he studied his wife's features. Her anxious face might have given him a glimmer of hope that she wasn't indifferent to him, *if* it hadn't been for the pitying look in her eyes.

Their leaf green color hadn't changed.

Everything else had.

"You're so pale, Nick. Are you feeling ill?" she whispered. "Please stay here for a while if you need to."

"I'm fine. We're just hungry for some ice cream, aren't we, Cody?"

"Yeah."

"If it's all right with you, Rosie, we're going to stop at Snelgrove's on the way home."

"Of course it's all right." Her voice actually shook.

She sounded hurt. He hadn't meant anything by the comment. He was just trying to be polite. Hell.

While they got back on the freeway, his thoughts digested the new information about his wife.

He had to admit she looked the epitome of the successful career woman. Earlier he hadn't quite known how to describe her to himself, how to describe the difference in her. Now everything made perfect sense.

"Nick, I've been thinking about the sleeping arrangements for R.T. Since your parents always stay in the guest room upstairs, he could sleep in the spare room down in the base—"

"I want him to sleep with me, Mom," Cody broke in before Nick could suggest the living-room couch.

Cody, Cody. You're not only wonderful, you're a quick study.

"My room has two beds. It'll be cool to talk to him about stuff."

Nick felt Rosie stir restlessly. Her gaze kept swerving to his hand on the wheel; she was obviously still in shock that he was minus the other. "He might not like to be questioned, Cody."

"He'll love it," Nick intervened. "Once you get him going, he won't know when to stop. The biggest mistake a person can make with a vet, particularly a POW, is to clam up on him. He needs to talk everything out, to validate what happened to him."

Do you hear what I'm saying, Rosie?

CHAPTER THREE

"W-WERE YOU AND R.T. put in the same cell?" she asked quietly, breaking the tension-filled silence.

That's a start, Rosie.

"No. Sometimes we were on the other side of the same wall. Other times we were separated by several walls. When the guards were lax, we could talk out loud. Otherwise we spoke to each other in Morse code by tapping on the wall."

"Do they still use that, Dad?"

"Some parts of the military do. But R.T. taught it to me in prison. It's a good communication system if all else fails."

"*Neat!* Do you think R.T. would teach me?"

"Of course. In fact, we'll demonstrate as soon as we get home. You can teach your friends. It's easy. I wish your mom and I had known how to use it in high school. We wouldn't have gotten into so much trouble passing notes in class."

That comment brought a bark of laughter from Cody. More importantly, Rosie's lips softened into a smile reminiscent of the old happy Rosie.

"What do you mean *notes?*" she challenged. "I hate

to admit it, but we were terrible, Cody. We had three classes together our senior year, and I didn't learn a single thing in any of them because your father wrote me these long letters I had to return."

"Yours were longer, and nobody *forced* you to do it, sweetheart."

Suddenly Rosie went silent and turned her head away.

For a moment they'd met on equal ground, enjoying a memory together.

Until the endearment had slipped out, triggering something so distressing his own wife couldn't face him.

Did the new man in her life call her "sweetheart," too? Was that the reason for her reaction?

"Tell me about your friends, Cody. I want to know their names and hear about the things you guys do when you mess around."

As he'd hoped, Cody kept up a running commentary until they reached Snelgrove's, in the heart of town. Nick learned that Jeff Taylor was his best friend and that you didn't say "mess around" anymore. You were supposed to say "hang out together."

"I guess you and R.T. know a lot about that, huh, Dad?"

Nick chuckled, in spite of his pain over Rosie's silence. "Yup. And you know what? We're still not sick of each other."

"Yeah, that's how it is with Jeff. We like the same things, and we never fight about anything. Did you have a best friend growing up, Dad?"

"Not the same way you do, Cody. I had a bunch of guys I spent most of my time with. I liked all of them for different reasons. But it was your mom who became my best friend."

"Really?"

That brought Rosie's head around. Nick could feel her eyes on him.

"You were my best friend, too," she whispered.

But no longer, Rosie?

"That's why we married out of high school, Cody. It's not for everybody, but it was for us. I was making investments in the stock market, so we struggled to make ends meet. Still, it was fun. I joined the army reserve to pay for college. Your mom worked part-time, and took night classes at the university. Then we found out you were on the way. That was one pretty terrific day."

"For me, too," Cody said.

Nick laughed again and was pleased to see the faint smile back on Rosie's face.

"I'll run in," Cody offered as they pulled to a stop in one of the parking spaces.

Rosie started to reach for her purse. It shouldn't have upset Nick, but it did. He forestalled her by taking out his wallet. Again he felt her eyeing him as he laid it across his thigh and propped it open with his bandaged arm, while he extracted some bills with his right hand. Then she hastily looked away. *Was the sight so abhorrent to her?*

"Is there anything you'd like, Rosie?"

She shook her head nervously. "But maybe you should buy some rainbow sherbert for your grandparents, Cody."

"Okay. I'll hurry."

He was out of the car like a shot, leaving Nick alone with his wife for the first time since the plane had landed.

Because he didn't know when they'd have this opportunity again before bedtime, he decided to face his worst nightmare right now.

"I've had years to think about what our reunion would be like, Rosie. How much would be the same. How much would be different. Seven years is too long to ask of any man or wom—"

"Nick!"

"Let me finish this, Rosie. I don't need details. To be honest, I don't think I could handle them right now. What I need is the simple truth."

A long silence. "I—I thought your parents or C-Cody would have told you by now."

So, there really is someone else in your life. Like a fool, I've been praying I was wrong.

"They didn't breathe a word about it, and our son has told me nothing, hasn't so much as hinted," Nick muttered, exhaling a painful breath. "You've raised a terrific boy who's sensitive enough, and intelligent enough, to leave that up to the mother he adores."

"He adores *you*, Nick." Her voice was full of tears.

His hand had been tapping Morse code on the steering wheel, but he hadn't even noticed until he saw her watching him. She could have no idea he'd been rapping out the same words over and over again, like a litany— "Is there a way out? Are the guards looking?" Old habits died hard. He stopped tapping.

"Who is he, Rosie? What's his name?"

Her body was trembling. Despite the distance separating them, he could feel it.

"He moved here from California two years ago."

Two years? They'd known each other that long?

"His name is Zach Wilde."

"Are you in love with him?"

She buried her face in her hands. "Please don't ask me that question."

Oh, Lord. He'd thought he could deal with this. But he was wrong.

"When I tried to reach you, Mom and Dad said you were on your way back from a Caribbean cruise with Cody. Was Zach with you?"

"Yes," came the muffled answer.

His teeth ground together. "If you've known each other two years, I'm surprised you're not married by now."

Slowly she lifted her head, but she wouldn't look at him. "W-we got engaged on the cruise. Not even your parents know about it yet."

His eyes closed tightly. "When were you planning to be married?"

"June twelfth."

You wanted the truth, Armstrong. Well, you just got it.

"Is Cody crazy about him, too?"

"No." Her voice shook with conviction.

"How come?"

"He didn't want another father if he couldn't have you. Your parents haven't been happy about it, either. They never believed you'd died in that explosion with the others," she explained in an emotional outburst, talking faster and faster, more like the old Rosie.

"I didn't want to believe it, either, but after this many years without mention of one POW still being held, I decided I couldn't live with false hope any longer."

So everyone remained loyal but you.

"Is Cody the reason you haven't married before now?"

She didn't say anything.

"Rosie?" He wanted the whole truth now, so there'd be no more shocks.

"He's…part of it."

"And the other part?"

"I couldn't let you go."

That's something, anyway.

"When did you change your mind?" he persisted, needing to hear it all.

She sucked in her breath. "Even though Cody couldn't accept Zach, I—I had a wonderful time on the trip. I never dreamed it would be possible to love anyone again after you, Nick." Her voice cracked. "But it happened, and I told him I'd marry him."

Nick felt the way he did after the first week of his captivity, when a select group of Saddam's henchmen took turns roughing him up every two hours for seven consecutive days because he refused to give them any information.

"I'll sleep on the couch tonight." He didn't want to think about tomorrow night.

"No!" she cried. "You can't, Nick. You deserve to sleep in your own bed. As if I'd let you sleep anywhere else!" Her cheeks had gone a fiery red.

That's your pity talking, Rosie.

"It doesn't matter where I sleep. I just don't feel like getting into the same bed you've shared with Zach."

"I've never been to bed with him."

Nick's head flew back in shock. *What did you just say?*

"After I'd been seeing Zach for a time, I made the decision that I wouldn't sleep with him, because I didn't want sex to complicate my feelings for him, whatever they were."

"And he's loved you enough to wait?"

She nodded. "Yes. H-he's a wonderful man."

Nick had been prepared to hate his guts. But he'd found out during the war that it wasn't possible to hate an honorable man.

Rosie might be in love with him, but she hadn't slept with him yet. There might still be a slim chance of winning her back. He'd have to start from scratch. Zach Wilde had two years' head start on him—and he'd won Rosie's love without Cody's cooperation, which meant he was the worthiest of adversaries.

Nick reminded himself that he had another advantage. He'd learned patience.

"Hi!" Cody climbed into the back seat and shut the door. "Sorry it took so long, but there was a group of tourists from that bus over there up ahead of me. Here's your malt, Dad."

"Thanks, son."

He reached for it, no longer worried that he'd have to throw it out when Cody wasn't watching because he was too sick to eat.

"Does it look good?"

Nick took several large spoonfuls, then couldn't stop. It was sheer ambrosia. "What I'd have given for one of these…"

While his wife and child looked on in wonder, he devoured the whole thing in a matter of seconds.

"Whoa, Dad!"

Nick flashed Cody a smile. "Does that answer your question?"

"I'd get a brain freeze if I ate mine that fast!"

"The trick is to eat it superfast so your brain doesn't have time to get frozen." He deposited his cup in the sack Rosie held open for him.

"Nick, don't tell Cody that!" she chastised. "In high school you used to pull that stunt on people all the time, and they'd imitate you—to their peril."

Rosie was pretending to be disgusted, but he saw that she was struggling not to laugh. Another tiny moment to cherish.

"Dad? You're awesome. I can't wait for my friends to meet you."

"I love you, too, Cody. Let's go home, shall we? R.T.'s been dying for one of these. It would be a sin to let it melt."

He backed the car out of the parking space, then merged with the traffic going east. Within minutes they'd reached Sunnyside Avenue, which ran past the zoo and into Emigration Canyon.

"You'll have to direct me now."

"Turn right on Twenty-second," Rosie murmured. "We're the fourth house on the left."

"This is a nice neighborhood." *Close to the university. Close to Zach?*

"There's Grandpa's car."

The redbrick home with white trim was a moderate-size, one-story rambler with a well-groomed yard and several large shade trees.

Out of nowhere came a deep fierce pride in his wife for making a solid life for herself and Cody. Though Nick knew his parents had lent Rosie their support, she'd had to live through these difficult years alone.

She'd been the one responsible for all the decisions, all the choices that had brought her and Cody to this point.

She'd been the one raising their son, making sacrifices to give him the best life possible. Nick felt profoundly grateful that such a woman was their son's mother.

The next time he got Rosie alone, he'd tell her as much.

"Come on, Dad! Let's find R.T. I want to show you the house and the backyard."

"I'm coming."

Nick got out of the car and went around to help Rosie, but she'd already alighted from the passenger side and had gone to the trunk to get his duffel bag. Was it because she felt sorry for him? Or because she'd grown accustomed to doing everything herself.

To Nick's mind, she'd become more independent.

Though it was a great reminder of how much time they'd lost together, he admired this new facet of her personality. He was also frightened of it.

"I'll take that." He pulled out his bag before she could, then shut the trunk.

Once again he faced the sophisticated-looking woman he couldn't quite reconcile with the wife he'd left behind seven years ago. Their gazes locked. She was getting better at masking her pity. Now he saw a hint of pleading in those lush green irises.

"Cody and I just got back from our trip last night, and there's literally no food in the refrigerator. Since we have a full house, I'd better run to the store at Foothill and get some groceries. I'll only buy what we need to get us through to tomorrow. What do you think R.T. would like for snacks? For dinner? What would *you* like?"

Her errand was a legitimate one, yet he could sense her eagerness to get away. She was going to call Zach, maybe even meet him, and there wasn't one damn thing Nick could do about it.

"Orange juice, whole milk—gallons of it. Eggs, fruit, corn on the cob, cauliflower, cheese, potato chips, cashews, bacon, sausage, ham, peanut butter, jam, French bread. A big Hershey bar, a Krackle. Any or all of the above will do for starters."

With every item he mentioned, her eyes filled a little more until the tears overflowed and ran down her cheeks.

On a half sob she cried, *"What did they do to you in there?"*

The old Rosie had come out of hiding for a minute.

If he could just find a way to keep her there long enough to make a real connection.

"I want to tell you. I need to tell you, but only when you're ready to hear it."

Her eyes closed tightly. "I'd be a liar if I said I wanted to hear what your life's been like for the last seven years. Ever since I heard the news that you'd been held prisoner all this time, I haven't allowed myself to think about the horror of it. But that's the coward in me talking. No one ever had a greater right to be listened to than you."

That's not the answer I want, Rosie. We're not talking about rights here! This is about love between a husband and wife. How far you've gone away from me, sweetheart.

"Take all the time you need, Rosie. Don't worry about me—I'll be here. With Cody."

NICK'S WORDS still reverberated in her head. He'd always had an uncanny ability to read her thoughts. If anything, his incarceration had sharpened his instincts.

A few minutes after leaving him, she sat numbly in her car, which she'd parked under the terrace opposite the supermarket. Nick had let her know that he was ready to share his story whenever she could handle it. But he'd said a lot more than that.

He *knew* she needed her privacy to make contact with Zach. In his own way, he'd given his permission.

It's not fair, her heart groaned. For years Nick had been locked in prison, and now that he was released, *she'd* locked him out. Unintentionally, inadvertently, but nonetheless she'd locked him out. There'd been too much change. And there was another man....

As for Zach, she could just imagine his pain. With one phone call, his happiness had been wiped away as if it had never been. She wanted desperately to talk to him, but she needed to call Linda Beams first.

There was a phone booth outside the store. Rosie looked up the number and punched it in. The base receptionist said that Linda wouldn't be in her office until the next day.

Trying to recover from her disappointment, Rosie explained her emergency. The receptionist commiserated with her situation and set up an appointment with Linda at nine the next morning.

Of necessity, Rosie realized she'd have to ask Chow Ping to teach her classes again and decided to make the call now before she forgot.

Finally she was able to phone Zach's office, but to her consternation, his secretary said he'd asked her to cancel all his appointments, that he wouldn't be in until the next day.

Rosie's hand shook as she placed a call to his condo, only a few minutes away on Wasatch Boulevard. All she got was the answering machine.

"Zach, darling? It's one-fifteen. I'm shopping for groceries at Dan's in Foothill. If you're home, or if you get home in time to hear this message, come and find me. I'll be here a half hour, no more. I've parked the car in my usual spot. I don't want you calling the house. If we miss each other, I'll phone you later."

Once inside the store, Rosie lost track of time as she went up and down the aisles in search of the items Nick had mentioned, plus a few he hadn't.

Chocolate-chip cookies. He preferred the dough to the baked cookies. He also loved doughnuts, tuna fish, nachos with cheese and refried beans, apple pie. He needed good food and lots of it. She would make certain he put on the weight he'd lost.

One of the friendly baggers, a young man named Dennis, teased her all the way to her car because he'd never seen her buy so many different kinds of groceries. She told him she had company.

If she'd confided that her husband had returned from Desert Storm, she would have been detained by dozens of questions. Not only couldn't she take the time, she felt a strange reluctance to let the world in on her secret—that Nick was alive and home again. Once people found out, their house would be deluged with visitors and phone calls.

Nick was the kind of man who had so many friends and contacts, you couldn't count them all. Everyone would besiege him. He wouldn't have a quiet moment to himself. This was his first day back. He'd want to spend it with family, no one else.

After stashing all the bags in her trunk, Dennis shook his head. "That must be some company. You practically bought out the whole store!"

It did look that way. Maybe she'd gone overboard, but she wanted Nick to eat to his heart's desire. Anything that appealed to him, she wanted him to have.

As she was opening the door to her car, she felt a pair of strong male arms slip around her waist from behind. *Zach.* She'd been so preoccupied, she'd forgotten he might have heard her message and come to find her.

In automatic response, she turned in his arms, seeking his comfortable, solid, familiar frame. But she'd just come from Nick's arms and would never forget how thin he'd felt beneath his uniform jacket. As for R.T.—

"I don't know about you, but I need *this*—" Suddenly Zach's mouth was on hers, claiming her love without hesitation because she'd given him that right when she accepted his ring.

But everything had changed, just as Zach had prophesied hours earlier.

No matter how hard she tried, she couldn't erase the memory of the experience in Nick's arms this morning. Worse, even though they were in a protected area of the parking lot, there were people around—maybe even friends—who would know soon enough that Nick was back and be shocked by her behavior with Zach.

Why on earth had she asked him to meet her here? Her husband was at home, waiting for her!

Fighting another spasm of guilt, she tore her lips from Zach's, but he refused to relinquish his hold on her shoulders. She knew what was coming next, and she couldn't look at him.

"Does he know about us yet?"

"Yes." She nodded. *Nick knows.* He'd known the

truth when he'd conducted a search of her soul and found the one thing she'd been dreading he'd discover.

"Rosie?" Zach gave her a gentle shake.

She could hear the questions he hadn't voiced, questions to which there were no answers yet, certainly not the answers he needed to hear.

His fingers kneaded her shoulders with more insistence. "I know you love him, darling, but you're in love with *me!*"

"I am," she said emotionally, "but it's an impossible situation right now."

"I realize that."

"No. I don't think you do." She stared up at him, dry-eyed. "Nick lost his left hand in the war, Zach. The buddy he brought home with him is blind in one eye from the same explosion. When they got off that transport plane, there was no family to greet R.T., so he's going to stay with us for a time. The two of them together would make little more than one of you."

"Lord."

In the next instant, Zach's arms provided the refuge she craved. A torrent of fresh pain over what Nick had suffered ripped through her body.

"We have to talk, sweetheart," he whispered into her hair, "but obviously it can't be here. Tell me what you want me to do. I'll meet you anytime, anywhere. Just don't leave me hanging. I couldn't stand that."

She didn't feel she could stand this untenable situation, either, but neither her pain nor Zach's could compare to Nick's and R.T.'s. "I'll call you."

"When?"

"When I can!" she cried. "Please let me go, darling. I should have been home ten minutes ago."

"Rosie…"

As she pulled out of his arms and got in her car, she took in his chiseled features and windburned cheeks. It dawned on her that he'd been out riding his bike to deal with his grief. How much more agony would all of them be called upon to endure?

"I promise I'll phone you before I go to bed tonight." It was a rash promise, but she owed Zach that much. *She loved Zach that much.*

His pain-filled gaze searched hers for endless moments. He didn't ask her if she'd be sleeping alone. She didn't tell him her intentions.

How could she? She wasn't sure of them herself.

Now that her husband was back needing all kinds of physical and emotional help, she could only function from one moment to the next. The future was terrifying to her.

"I love you," he said in a fierce whisper, leaning inside to capture her mouth one more time before she drove away.

CHAPTER FOUR

NICK NOTICED that a lot of the furnishings in the traditionally styled house were new—but she hadn't gotten rid of their king-size bed.

Were the memories of the passion they'd shared there too precious for her to part with?

Or had she been planning to sleep in it with Zach as soon as they were married—

"Hey, Dad?"

Nick heard his son's voice in the hall and turned swiftly toward the bedroom door. His body had gone clammy from another cold sweat; it had broken out at the thought of Rosie loving another man.

"In here, Cody. Where's R.T.?"

"He's out in the yard with Grandma and Grandpa eating his malt."

"Good."

"Mom let me keep your clothes in my closet. Here they are!"

Cody came into the room carrying Nick's black-and-gray parka, his midnight blue gabardine winter dress coat, a half-dozen of his old pullovers and crew-neck shirts, sweaters, khaki trousers and jeans, all of which would hang loosely on him for some time to come.

Unfortunately, in his naïveté Cody had thought that of course his mom and dad would pick right up where they'd left off and begin sharing a room again. Sharing a bed... Before Nick could suggest that he leave everything as it was for the present, Cody had gone off again, coming back minutes later with another armload of clothes.

"I kept all your T-shirts and shorts so I could wear them when I grow up."

Nick's throat swelled with love and gratitude for this son who filled so many of his needs right now.

"I bet you're tired of all that military stuff, Dad. Why don't you put on something else?"

If he'd thought his old clothes would fit, there was nothing Nick would have liked better. But Cody was so anxious to be of help, Nick couldn't disappoint him. He had no desire to see that eagerness disappear from his son's eyes. "Do you have a belt?"

"Sure. I'll get it!"

Once more he raced out of the room, leaving Nick to deal with the thousand and one memories associated with these clothes—especially the thin T-shirts Rosie used to put on after a shower to entice him away from whatever he was doing in the middle of a lazy Saturday afternoon....

One look at her long slender legs, the way her damp curves transformed the shape of the material, and he forgot the world in the wonder of making love to his gorgeous, giving wife.

He'd experienced enough of life, had heard enough male talk among the men in the reserve long before his capture, to know that his and Rosie's marriage had been exceptional.

It had taken Rosie until the cruise to get engaged again. That had to mean something, didn't it?

Deep in thought, he removed his uniform and shrugged into a long-sleeved navy pullover the sleeve of which could hang down over his damaged arm if he wanted. A glance in the mirror above Rosie's dressing table told him he looked like hell. If anything, the folds of the material emphasized his thinness.

Cody came in as Nick zipped up the old jeans Rosie used to like so much.

"Here you go, Dad." He offered him the belt when he could see that the jeans wouldn't stay up. It made Nick more determined than ever to get some flesh back on his bones.

Cody helped him fasten the buckle. "What do you think, son?"

"You look good, Dad."

Nick flashed him a smile, then pulled Cody onto the bed to wrestle with him. "Liar."

When their wrestling eventually had them on the floor, Cody cried out, "You may be skinny, but you're strong! I quit, Dad."

"Yeah?" Nick sat up, grinning.

"Yeah."

"Say it like you mean it."

"I surrender!"

After Nick released him, a broad smile lit Cody's face. "Your arms and legs are like steel bars."

"That's because R.T. and I worked out on a regular basis."

A haunted look crept into Cody's expression. "I heard the Iraqi guards tortured prisoners for doing that."

They did, Cody, in ways you don't want to know about and will never hear from me.

"Yeah, well, R.T. and I were smart and did our exercising at night when they got lazy and couldn't see us very well." It was time to change the subject. "You know, you're pretty tough yourself."

"No, I'm not. But someday I'm going to be just like you."

Nick's emotions were spilling out all over the place. He stood up and grabbed his son in a bear hug. "I love you, Cody. I'm a lucky dad. From now on, we're going to spend a lot of time together." He paused. "For starters, I thought we'd join a gym and work out together in the evenings after you've finished your homework."

"Cool! And when summer comes, we'll go on a whole bunch of backpacking trips."

"I'm planning on it. We'll take some of your pals and camp up by Mirror Lake in the Uintahs."

"Jeff's dad loves to do stuff like that, too. You'll like him a lot. I can't wait for you to meet everybody!"

"I can't wait, either."

"I guess we won't be able to do much in August because I have football practice. Will you come to my games?"

"I'll never miss another one."

"But, Dad, you're still in the reserve, aren't you?"

Nick shook his head. "No, Cody. I'm through with all that. I'm home forever."

"Yippee!" Cody burst out before hugging Nick again.

Catching sight of the messy bed, Nick let go of his son and suggested they clean things up before Rosie got home. "I'll hang what I can in the closet while you stack everything else over there in the corner. I'm sure your mom will have her own ideas about where my stuff's supposed to go."

"She's sure taking a long time," Cody grumbled.

"That's because I was so hungry I gave her a huge list of groceries to buy."

"Dad?" he murmured tentatively.

Here it comes.

Nick finished hanging his coat and parka in the closet next to Rosie's pink quilted robe, the one he'd bought her the last Christmas they were together. "Yes?" he answered without turning around, burying his face in the soft fabric. It smelled of the bath oil she always used and brought back a flood of intimate memories.

He heard Cody expel a troubled sigh. "I forget. Never mind."

"Cody?" Nick closed the closet doors and faced his son. "If you need to talk to me, then I want to hear it. I guess I hate secrets about as much as I hate anything."

"Me, too." Cody bowed his head. Nick realized he was trying hard to find the courage to broach the one subject guaranteed to exacerbate his father's pain. He needed help.

"I understand you just got back from a Caribbean cruise with your mom and Zach Wilde."

At the mention of the other man's name, Cody's dark head reared back. His tanned face reflected astonishment. "You know about him?"

Nick nodded. "Your mom says they're engaged and planning to be married in June."

His son's eyes glittered with unshed tears. "But you're home now, so she *can't* marry him."

My feelings exactly.

"I wish life was that simple, Cody, but it isn't."

"I *hate* war!" Cody shouted unexpectedly, pounding the wall with his fist. "I hate Zach. She's probably over at his condo right now." He broke down, trying to smother his sobs.

Nick had assumed as much, too, and the knowledge was killing him.

"If Mom marries him, I'm never speaking to her again."

It was starting. The thing he'd been dreading had started. Right now, Cody's justifiable anger terrified him. He had to do something to alleviate his son's pain.

"Do you have a bike? And did your mom keep my old one?"

Cody stared at him in bewilderment. "Yes." His shoulders were still heaving. "Both."

"We can't talk here. Let's take a ride down to Sunnyside Park."

With that suggestion, Cody wiped his eyes, which

had begun to look a little less wild. "Okay. I'll get them out of the garage and meet you in front."

"Good. While you do that, I'll let your grandparents know where we're going so they won't worry."

Cody dashed from the room. Nick followed at a slower pace only to discover Rosie in the kitchen, her arms loaded with groceries.

Their eyes met. She was the first to look away, guilt written all over her face as she started emptying the bags. He studied her mouth, wondering if Zach's kiss had blotted out the memory of the one he'd given her at the base earlier in the day.

"Are there more of those?" He nodded to the bags she'd put on the counter.

"Yes."

"I'll get them."

In the space of a heartbeat, her glance flicked to his left arm, then she averted her eyes. "Nick… please… This is your first day home. Let me wait on you."

"I'm not an invalid, Rosie."

She wheeled around to face him, her cheeks on fire. "I know you're not."

"Then don't treat me like one. Where did you park the car?"

She moistened her lips nervously. "It's behind your parents' car."

He stole an apple from one of the sacks and bit into it. "I'll be right back." Finishing it in a few bites, he headed out the door. Cody was waiting in front of the house, straddling his mountain bike. Nick's old bike lay on the lawn beside him.

Nick reached into the trunk of the car for the groceries. "I'm going to run these in to your mother, then we'll go."

"Okay," he answered quietly.

"Hey— Catch!" He tossed a couple of packages of Twinkies at his son, producing the smile he was looking for. "I'll hurry."

When he reentered the kitchen, Rosie was peeling potatoes. She murmured a cordial thank-you, but her rigid back, the set of her beautiful golden head, betrayed the growing tension between them. He put the bags on the counter.

"Cody's going to take me on a little tour of the neighborhood. We'll be back before the food's ready."

She turned to him, a hint of pleading in her shadowed green eyes. "I—I think that's a good idea."

Nick's chest constricted. "I thought it might be," he bit out, hurting like hell.

"Please don't be sarcastic, Nick. I didn't mean it that way. It's just that Cody has wanted his father for so long now…." Her voice trailed off.

"Shall I apologize now for granting him his wish?"

"What are you talking about?" He could see she was fighting tears, but he couldn't control his feelings any longer.

"I thought it was obvious. My unexpected return from the dead has destroyed your dreams."

She flinched as if he'd slapped her. *"Nick!"* Her face

lost all its color, and he felt her pain, her confusion and guilt. But the white-hot heat of his own pain had consumed him; he had to get out of there. He left the kitchen on a run, ignoring her pleas for him to come back.

If Cody was surprised at his quick return, he didn't say anything. Instead, he put a Twinkie in his father's mouth. "I bet you haven't had one of these in a *long* time."

After the gut-wrenching scene in the kitchen, Nick didn't think it would be possible for him to smile again, but he did. "I bet I haven't, either," he responded, his mouth full of cake and filling. The taste took him back to his childhood. "It's nice to know that some things never change." He managed another smile.

"Let's take off, Cody. I think I can still remember how to ride one of these contraptions."

Levering himself onto the seat, he grasped hold of the handlebars, almost forgetting that his bad arm wouldn't be of any use on the hand brake.

"You may have to help me when we need to stop."

"Gotcha, Dad."

Once again Nick found himself thanking God for his son. The bond between them was growing stronger with every passing second.

Side by side, they pedaled to the corner and headed down Sunnyside Avenue, picking up speed. After several blocks they had to stop at a semaphore. On cue, Cody's left hand reached out to Nick's brake. While they waited for the light to change, he asked, "Was it okay with Mom?"

After a slight hesitation, Nick answered. "Sure. She and Grandma won't have our meal ready for an hour at least."

"Dad?"

There was that tone in his son's voice again. Nick took a deep breath. "Yes?"

"Are you and Mom going to get a divorce?"

"MRS. ARMSTRONG? Can I be of any help? Peeling vegetables was my strong suit during KP duty."

Rosie took a shuddering breath. She hadn't heard R.T. come in the back door and prayed he couldn't tell she'd been crying. "Thank you, R.T. I've already put the scalloped potatoes in the oven. But if you'd like to finish the carrots, I'm going to put on some jeans and a T-shirt. I'll just be a few minutes."

"There's no hurry."

She had a feeling he wasn't talking about her change of outfit. Everyone had given her and Nick a wide berth, including his parents. Through the window over the sink she could see them on the porch swing, their heads close together in avid conversation.

They hate me. They hate what I've done to their son.

Who could blame them?

I hate myself.

At the door to the hall Rosie paused and said, "Please. Consider our house your home. Help yourself to anything that looks good. Day or night."

"I'm glad you said that. I've been thinking about a peanut-butter-and-honey sandwich for hours now."

"They're both in the right-hand cupboard, and the bread is in the fridge. I bought you your own gallon of milk."

"I'm your slave for life, Mrs. Armstrong." He opened the cupboard and took out the two jars.

"Call me Rosie."

"Deal."

After another pause, she murmured, "R.T.? H-how long were you married?"

He'd already made his sandwich and was in the process of devouring the second half.

"A year. I could be wrong, but I'm pretty sure Cynthia's remarried by now and probably has a couple of kids. Even if I could've reached her by phone, I didn't really think she'd be there to meet me. We didn't have that long a history together, not like you and the sar—" He stopped for a second, then amended, "Not like some married couples."

Rosie's eyes closed tightly. R.T. and Nick were as close, emotionally, as two people could be. There were no secrets between them.

"I—I've hurt Nick," she confessed on a half sob.

"I know."

"What am I going to do?" she whispered in agony.

"What do you *want* to do?"

"I want to set the clock back seven years."

He made a sound of exasperation and shook his head. "Rosie, you don't get it. *You're* the only reason he's alive! The only reason he *stayed* alive!

"Because of him, *I'm* still alive. Talk to him, dammit! After six and half years rotting in an Iraqi hellhole, he needs to talk about it. He needs to talk his head off about everything that happened to him. He deserves that much from you—from all of you—but he can't do it with everyone tiptoeing around him, treating him like he's a piece of glass that's going to shatter.

"Good Lord, he was a superman out there! Anyone else would have left me for dead, but not the sarge. Without me, he could have gotten away and been picked up by our own soldiers.

"Instead, he dragged me from the explosion site and carried me through the rest of that minefield. He didn't even know how bad his injury was. His *hand* was blown off." R.T. swallowed several times, convulsively.

"No one expected the reserve units to see action. None of us was adequately prepared to be so rapidly activated and torn from our families. Yet the way your husband stood up to the torture and never broke, you'd have thought he'd been trained for the military all his life." R.T.'s face screwed up as tears fell unashamedly down his pale cheeks. "I wouldn't have made it without him. He's the best of the best.

"Don't you see it's no good wishing to put back the clock? He's done his time, Rosie. If nothing else, he's earned the right to a full hearing from the woman who sent him off to war a whole ma—"

"Dear God, R.T.—"

"Hey." He pressed his forehead against the cupboard. "I'm sorry for going off like that."

"You had every right!" she cried, ashamed of her inability to understand. His words had given her a glimpse into the living nightmare of their past. Selfishly, she didn't want to see anymore. What kind of monster *was* she?

"No. You're as much a victim of the war as we are. You might as well know now. I was the one driving the truck when we hit that mine. If it hadn't been for me, and if your husband hadn't stayed with me, hadn't saved my life, he would have returned home to you with the guys who survived the explosion."

"Don't talk about blame, R.T. All I hope is that you don't hate *me* too much."

He shook his head again. "I've stricken that word from my vocabulary."

"Then you're a far better person than I am. Excuse me," she whispered.

She hurried into her bedroom feeling sick to her stomach. The sight of Nick's old clothes stacked in the corner gave her another jolt. Cody hadn't wasted any time. His father was back, and life would resume as if the war had never taken place.

Swallowing the bile rising in her throat, she rushed over to the closet to change clothes. She gasped when she opened the doors and saw more of Nick's things hanging next to hers.

Unconsciously she reached out to touch the clothes she'd thought she'd dealt with for the last time.

Nick had always been physically perfect to her. In his topcoat, he'd looked sophisticated and rakishly handsome. She groaned. If she allowed memories to intrude, she'd never be able to cope.

Stop it, Rosie. This is sick. You're still thinking of him as dead. He's alive! Why can't you believe it?

Because he doesn't look the same? Because he's not physically perfect anymore and you're repulsed?

Because you're in love with Zach and don't want *to believe it?*

That's what Nick thinks.

Is that what you *think, Rosie? Do you even know what you think?*

If you're this shallow and insensitive to another human's suffering, if you're really this cruel and selfish, then you need help, Rosie Armstrong. The kind of professional help not even Linda Beams can give you.

Please, God. Make it possible for me to listen to him tonight. Give me the strength to get through the next twenty-four hours without losing my mind....

Rosie stood there on shaky legs trying to gather the courage to phone Zach and tell him she couldn't see him or talk to him for a couple of days.

Now was the time to call him, while Nick was out of the house. Then maybe she'd be able to concentrate long enough to put dinner on the table. *Nick's first home-cooked meal in seven years.*

Quickly, before any more time was lost, she changed out of her suit into jeans and a cotton top. After exchanging her high heels for leather sandals, she sat on the edge of the bed, picked up the phone and punched in Zach's number.

When she got his answering machine, she let out the breath she'd been holding. To her horror she recognized it for what it was. Relief.

Relief because she wasn't ready for the kind of pressure she knew Zach would apply when she told him her plans.

He would try to break down her resolve, change her mind. And because of her love for him, she was too vulnerable right now to withstand all the emotional arguments he'd use.

"Zach?" She couldn't prevent her voice from shaking. "I'm keeping my promise by phoning you now. There won't be a chance later.

"I've had a little time to think and I've come to a decision. I—I'm not going to see you for a while. Please don't ask me for a timetable, because I can't give you one. I owe Nick my undivided attention while he adjusts. Cody's emotional state is fragile. So is mi—"

"And what about mine?" an angry male voice broke in, one she hardly recognized as Zach's. He was at the condo, after all.

She jumped to her feet, trembling from head to toe.

"You can't do this to us, Rosie. You shut me out for too damn long as it is. I'm not trying to be unreasonable. All I ask is that you fit me in for at least a few minutes every day so you don't forget what I look like!"

She gripped the receiver more tightly. "That can't happen and you know it. I love you, darling. But think— Nick's been deprived of his life for seven years. *Seven years.* Now I have to spend a few days helping him to put some of the pieces back together. I'm the only one who can do that—but it'll be impossible if I allow myself to see you."

She heard a deep groan.

"No one told him, but I'm positive he knows we were together today. I can't hurt him like that again, Zach. I can't!"

There was a dreadful silence. "But you can hurt *me*."

Her face went hot. "That's not fair, darling. I'm trying to do the right thing. But to sneak behind his back would be cowardly. It's not worthy of either one of us."

"I thought you told him about us!"

"I—I have."

"Then he knows the situation and he'll have to understand that you and I need time together, too."

"You're asking for understanding from a man who was left to rot in underground prisons for six and a half years?" she asked. "Have you forgotten I'm still his wife?"

"That's funny," he lashed out. "Until this morning, I thought you were my fiancée."

"Zach…you know what I meant."

"I'm afraid I do," he muttered. "If you ever figure out who you are, let me know. See you around."

"No, Zach. Don't hang up! Please—"

But the line was dead.

"Rosie?"

No…

She whirled around, the phone still in her hand. "Nick—"

"I didn't mean to eavesdrop."

She swallowed hard. "I'm sure you didn't. I—I was calling Zach to tell him I couldn't see him for a while."

"It's okay," he murmured, still standing in the doorway. "You don't owe me any explanations. If I were in his shoes, I probably would've charged my way over here long before now."

Knowing the old Nick, he probably would have, she admitted to herself, not wanting to acknowledge the ghost of a smile hovering at the corner of his mouth. For a fraction of a moment she could remember other times when he'd smiled like that. It made her feel light-headed.

"From my standpoint, Zach's self-restraint is highly commendable. According to Cody, he's 'pretty cool, a great guy. I just don't want Mom to marry him.'"

That was quite a heart-to-heart they'd had during their bike ride.

Tears stung her eyes and she looked away.

"Rosie, now that I'm back home to father our son, Cody isn't going to be as difficult. Do you hear what I'm saying?"

She could hear what he *wasn't* saying, and it confused her.

Nick was being so understanding it had caught her off guard. On the other hand, Zach was acting so completely out of character she couldn't explain it.

"Mom and Dad have taken over in the kitchen. We'll all get along fine if you want to use this time to drive to Zach's condo and make peace with him. Judging by your end of the conversation, the man's going through hell. He has a right to be put out of his misery."

A slow burning anger held her in place. "Don't say any more, Nick."

He frowned. "Say what?" he demanded.

She dropped the receiver back on the cradle. "You know what I mean."

"I think you're going to have to tell me."

Shades of the old Nick were surfacing faster than she could assimilate them. She whirled around to face him. "Hell is the place you've just come from. To use the word in any other context is ludicrous, and you know it."

His eyes narrowed. "Hell is a place. I agree. But it's also a state of mind."

"Stop it, Nick!" she practically shouted at him. "You can't compare what you've lived through to my state of mind or anyone else's. If you're trying to destroy me, you're doing a stellar job."

He moved away from the doorjamb and stepped closer. "Anything but, Rosie. You have to understand that I took a calculated risk in coming home without giving you advance warning.

"My superiors in Germany cautioned me that it would be better if we had our first reunion over there, to give everyone some time to come to grips with the fact that I didn't die in the war."

Rosie shuddered in renewed pain to hear him say those words so matter-of-factly.

"I thought I knew better." His voice sounded gruff. "I was so anxious to get home to you and Cody I refused to listen to professionals who knew what they were talking about. Poor R.T. thinks he owes me his life because he has some misguided idea that I saved his, so he was willing to do whatever I wanted.

"The poor devil deserved to know his fate long before he got off that plane this morning. That's the other regret I'm going to have to live with." There were tears in his voice. "Not one damn person was there to let him know he'd been missed, to acknowledge that he'd ever fought for his country…"

"Oh, Nick." She moved toward him. But his body had gone rigid. She sensed he'd reject any comfort she tried to offer.

"The timing couldn't have been better, could it?" he asked with evident self-loathing. "If I'd done the right thing, you and Zach would have heard the news about me several weeks ago and you could've had time to talk things out and come up with some kind of strategy before you had to face me again.

"Instead, I burst in on what was probably one of the happiest times of your life. We both know Cody would've eventually accepted Zach as his stepfa—"

"There is no wrong or right time!" She interrupted him before he could say another damning word. "Three weeks or nine hours could make no difference to the fact that you're alive and you've come home! That's all that matters. All that's important!"

One dark brow lifted. "Not true, Rosie. We all need time to get our bearings. After dinner, R.T. and I will move to a hotel for a week or two, maybe the University Plaza Hotel. Cody and I passed it on our bikes. It's two minutes from the house. That close, I'll be accessible to him after school—"

"No!" In the next breath she'd closed the distance

between them and grasped his shoulders. "Don't you dare talk about moving out! *This is your home, Nick.* I want you here!" She shook him.

His eyes took on a faintly glacial sheen. "But not in your bed."

"*Yes,* I want you in *our* bed," she fired back.

The cord in his neck throbbed. "Tonight?"

His question pulsed in the air like a live wire. Their gazes collided.

One wrong word and Nick would leave. She could see it in the savagery of his expression.

If she let him walk away now, something told her the painful consequences of that action would haunt her for the rest of her life.

Forgive me, Zach, but this is something I have to do.

"Yes," she whispered. "Tonight. Please, Nick. Promise me you won't move out."

CHAPTER FIVE

THE FEAR IN THOSE pleading green eyes wasn't something Rosie could fake. No doubt their son's welfare figured heavily in her panic-driven petition.

Cody was one terrific kid. But he was fragile right now, and there was a limit to his ability to cope with their hellish situation. Having just heard his son spill his guts, Nick shared Rosie's concern.

Her fear, rather than the touch of her hands on his shoulders or the words she'd felt compelled to say for decency's sake if nothing else, made Nick reconsider his decision to move out.

"There have been enough shocks for one day. I have no desire to create another crisis for Cody. He's already torn apart by conflicting loyalties. I'll stay."

"Thank you," she said quietly. She seemed unaware that her fingers dug into his skin through the pullover as her eyelids fluttered closed. They drew his attention to the faint purple smudges beneath her lashes, evidence of her trauma, the lack of sleep.

New lines radiated from the corners of her eyes and around her generous mouth. The shape of her facial features was a little more pronounced, giving her a more womanly aspect, evidence of the passage of years he'd missed. Years they could never recapture as a joint memory of living together and loving.

To resolve your grief, you must accept the fact that what was will never be again. Then you must give yourself permission to grieve over your grief.

Those words—reiterated by the hospital staff on a daily basis—were so easy to say. So impossible to act on, Nick moaned inwardly.

How do I accept the fact that the stranger in my arms was once blood of my blood, flesh of my flesh, soul of my soul?

How can I bear it that she loves another? How do I stand that?

"Mom? Dad? Grandma says dinner's ready."

"We'll be right there," they both answered at the same time.

As Rosie pulled away from him, her wan little smile came and went too fast for Nick to believe they'd shared a moment of spontaneous humor.

He followed her out of the room and down the hall. Though she was a good fifteen pounds thinner than he remembered her, the shape of her body had grown more svelte and womanly. She looked toned. *She looked terrific.* No doubt Zach was her match in all the ways that counted.

Nick had thought he'd want to see his successor. But certain images of Rosie with the man Nick's mind had conjured up brought on such an intense spasm of jealousy it made him think again.

"I hope you still love ham and scalloped potatoes," she called over her shoulder.

"Why would that have changed?"

At his question, she faltered in her stride and turned to him. "I don't know. I was just trying to make pleasant conversation."

"Hell, Rosie. You know I didn't mean it the way it sounded."

The pinched look on her face told him he'd really hurt her. "Then why did you ask it?"

That's a good question, Armstrong.

"Maybe because once upon a time you would never have felt forced to 'make' conversation with me. Maybe because it was a too painful reminder of the years we've missed, and for a little while I wanted to forget the past. Maybe because you made me feel like a long-lost uncle, instead of your husband. Maybe because I'm aware you'd rather be with Zach right now than here with me. Is that enough truth for you?"

Her eyes filled, but not one tear fell. "I'm sorry. In the future I'll try to be more careful."

"That's the point, Rosie. I don't want you to *try* to do anything. I'm the one who should apologize for being so damn touchy." He expelled a deep sigh. "Just ignore me and be yourself."

Her gaze didn't quite meet his. "I don't know who 'myself' is anymore."

"That makes two of us. Aside from Cody, it appears to be the only common ground between us. Perhaps because this is brand-new territory for both of us, we can agree to forgive each other ahead of time for any unintentional slings and arrows that find their mark."

Her face crumpled in despair. "You talk as if we're enemies."

"No, Rosie. The exact opposite, I think. An enemy desires to harm. You and I, on the other hand, keep making wider circles to avoid hurting each other. But somewhere in that process, we continue to alienate all the same."

She averted her head. "How are we going to get through the rest of this day without doing more damage?"

"I suppose by accepting the fact that we're both painfully aware of how easily our psyches can be bruised with one wrong word or glance."

"I don't want to hurt you, Nick." Her voice sounded tormented.

"I don't want to hurt you, either." He gestured toward her with his good arm. "Come on, let's go eat."

Unaccountably relieved that they'd survived the latest skirmish, he trailed her into the small formal dining room off the kitchen.

"There you two are," his father said. Nick detected satisfaction in his tone, as if seeing Nick and Rosie together meant everything was getting back to normal in a hurry, and they could proceed with life as it used to be.

His mother fussed around R.T., but Nick recognized the approving gleam in her eyes as he and Rosie emerged from the hallway. That gleam revealed all her hopes and dreams for a happy future.

Nick stood in awe of his parents' incredible optimism. When everyone else had given up, *even*

Rosie, they, along with Cody, hadn't believed in their hearts that Nick had been killed in the war.

Was it any wonder they assumed he and his estranged wife would have little difficulty weathering this final storm before ending up in the sunshine again?

When Nick had called them from Germany, there was no mention of Zach. Not until Rosie's kiss did he realize another man had entered the picture.

At first he'd thought his parents had purposely left Zach's name out of the conversation because they didn't want to deliver any blows that might mar his homecoming. But since this morning, he'd had time to reflect on his parents' silence about Rosie's fiancé, and he'd come to a different conclusion.

They hadn't said a word to him about Zach because they refused to face the fact that Rosie could love anyone except their son. Period.

Probably because he was an only child, Nick's parents had a fatal blind spot where he was concerned. If they chose to believe that something was so, then no power on earth could change their belief.

Nick loved them for that astounding quality—for loving him without qualification—but he also wept for them because in their denial, they were going to reap the proverbial whirlwind.

"Sit up here, Dad," Cody said excitedly.

The head of the table. How many times in the past seven years had he dreamed of moments like this?

Stop it, Armstrong. The past is over.

"Don't mind if I do." He tousled Cody's hair, then

pulled out the chair on the left, next to his own. His gaze
darted to his wife. "Rosie?"

"Thank you."

As he guided her, he knew his hand rested a little too
long on her shoulder, but her warmth and softness had
seeped through his palm, grounding it.

She was so alive. Her energy infiltrated his starving
body, reminding him how much he craved her touch.
Lord help me.

Somehow he'd thought he was prepared for this
moment, with all his family gathered around the table
anticipating this most special of thanksgiving feasts.
But as he took in each beloved face, he felt his throat
close up. His heart hammered so painfully in his chest
he couldn't breathe.

"If you don't mind, I'd like to say grace," R.T. said,
intervening at the precise moment Nick thought he'd
have to excuse himself from the table.

During their years of captivity, R.T. and Nick had
become extensions of each other. When one cut himself,
the other bled. Right now R.T.'s steady brown gaze was
focused on Rosie, seeking her permission.

Her face softened as she responded in a tremulous
voice, "I wish you would."

"Let's all join hands."

Cody grabbed Nick's right hand and clung. It was
purely accidental that Rosie was sitting at Nick's left,
which meant that she'd have to hold on to his bad arm,
above the wrist. He had to admit she hid her revulsion
well. So well, in fact, that he could almost believe she

wasn't aware of it. No doubt shock had settled in and she wasn't feeling much of anything.

"Dear Father, we thank you…" Nick heard the crack in R.T.'s voice, then a pause. "We thank you for life itself. For the beautiful circumstances in which we find ourselves this day. For the many prayers offered in our behalf, which led to our being freed. Help us find the strength to use this freedom in wise ways, meaningful ways, which might help others.

"Bless this house with every needful thing. Bless the hands that prepared this food, that it will nourish—" his voice trembled "—and strengthen our bodies.

"At this time, Father," he continued, his voice dropping to a lower register, "I wish to thank you for my buddy, Nick, Sergeant Armstrong. He was your servant, your instrument. If it weren't for him—"

Nick felt Rosie's hand slide up his forearm and squeeze it hard before R.T. whispered, "Amen."

"Amen," Nick's father pronounced in a suspiciously thick tone. He picked up the carving knife and began to cut large slices of ham. "Let's eat. You first, R.T."

"Amen," Rosie murmured, staring straight into Nick's eyes before she allowed her hand to fall away. At this moment, he could read admiration in those green depths. The kind of respect one would have for an exceptional human being, whether male or female.

But definitely *not* the look of the impassioned lover he'd left behind seven years ago, the besotted wife who'd once worshiped the ground he'd walked on, just as he'd worshiped everything about her and still did.

No. These days Zach Wilde was the person upon whom she lavished her desire.

Nick's stomach churned.

In his haste to reach his drink, he knocked over the glass, sending the milk splashing all over himself and Cody, not to mention the attractive paisley tablecloth he'd never seen before.

While Cody dashed to the kitchen for paper towels, Nick got to his feet in time to see his mother come rushing toward him with an anxious face, napkin in hand. "What's the matter, Nicky? If you didn't feel well, you should have told us."

"No need to get alarmed, Mom. I'm just clumsy." He walked her back to her chair, then returned to his place to help Cody clean up.

"That was one of the pluses of living in a cell," R.T. piped up. "If we spilled our food, it didn't matter."

Cody looked at R.T. "What kind of food did they give you?"

R.T. paused before taking a bite of ham. "I never did figure it out. Did you?" He switched his gaze to Nick who could never thank R.T. enough for defusing another unpleasant moment.

"Nope. In fact I'm not sure that's what you'd call it."

Neither his parents nor Rosie, especially Rosie, seemed to find his comment funny. R.T. and Cody, however, laughed out loud.

"Forget all that, son," George muttered. "Now here's a real meal you can sink your teeth into."

Nick shook his head at the heaping plate of food set

in front of him. If he got through a third of it, he'd be surprised. He and R.T. shared an amused glance. No matter how good everything looked, their stomachs had shrunk. The doctors had told them to eat lots of small meals throughout the day.

"Grandma makes the best biscuits in the whole world, R.T. You can't stop with just one."

"I'm finding that out, Cody."

For a few minutes there was a lull in the conversation while everyone ate. Throughout his marriage to Rosie, Nick had been served this same meal many times. But he'd never appreciated it in quite the same way, especially the scalloped potatoes. He was glad she'd made enough for an army because he had trouble sleeping at night and planned to raid the refrigerator.

Suddenly the sound of a high-pitched siren rent the air. Both Nick and R.T. covered their ears and leapt to their feet. In the process, Nick's cob of corn dropped to the plate with a thud and his chair fell backward on the carpet. But until the din finally subsided, he was rooted to the spot.

"Dad? It was just a car alarm…."

Cody's anxious expression was superseded only by the horrified look in Rosie's eyes.

Slowly Nick lowered his hand. "Sorry," he murmured, then righted the chair and sat down again. "We didn't mean to scare you. I'm afraid R.T. and I are going to be doing a lot of strange things for a while."

His mother started to cry, but his father patted her hand and she caught herself. Looking around, he said, "Who wants more ham?"

R.T. was still on his feet. "I don't think I could, sir. If you'll excuse me for a minute, I'm going to try to find out if someone knows where my aunt is. But I'll be back for dessert. Since I heard we're having strawberry shortcake, I haven't been able to think about anything else."

Nick flashed him a private signal. *Get out of here, R.T., before you jump through the ceiling.*

His gaze followed R.T.'s progress from the dining room before he realized that Rosie's complexion had paled to alabaster. She sat rigidly in her chair. "What just happened, Nick? And don't make light of it."

For the first time all day, he felt that maybe he had her attention.

After a brief hesitation, in which he weighed the wisdom of letting Cody hear this, he said, "All right. Part of our harassment in the bunkers was to be awakened in the dead of night by a long blaring siren set at decibels high enough to puncture an eardrum. That only happened once before we learned to stuff our ears with whatever was available, because you never knew when they were going to pull one of their stunts."

Just reliving the memory, Nick felt sweat break out on his forehead. "It happened to us on the fourth night of our incarceration. Up to that point they hadn't fed us, given us water or let us go to sleep. We'd been put in cages too small for us to stand or lie down. There was nothing we could do but sit or stand in a bent position."

"No, Nicky!" his mother wailed. "I can't bear it." She ran from the room, sobbing.

"Janet?" Nick's father pushed himself away from the table and hurried after her.

By now Cody's pallor matched his mother's. His eyes filled his whole face. "They were trying to break you down so you'd give them information, huh, Dad?"

"That's right, son. But R.T. and I kept our mouths shut. After four days and nights of torture, we didn't care what they did to us. We were too exhausted and just passed out where we were. That's when they used the siren on us.

"As I said, the first time it went off, I woke up thinking the bunker had been bombed. Because we couldn't get out of our cages, we figured we were goners. But we soon learned that it was a routine tactic to make us talk. When that didn't work, they roughed us up on a fairly regular basis, but between sessions, we were at least given cells large enough to lie down in.

"I'm afraid the siren we heard a few minutes ago triggered a reaction that's going to be hard to change. Our nerves have been shot to hell, but give us time. One day we'll be able to sit as calmly as you did."

Which was probably a lie. But it sounded good and seemed to satisfy Cody for the moment.

Rosie's state of mind was another matter. She looked ill. So ill, in fact, that Nick thought she might faint.

"I—I'm going to fix the dessert. Cody? Will you start clearing the table?"

He nodded.

"We'll both help," Nick offered.

"No!"

Her pleading eyes belied the sharpness of her tone. "I'm worried about R.T. Go to him. He mustn't be alone right now and you'll know how to comfort him. After what you've just told us, I don't think anyone else could."

Maybe he'd gotten through to her a little.

"He'll be all right. If anything, he's embarrassed. I'll talk to him, and then we'll be back in for dessert."

"Your mom's going to need help, too."

But not you, Rosie?

A helpless anger raged inside him. "She's got Dad. That's what a husband's for."

Rosie turned away.

In an instant, he'd destroyed the ephemeral rapport between them. *Another sling, another arrow. More regrets. Hell.*

"MOM?" CODY HAD JUST walked into the kitchen with a load of plates. "Are you okay?"

No. I'm not. I don't think I ever will be again.

"Not really." Her voice shook. "I'm sorry you had to hear those things." Appalled was more like it. Didn't Nick care that those graphic details of his torture would give their son nightmares?

"Jeez, Mom, I'm not a baby. We've learned about a lot of horrible things in my world-history class. Dad's so cool not to break. I love him, even if *you* don't!'

"Cody—"

"It's true!" he blurted, tears gushing from his eyes. "Dad figured out where you went today. He's not dumb."

Before she could demand he apologize, Cody

dashed into the dining room for another load of dishes. The violence of his emotions almost immobilized her. She swayed against the counter where she'd been putting whipped cream on the strawberries. Her chest pains felt real.

"I'll tell you one thing," Cody began in that aggressive tone the second he came back in with the ham platter and biscuit tray. "I hate Zach. I *hate* him. If you marry him, plan on me living with Dad."

Rosie felt as though she was going to die. "Cody…Cody…" In despair she reached for him, desperate to prevent the fissure from cracking wide open. But for the first time in their lives, he jerked his body away from her and flew out of the kitchen.

She didn't have to wonder where he'd run. Suddenly her home had turned into an armed camp, and Cody had chosen sides. In less than twenty-four hours she'd managed to alienate everyone she loved….

Rosie hid her tear-wet face in the nearest dish towel. There shouldn't have to be a division. Life wasn't supposed to be like this!

"Rosie, honey?" George said gently. She hadn't heard him enter the kitchen.

"Dad… How's Mom?" she asked in a dull voice.

"Pretty bad. She's lying down. Nicky's in with her. I guess you didn't hear the doorbell. Do you want me to get it?"

Zach? With the circumstances so precarious, he wouldn't come over here now. *Or would he?* Was that what her father-in-law thought?

Nick had said that if he'd been in Zach's position, he wouldn't have let anything stop him. Had she underestimated Zach's pain? His desperation? If he *was* at the door, she didn't want anyone else answering it.

"No," she said, wiping her eyes. "I'll go. Thank you."

He touched her arm to detain her. "Honey…" he began, then seemed to think better of it and fell silent.

It didn't matter. Rosie knew exactly what he wanted to say. *Don't hurt my boy. You mustn't hurt him. How can you hurt Janet and me this way?*

The bell rang again. Her heart had dropped to her feet before she reached the foyer and opened the front door, expecting to see Zach.

Instead, a slender petite brunette with short hair and a pretty face stood anxiously on the porch. Her blue-gray eyes seemed to be searching past Rosie.

"Yes?" Rosie said. "May I help you?"

"I hope so," came the fervent reply. "I'm Cynthia Ellis, R.T.'s wife. I heard he was here," she said in a trembling voice. "R.T.'s aunt phoned with the news a little while ago. I drove up from Orem as fast as I could." She sounded completely out of breath. "Is it true? Is he really alive and home?"

There were no shadows here. No conflicts. This woman radiated a fullness of joy. Her eyes shone like stars.

At a glance Rosie saw what Nick had expected to see—what he had deserved to see—when he'd gotten off the plane this morning.

It couldn't have been just this morning, could it?

Confronted by the immensity of her own betrayal,

she felt as though another dagger had pierced her heart. In loving Zach, she'd deprived Nick of a pearl beyond price at the most crucial point in his life.

She could only imagine what seeing Cynthia's shining face would mean to R.T.

"Yes. I'm Rosie Armstrong. My husband was in prison with him."

"I know. His aunt told me. It's unbelievable, isn't it?"

Yes. Unbelievable.

"Come in. Please."

The other woman stepped over the threshold and Rosie shut the door. "Wait right here and I'll go get him."

"All right." Cynthia nodded. "But I'm so excited I'm sick. I still can't believe he's alive, that he's here!"

"He's not going to believe you're here, either," Rosie murmured. "Just a minute."

Rosie turned and flew down the hall to Cody's room. When she entered, she saw R.T. and Cody sitting on the twin beds facing each other.

She was pretty sure R.T. was demonstrating Morse code to her son. Cody avoided looking at her, but R.T. got to his feet.

"Sorry I ran out of the dining—"

"No one blames you," she interrupted him gently. "R.T., you have a visitor. She's in the front hall."

Obviously her news stunned him. "Aunt Laura?"

"Why don't you go find out?"

Immediately his face paled. She saw his hands begin to shake.

Out of pure compassion she moved to his side and

put her arm around his shoulders. "Everything's going to be fine. Come on. I'll walk with you." He flashed her a look of gratitude, and they made their way out of the room.

The second they stepped into the front hallway, Cynthia Ellis's cry of love reverberated throughout the entire house. R.T. flew into her arms. They clung to each other with a fierce desperation that was too private, too beautiful to watch, but Rosie couldn't look anywhere else.

Nick, what have I done to you?

It might have been five minutes before either R.T. or his wife spoke. "You've come back to me," Cynthia Ellis said. "I can't believe it. It's a miracle. Oh, R.T, I love you!" she cried over and over again.

"I don't see how. Half of me is gone, and I—I've lost one eye, Cyn," he sobbed into her neck.

"Do you think I care about that? You're home, and I'm going to take care of you, soldier."

"I can't believe you're not married."

His words crucified Rosie; whether R.T. knew it or not, the reception she'd given Nick had convinced R.T. that his wife would never have held on this long.

Like rocks thrown in a still pool, the ripples continued to spread, doing their damage.

"I *am* married, you goof. To *you*. You know you're my guy, don't you?"

"Ah, Cyn, you don't want an old wreck like me."

"How about me, R.T? I'm a much worse wreck. After seven years, I've got the battle scars to prove it.

We'll compare wounds all night, shall we? And we'll kiss every one better, okay? Unless I'm not your girl anymore. Did you find someone else over there?" Her voice caught, revealing the depth of her emotions.

"Ah, Cyn," was all R.T. could answer, he was drowning in so much happiness.

"Go on home with her, soldier. Go home *now!* That's an order."

At the sound of Nick's authoritative voice, Rosie wheeled around in shock. She'd no idea he'd been standing there all this time.

A beautiful smile meant for R.T. alone illuminated his face. He moved past Rosie and put his arms around both of them. She saw him tousle Cynthia's dark curly locks—and felt the hairs on the back of her neck prickle.

"In case you didn't hear him say it yet, he loves you, Cyn. I know because he called out your name in his sleep every night for six and a half years. Maybe tonight *I'll* finally get some sleep."

There was more laughter, more tears of joy as they all hugged. Their own private fraternity to which no one else belonged. Rosie hadn't given the proper password, so she couldn't enter.

She'd never felt so bereft in her life. She had to do something fast, or she was going to lose it in front of all of them.

"Cody?" she called to her son, hurrying down to his room. When she entered, he looked up with accusing eyes. If an expression could wither, she'd be shriveled.

"R.T.'s wife has come to take him home. Would you help me pack his things and carry them out to her car?"

He blinked. Obviously such an eventuality hadn't occurred to him. "But he thought she was married to someone else by now!"

"I know."

"So she *did* wait for him, like he prayed."

Another blow. Any more, and Rosie wondered if she'd still be alive come morning.

"Yes."

Cody's face clouded in pain before he jumped to his feet. "He didn't unpack anything. I'll bring his duffel bag."

"Thank you, honey."

"I'm doing it for R.T. Not you." He grabbed it from the corner and lugged it out of the room. Rosie followed him down the hall on unsteady legs, wishing the mountains would collapse on her to bury her pain.

By the time she reached the foyer, Cody was being introduced; then they all started out the front door. Suddenly R.T. looked around, and his searching gaze found Rosie's.

He left the group and hurried toward her. But he seemed to be having trouble finding the words. Finally he gave up trying and they hugged.

"Thanks for everything, Rosie."

"There's no reason to thank me, R.T. I'm just so happy for you."

He embraced her harder. "I'll pray for you and the Sergeant."

Her body shook. "I—I'm afraid we're going to need

those prayers. So will Cody. Come and see us soon? You're only forty-five minutes away. Nick won't know what to do without you."

"Yeah. We're both going to have problems for a while."

She smiled sadly. "Take care, R.T."

"For what it's worth, your husband's the greatest. I know you know that, or you wouldn't have married him in the first place." He paused. "I guess that means your fiancé's pretty exceptional, too."

"He is," she whispered, dying a little more.

"Please remember one thing. If you need help, if you need to talk, you'll always have a friend in me."

"I don't deserve that kind of loyalty, but I'll probably take you up on it just the same," she murmured with tears in her voice. "Bless you, R.T."

CHAPTER SIX

FOR A MONDAY EVENING the Alpine Club was relatively empty, Zach noted, as he entered the dimly lit bar and sat at the nearest vacant table.

"Hi, there," one of the cocktail waitresses greeted him, a warm smile evident. "What'll it be?"

With a grimace Zach put a ten-dollar bill on the table. Then he took a piece of paper from his trouser pocket and handed it to her. "All I need is for you to dial that number for me and ask for Rosie. If they want to know who's calling, tell them it's Fran. If and when Rosie comes to the phone, tell her just a minute, then hand the receiver to me. Can you do that?" he asked with barely controlled intensity.

She eyed him speculatively. "Sure I can. Follow me."

Pocketing the money, she headed for the phone booth next to the rest rooms. He fed a quarter into the slot and waited while she punched in the numbers. The unrelenting throb at his temple was finally playing havoc with his stomach.

After about ten seconds had passed he saw her straighten. "Hi. May I please speak to Rosie?" There was a pause, then, "Yes, it's Fran."

Zach swallowed hard. This probably wasn't going to work. If by any chance Rosie's husband had answered the phone, he'd want to know all about Fran. Rosie would have to think fast since Zach had pulled that name out of thin air. Surely she'd realize what was happening and play along until he could talk to her.

"Just a minute, please," the waitress murmured. She handed the phone to Zach, giving him the victory sign as she walked away.

"Rosie—"

"Yes?" came a troubled voice. It didn't sound like his Rosie.

"Don't say anything. Just listen. I'm taking a Delta flight to California tonight—I'm on my way to the airport now. If and when you decide you want to get in touch with me, call Barb at the office and she'll know how to find me. Until later, sweetheart."

Before he could change his mind and beg her to talk to him, he jammed the receiver back on the hook and left the bar in a few swift strides. Once outside, he got quickly into the Passat, one of his company cars, and headed for the freeway.

Reaching for his cellular phone, he called his assistant manager, Mitch Riley. They talked business until Zach reached the huge airport parking lot, from which he could take a shuttle to the terminal.

Mitch would have to handle things until Zach got back. Unfortunately he had no idea when that would be. It was killing him to leave, but it would kill him to stay. But putting a thousand miles between him and Rosie ensured that he couldn't go storming over to her house in the middle of the night demanding her time regardless of her husband's feelings.

Zach's own feelings bordered on the primitive. He could all too easily imagine dragging Rosie off someplace—someplace they'd be alone.

After he'd parked the car, he grabbed his suitcase and climbed into the shuttle van. The flight to L.A. wouldn't be leaving for an hour. He'd purposely told Rosie which airline he was using on the outside chance she'd drive out to the airport to see him off.

But as he checked his bag and made his way to the departure lounge, he realized that such hope existed only in his most delusional fantasies. No matter how much Rosie wanted to be with Zach—and he *knew* she wanted to be with him—she couldn't and wouldn't leave her husband on his first day home from the war.

Zach's rational mind agreed that such an act would be an inhuman thing to do to anyone.

That was why he had to get out of there. His last spark of humanity had been extinguished the moment Rosie said she wouldn't be seeing him for a while.

Since he wasn't fit company for anyone, he'd take out his sailboat. Once at sea, no one would be able to reach him or disturb him, not even his family. Until he'd made contact with Barb, that was the way he wanted it.

"HEY, YOU TWO. In bed already?"

"Nicky!" both his parents said at the same time.

"Come in, son." His father beckoned with his hand, while Janet gave him a faint smile.

Nick approached the foot of their double bed, trying not to think about the agonized look on Rosie's face after Cody had called her to the phone a few minutes ago. It had been a one-sided conversation. Whatever Zach Wilde had said to her, it was enough to drain the color from her cheeks and convince Nick that his wife was in dire pain.

"Mother? I'm sure you've conjured up some horrible images about my imprisonment, but just remember that I survived it, and I've come home."

"To what?" she cried angrily. "I'll never forgive Rosie for what she's done to you."

He gritted his teeth. "Don't blame Rosie. The war changed all our lives."

Ignoring Nick's comment, George patted his wife's arm. "This business with Zach will soon pass. Now that Nicky's back, our Rosie wil—"

"No, Dad," Nick broke in. If he didn't get through to them now, they might never face reality. And maybe saying the words would help *him* chart the precarious course ahead.

"To be honest, I have no idea where Rosie and I are going. We've lost seven years. We're like babes in the woods, floundering around, trying to make sense of everything.

"If Rosie was the cruel insensitive creature your anger is making her out to be, she wouldn't have come to Hill this morning to face me, let alone to tell me the truth about Zach. But she did, and under the circumstances, that kind of integrity is as much as I could've hoped for."

His mother sat up straight in the bed, her eyes red-rimmed. "How can you stand there and defend her?"

Nick expelled a long sigh. "How can I not when she's made such a wonderful home for Cody, not to mention an impressive career for herself?"

"She couldn't have done it without *our* help!" His mother's sharp words rang through the room.

"Your mother's right, son."

"Has she ever shown either of you anything but the profoundest gratitude for all you've done?" Nick fired back, feeling the heat of anger sweep over him.

Neither of them met his gaze.

"When she heard I was MIA and presumed dead, a lesser woman might've gone to pieces and never succeeded, no matter how much help she'd received."

"She gave up on *you!* We *never* did."

The truth of his mother's words hit him like the second shock wave of a bomb blast. Then she was sobbing.

He moved to the side of the bed and embraced her. "That's because you're such wonderful parents, and I love you for that. But the fact remains Rosie has done a fantastic job with Cody. For that I will always be grateful."

His father stirred restlessly. "I think what we all need is a vacation together. Why don't we pack up the Buick in the morning and head for Yellowstone country?"

Grim-faced, Nick got up from the bed, realizing his arguments had made no impact on his parents.

"Good as that sounds, Dad, I can't go anywhere until I see about getting a prosthesis of some kind. As for Rosie and Cody, they've still got school. I'm afraid that for a while we're going to have to take things a day at a time."

Most likely there are going to be many changes you'll fight, but it can't be helped.

His mother lay back against the pillows. In the soft light of the bedside lamp, Nick could see how much his parents had aged, though they were still a very handsome couple. He loved them and always would, but he was painfully aware that their single-minded devotion to him had created a breach with Rosie, one he wasn't sure could be mended.

Suddenly there was a knock on the door, and Cody poked his head inside. "Hey, you guys? Can I come in?"

"Of course you can." George chuckled and extended his hands to Cody, who ran toward him. They hugged joyfully while Nick looked on. "This has to be the happiest night of our lives, having your dad back."

"It sure is!" Cody exclaimed, then ran around the other side of the bed to kiss his grandmother good-night.

Nick noted that the three of them were exceptionally close. Because of his parents' love and Rosie's, Cody seemed to be in the best emotional shape of any of them. Again he sent up a silent prayer of thanksgiving that, in his absence, his son had been blessed with such a strong supportive mother and grandparents.

In a few minutes, he'd be alone with his wife for the rest of the night. Before they hurt each other any more—which would happen inevitably, despite their most compassionate intentions—he'd offer Rosie his gratitude.

"Come on, Cody. Time to let your grandparents get their rest."

Nick gave his parents each another hug and said he'd see them in the morning, then ushered Cody from the room, his arm around the boy's shoulders. "You need to get to bed, too. School's going to come early in the morning."

"I don't want to go school tomorrow, Dad. Please let me stay home with you one more day."

"That's for your mom to decide," he murmured as they entered his bedroom.

Right now Cody had a serious case of hero worship where Nick was concerned; he felt so hurt and angry about Zach he was taking it out on Rosie. It would be very easy for Nick to play on his son's vulnerability and make it impossible for Rosie to wield any influence. *The last thing he wanted to do...*

Cody scuffed his toe against the carpet. "Mom'll make me go."

"It's probably for the best, son. I'm going to be at the Veterans' Hospital most of the day seeing about a new hand. But I'll tell you what. I'll pick you up after school. Bring some of your friends along. We'll get a malt together and talk football."

Cody's eyes lit up. "All right!"

Relieved that his son hadn't objected, Nick added, "Maybe after dinner we can find a gym where we can work out."

"There's one in Foothill!"

"Really?"

"Yeah. I go there sometimes with my friends."

"Okay. We'll do it. Now, have you said good-night to your mom?"

A sheepish expression crossed Cody's face. "No."

"I'll bet she's waiting. Why don't you go give her a kiss, then come on back to bed."

Cody's eyes clouded. "I'm so glad you're home, Dad."

Again Nick felt that thickening in his throat. "Ditto, son."

Cody wiped his eyes with his arm. "I'll be right back. If you want, you can look at my junior-high yearbook from last year. Here. I was showing it to R.T. I'm in three pictures, but they're kind of dumb. I've grown a couple more inches since then."

Nick took the yearbook. "You've grown about five more *feet* since I last saw you." He winked at his son. "I'm anxious to look at every picture taken while I was away so I can fill in the blanks. When you and your mom saw me off, you were this little curly-headed guy who liked to ride on my shoulders."

Cody made a face. "I looked like a girl."

Nick chuckled. "Did you ever see pictures of me at five years of age?"

"Yeah." Cody grinned. "Grandma has a zillion of them. You had a whole bunch of curls and looked like a girl, too."

"Well, nobody would ever take us for females now."

Their eyes met in mutual understanding and they hugged. "I'll be right back, Dad."

"While you're at it, you might thank your mom for being such a great mother all these years without any help from me."

Cody's grin faded and he looked away. Nick knew his son wanted to say something negative, but at the last second had thought better of it.

As soon as he'd left, Nick flipped through the pages, painfully aware of the years when he hadn't been part of Cody's life. *Or Rosie's.*

For so long, R.T. had been Nick's only link with reality. It seemed strange to think that the man who was closer to him than a brother no longer lived on the other side of the wall, and never would again.

All that time, R.T. had been Nick's immediate concern. On their flight from Germany, Nick hadn't really believed Cynthia would still be there, waiting for her husband. A marriage of only one year and no children… But by some miracle, Cynthia hadn't met—or worse, married—anyone else.

Happy as he was for R.T., it was hard to see him drive off with his wife, who was obviously still very much in love with him.

Nick set the book on Cody's desk and stood up. His palms had gone clammy. He started getting the shakes.

You miss him, Armstrong. You miss him like hell.

And you're afraid to be alone with Rosie.

"Dad? I'm back. Did you see the picture of me during the assembly?"

"You mean the one where you're all in grass skirts and bikini tops?"

"Yeah." Cody grinned.

Nick grinned back. "Did you borrow your mother's bathing suit?"

"Yeah."

"Well, I have to say she looks a lot better in it than you do. In fact, I bet your mom's still the best-looking of all your friends' moms."

There was a long silence before Cody nodded. "You love her a lot, Dad, don't you?"

Nick sucked in his breath. "I fell hopelessly in love with her when I was eighteen and that's never changed. We had a wonderful marriage, closer than most."

"Then…"

"Then how come she fell for Zach?"

Cody nodded again.

"For one thing, she thought I'd been killed in the war. For another, you said yourself he's a great guy. For a third…well, it's my opinion that people who've been in a bad marriage are often frightened to repeat the experience for fear they'll make the same mistakes.

"Since she'd been so happy in our marriage, she probably wanted to have that experience again and decided Zach could enrich her life. In a way, it's a compliment to what she and I had shared. Can you understand what I'm telling you?"

I'm not sure even I understand it, Cody, but it's the only explanation I have for the moment.

"But n-nobody's like you, Dad," the boy said

brokenly, tears gushing down his cheeks. "Mom always used to say that. How come she can't feel that way now?"

Cody, Cody. If I had the answer to that question...

"The heart's a funny thing, son. You can't order it to feel a certain way. It does what it wants. You can't get mad at it."

Cody blinked and stared across at Nick. "You mean you're not mad at Mom?"

"I was this morning," Nick confessed quietly. "I won't lie to you about that. The truth is, I'm in a lot of pain, just like you. Just like your mom. There's a great deal to work out, and today is only the first day. We're going to have to be patient."

ROSIE THOUGHT she was going to jump out of her skin with anxiety as she waited for Nick to come to bed. She'd busied herself cleaning the house, locking all the doors, turning out the lights.

While he was with Cody and his parents, she'd emptied his duffel bag and made room for his things in her closets and drawers. A clean pair of pajamas they'd given him in Germany lay across the foot of the bed. After showering, she'd put on a nightgown she hadn't worn since before he'd left for the war, then slipped into the pink robe Nick had given her eight Christmases ago.

Finally she'd gone to bed, forcing herself not to think about Zach flying to California. His terse communication had created a sense of loss that made her feel as if her only friend on earth had suddenly deserted her.

But in another sense, she was glad he'd gone to be with his family. He was particularly fond of his older brother, Richard, who could provide needed comfort right now.

Rosie had never had brothers or sisters and could only imagine what a luxury it would be to run to a sibling in a crisis. For that matter, Nick had been an only child, as well. Throughout their marriage, they'd been each other's best friend, had relied on each other for everything.

She and Nick had married right out of high school, their passion too flammable to endure a lengthy engagement. Nick had been her one and only lover. To Rosie, the physical side of their marriage had been pure ecstasy. But when she thought of making love to him now, she couldn't summon any actual memory of what those feelings were like.

It was like looking back thirteen years to Cody's birth—forty-eight long hours of labor. She had an almost abstract awareness that there had been intense physical pain; at the time, she'd thought she would never forget it. But she *had* forgotten those pains, and until she had another baby, there was no way she could ever relive them.

When Zach entered her life, everything was different. Her feelings had taken a long time to get to the point that she wanted him in her bed. She'd heard too many stories of widows and divorced women who'd remarried and then discovered that after their physical needs had been satisfied, there was little else holding the marriage together.

Rosie had been determined to build a rock-solid relationship before she allowed herself to respond sexually to Zach. She'd never felt out of control with him the way she had with Nick. In all likelihood it was because she was much older and because she'd gone through a long period of mourning. Not only that, there were Cody's feelings to consider. The combination of circumstances had made her cautious. Fortunately Zach had loved her enough to wait until they were married before they consummated their relationship.

Bothered by a headache that had begun during dinner, she got up and padded to the kitchen for some painkillers. While she was putting the bottle back on the shelf, the phone rang, startling her.

The only person she could think of who'd be calling this late was Zach. Was it possible he'd changed his mind and hadn't gone to California, after all?

She was afraid to pick up the phone, afraid they'd go through another excruciating emotional battle. But the continued ringing would wake the whole house. After another moment's hesitation, she answered.

"Hello?"

"Rosie? It's R.T."

She blinked. "R.T.? Are you all right?"

"Yes. Could I speak to Nick?"

He wasn't all right at all.

"Of course. I'll get him. Hold on."

Laying the receiver on the counter, she ran to find Nick, who was just coming out of Cody's bedroom. In the near darkness, his tall body was little more than a silhouette.

For an instant, it reminded her of other times when he'd come from the shower toward their bed, a shadowy figure intent on making love to her. She reeled from the impact of such a deeply buried memory that suddenly, unexpectedly surfaced.

"R.T.'s on the phone."

"I thought he might be calling."

"If you want privacy, take it in the kitchen."

"Thank you," he murmured and strode past her.

Rosie hurried to the bedroom, still disturbed by the strange experience outside Cody's door. She suspected Nick would be talking to R.T. for a while and decided she'd try to reach Zach on the phone line hooked up to the computer downstairs in her office.

He would be with his family by now, and it was an hour earlier in California. She felt as if she'd lived ten lifetimes in one day; she needed to hear his voice again, if only to say good-night.

Without any further hesitation she darted into the hall and flew down the stairs to the basement. She kept a directory of her personal numbers in her desk drawer.

But a call to his family's home revealed that they had no idea he was coming to California. He hadn't phoned them. Maybe he was still on his way home from the airport.

With the assurance that they'd have him call as soon as he arrived, his mother hung up. Rosie replaced the receiver with the awful premonition that Zach didn't want his family to know any of this. In fact, she was pretty sure he hadn't told them about the engagement yet.

Maybe he hadn't gone to California. Maybe at the last minute he'd changed his mind. He could be anywhere. Only his secretary was privy to that information, but it was too late to disturb her. Rosie would have to wait until tomorrow.

On the slight chance that he'd decided not to leave Salt Lake, after all, she phoned his condo, but all she got was the answering machine.

Was it possible he'd gone off somewhere on his racing bike? Whenever he was upset or needed to think, he usually went cycling for a few hours. He'd been training for the Tour de France in Park City when she'd first met him. At the time she'd been unaware that he'd been grieving over the loss of his fiancée.

Rosie, along with Cody and a couple of his friends, had rented bikes to wheel around the restored mining town high in the Wasatch Mountains. It was early in the morning, and they'd come to an unused stretch of road, or so they'd thought. As they rounded a sharp curve, there was Zach, headed toward them with the speed of a torpedo.

Only his expertise prevented a serious accident. Instead of being angry at having to skid to a stop to avoid collision when it was their fault for being all over the road, he graciously apologized and struck up a conversation. Once they found out he was in training, Cody and his friends were in awe of him, besieging him with questions.

What began as a chance meeting turned into an all-day excursion. Zach led them on an eventful ride to Bridal Veil Falls, where they hiked and picnicked. No one wanted the fun to end, so they ended up having dinner together, as well.

It was the first time Rosie had been in another man's company—outside of school and work—since Nick's death. When Zach asked if he could take her and Cody out to dinner the next time he drove down to Salt Lake, she found herself saying yes.

Cody thought it was cool, and the three of them had a lovely evening out. But then it became clear that Zach was attracted to his mom, that he wanted to start seeing her on a regular basis, and Cody became difficult. The problems began.

He'd been difficult ever since. Right up until tonight. Now, suddenly, he was a different child. After the explosion in the kitchen earlier, she hadn't expected him to come near her, let alone say good-night and give her a hug.

Nick's influence, surely.

Nick. By now he'd probably be off the phone.

With a guilty start, she replaced the receiver and ran up the stairs to the bedroom. The door stood ajar. She could see him in the middle of the room, tying the ends of the belt of his old striped bathrobe around his waist. His pajamas still lay at the foot of the bed.

There was an odd fluttering in her chest as she made her entrance.

His enigmatic gaze swerved to hers and narrowed. "Obviously, the prospect of sleeping with me was a little too daunting, after all. If you want me to stay on the couch, just say so. No lies, Rosie. At this point, all we've got going for us is the truth."

Nick, I'm not trying to hurt you.

"I was taking advantage of the time you were on the phone with R.T. to call Zach. He left for California in a lot of pain, but it seems I can't locate him. Is that enough truth for you?"

"It's a start," he muttered, drying his hair with a towel.

He must have just come from the shower. She could smell the scent of her soap on his skin. Another flood of memories unexpectedly assailed her, confusing her.

She scrambled into bed and pulled up the covers. "H-how's R.T.?"

"He's terrified."

"Of what exactly?"

"Cynthia wants to make love and he doesn't."

"Why? They adore each other."

"That's why," he ground out, tossing the towel onto the nearest chair. Then he turned off the light. "He's afraid he won't be able to perform as he once did. He's afraid she'll be turned off by his skinny body. He doesn't look like he used to, and he's afraid she's only pretending to love him out of pity."

"She sees past that," Rosie said with conviction. "You saw, you heard her joy when R.T. appeared in the foyer. Pity was the last thing on her mind."

"It doesn't matter what we know." She felt his side of the bed dip as he slid beneath the covers. "R.T. isn't convinced."

Nick's tone of voice haunted Rosie. "What advice did you give him?"

"To ask her if it would be all right if they just held each other all night because he needed time to realize that this is real, not a dream."

Hot tears squeezed out of her eyes. "Do you think he'll take your advice?"

"He always does. I'm figuring Cynthia's a smart woman. I imagine ten or fifteen minutes is all she'll need to convince him of her love…as only a wife who has known her husband intimately can do."

A tight band constricted her breathing. "D-do you want to hold me, Nick?"

"No. The idea of a sacrificial lamb has never appealed."

She winced in pain at the swift retort. It didn't seem possible that they could be saying such hurtful things to each other, not after the kind of marriage they'd once shared.

"The next time I hold a woman, it will be because our love is mutual."

A woman? What did he mean?

"I still love you, Nick," she whispered. "I always will."

"I believe that. It's the only reason I'm lying here right now. But the difference is I'm still in love with the Rosie I left behind. The new Rosie is a stranger—one, furthermore, who's in love with another man. I've had all day and night for the dream to die.

"Tomorrow morning, after I've been to the hospital, I plan to consult a good divorce attorney."

"Divorce?"

She cringed, her heart pounding. She hadn't even considered such a thing. She hadn't been able to think beyond the moment.

"It was the first question Cody asked me on our bike ride today. He wanted to know if we were getting a divorce. When I thought about it, I realized it was a perfectly natural question. You can't marry Zach while you're still married to me." A long silence ensued. "Rosie?" he prodded. "Did you hear what I said?"

"Y-yes," came her ragged whisper. He hadn't been home twenty-four hours. Could he really be discussing divorce—and discussing it so…so unemotionally?

"Then we need to get it under way as soon as possible. I can't promise you'll be free by the wedding date you've chosen, but I'll do everything in my power to get our divorce through quickly. I should think that seven years of no history between us will speed up the process.

"As for our son, gut instinct tells me it might be better if I stay here for a while longer. It will give Cody a little time to accept our situation. But I'll leave that decision up to you."

Cody'll never accept it.

I don't accept it.

All at once a terrible anger caused her to throw back the covers and jump to her feet. "Nick, why are you talking about this on your first night home?"

"Why do you think?" he responded blandly. "You should know me by now. At least, you *used* to know me. I've always been a realist. In that regard, I haven't changed. You're engaged to be married, and I came back from the dead. Two irreconcilable facts."

Rosie started to shake and couldn't stop. "It's too soon to talk about…about these things. Y-you need time…therapy…"

"I agree we can all benefit from therapy, but I'm not in the mood right now." He got to his feet and they faced each other across the bed in the darkness.

"As for time, I've had seven years to think. What I want at this point is to build a new life for myself. Since I've lost my wife, naturally I'm eager to start dating other women with the hope of remarriage and more children down the road. Can you understand that?"

Oh, yes, she could understand that. It sounded like he couldn't wait! And there wasn't a woman alive who'd be immune to his charm.

Hardly able to breathe, she murmured, "Of course."

"There's just one problem, Rosie. The kind of woman I want to end up with wouldn't dream of dating a married man. Therefore, like you, I need to be free first. In both our cases, there's no time to lose."

She couldn't fault his reasoning or his needs.

They made perfect sense.

He had every right!

She had absolutely no right.

She was devastated.

CHAPTER SEVEN

THE SILENCE FROM ROSIE told him he'd hit a nerve. But after weighing the situation carefully, he'd decided there was only one way to stop his pain. His marriage to Rosie had been too wonderful to consider enduring anything less. It was all or nothing.

"Rosie? There's something else I want to make clear right now. I have no hard feelings against Zach. On the contrary. Since he's going to be the other man in Cody's life, I'd like to meet him sometime. You can tell the poor devil he doesn't have to tiptoe around me. The more civilized we all are, the better it'll be for our son, whom I firmly believe should live with you after the divorce.

"Speaking of Cody, will it be all right if I pick him up after school tomorrow? Don't worry. I know you have classes to teach and you'll need your car. Mom and Dad will be here for a few more days, and I'll use theirs."

"Nick—stop it!" she blurted, her cheeks fiery hot. "Tonight isn't the night to talk about the future. I'm not going to work tomorrow. I want to hear about your life. I want to help you."

"I know you do. But I told you pretty much everything at the dinner table. Anything else isn't fit for human consumption. The ways people have figured out to torture one another aren't worthy of remembering. I promised myself that if I ever got out of that cell, I'd embrace life and never look back."

"How *did* you get out?"

Pleased she'd thawed enough to be curious, he said, "I suppose when the United Nations inspection teams started snooping around Saddam Hussein's installations after the war, word got out that he'd kept some prisoners no one knew about. R.T. and I were two of the lucky ones released."

"You mean there could be more?" she said, aghast.

"Maybe."

"Oh, Nick! That's so horrible, so awful!" He couldn't see her face, but she sounded as if she was crying.

For a moment, the old Rosie was back in the room, her compassionate heart bleeding all over the place.

"It could drive me mad if I ever really thought about it, which I'm not going to do. Instead, I plan to raid the refrigerator. Do you mind?"

"No," came her pain-filled whisper. "This is your house, too. Bought and paid for with money you earned for us.

"Nick, instead of consulting an attorney tomorrow, why don't you call Jerry Moore and see about getting your old job back at the brokerage house? You were their whiz kid before. I'm sure that with a little refresher course you'd work your way to the top again."

"I appreciate your confidence in me, sweetheart. If

that was what I wanted to do for the rest of my life—if Salt Lake was where I intended to put down new roots," he said, taking an enormous plunge, "it's possible that would all work out."

Another long silence. Another curve ball she hadn't seen coming. This was one time, he reflected, that her keen mathematical mind was of little use to her. But he had to move on with his life. *So did she.* Her life had been a living hell, too. It was time for all the pain to end.

"Are you thinking of moving?" She couldn't have feigned the alarm in that question. It was something to cherish.

"That's right."

"But St. George wouldn't give you the broad base of clients you need."

"Who said anything about St. George?"

She sounded at a total loss for words. "I—I just assumed that if you were going to relocate, you'd probably want to be near your parents."

"St. George is too close a reminder of the desert. In the last seven years I've lost my taste for it."

"I'm sorry," she rushed to apologize. "I didn't think— Forgive me, Nick."

"There's nothing to forgive. Are you hungry for some scalloped potatoes?"

"No." The word sounded abrupt, as if she'd lost patience with him.

"I could eat the whole pan."

"Wait—"

Nick paused at the door. She sounded almost frantic, a sign that he was still rocking her foundations.

"What do you plan to do for a living? Where will you go?"

"I want to work in the out-of-doors."

Quiet again. Then, "You're kidding."

"Not at all."

She made a sound of exasperation. "Doing what?"

"Maybe working a small ranch somewhere in the mountains. I have several ideas, but that's all they are right now."

"But you know the market like the back of your hand! Be serious, Nick!"

"My days of sitting in a claustrophobic office watching stocks fluctuate on my computer are over. That's not living, Rosie.

"Before I say good-night, there's something else I have to tell you." He paused, gathering his resolve. "I may have only spent one day with Cody, but it was enough to realize what a superb mother you've been to our son."

His voice was shaking, but he had to finish saying what was in his heart.

"I'm proud of you, Rosie. Proud of what you've accomplished and become, proud of the beautiful home you've made. I love you for keeping close family ties with my parents, for giving them the opportunity to stay in your life. I'm sorry everyone has fought you so hard where Zach is concerned.

"Now that I'm home, all that's going to change. Don't worry about Mom and Dad or Cody. Just give me a little more time with them, and everything will be fine.

"Since I have trouble sleeping, I'll probably stay up half the night watching TV in the living room. Ignore any weird noises coming from there. R.T. tells me my dreams get pretty wild, but I doubt they're any worse than his. I suppose Cynthia is going to go through her initiation tonight. At least I can spare you the worst of it. See you in the morning."

"GOOD MORNING. I'm Rosie Armstrong. I have an appointment with Linda Beams."

"She's expecting you, but she's with someone else at the moment. She asked me to give you this to read while you wait."

Rosie thanked the uniformed officer at the front desk and sat down with the small leaflet. Her eyes were swollen almost shut from crying. At first she had to squint to make out all the letters.

FOR FAMILIES OF LOVED ONES COMING HOME FROM WAR.
STRATEGIES FOR HELPING MY LOVED ONES AND MYSELF.

1. Educate yourself on what to expect when your loved one returns home. Acknowledge your fears that he or she may come home as someone who is "different" in certain ways.
2. Recognize the veteran for participating honorably in the war.

3. Communicate an attitude of "I care," and "I am here for you."

4. Be an empathetic listener. Sometimes the individual may not feel the full impact of what has happened for days, weeks, months or sometimes years. When your loved one is ready to talk or "debrief," listen without making judgments, moralizing or trying to "make it better."

At times, loved ones will prefer to debrief with professionals or other veterans, instead. This is often necessary because they fear what may happen if they open their hearts too fully to the pain. They may also want to protect their loves ones from this pain.

5. Allow the returnee to adjust and reenter at his or her own pace.

Recognize that change comes slowly. Be supportive, but don't push.

6. Become involved in support groups as quickly as possible.

7. Some common questions and responses you can pose to returnees include:

"What are you feeling?" vs "Are you okay?"

"You must be experiencing all kinds of emotions now."

"I know this is hard to talk about, but it's important to talk."

"What was the hardest part of everything for you?"

Many returnees will find it hard to respond to these questions, and many will avoid such discussions sometimes. Yet, the process of debriefing on some level—whether with family, friends or in a structured support setting—is crucial to a healthy reentry and healing process.

9. Become aware of the many emotions you yourself are experiencing and find healing ways to release these feelings. Prepare your family in advance for what they may experience with the returning veteran.

10. Keep a daily journal of your thoughts and feelings.

11. Pray. Talk to your clergy if you find it comforting.

12. Seek professional assistance whenever you feel overwhelmed and debilitated by the stress and emotional impact of the changes you are experiencing.

13. Observe children and adolescents carefully for signs of emotional distress. They may feel guilt, confusion, anger and a sense of helplessness around the returning veteran. They may feel loneliness and a sense of emotional abandonment.

14. Exerci—

"Hi, Rosie. It's been a long time."

At the sound of Linda's voice, she lifted her head.

"Thanks for seeing me on such short notice."

"Anytime. Come on in."

She followed the older woman into her office and sat down opposite her desk. Linda eyed her frankly.

"Your message was bittersweet. Out of the blue your husband has miraculously returned—minus a hand. And at the same time you're on the brink of being married again. I'd say that the stress in your lives has been magnified a thousandfold overnight."

Rosie nodded, rocking back and forth on the hard chair, her hands clasped around her knees. "According to the leaflet, I've committed almost every major sin in the lot, including one not even mentioned."

Linda's brows lifted expressively. "The leaflet addresses the issues facing a returning vet, not necessarily a POW. There are some differences.

"In your case you had no advance warning that he was alive, no time to prepare for his arrival. You need to forgive yourself for any mistakes you feel you've made, and learn from them. You also need to forgive yourself for falling in love with another man.

"If that becomes impossible to do, then I suggest you seek psychiatric help. Though I'm here for general support, my work as a thanatologist deals mainly with grieving veterans and their families. You need a specialist to help you cope with your new situation. But let's put those considerations aside and discuss where you are emotionally and mentally at this moment."

"I wish I knew, Linda."

"How is your fiancé reacting?"

"He's in agony. He left for California yesterday. I need to phone him, but…"

"But you don't know what to say," Linda finished for her. "At this stage, you can't possibly have answers since you don't even know the questions."

"Exactly."

"Some time apart won't hurt your relationship, and it will give all of you space to think. Let's talk about PTSD—post-traumatic stress disorder. Turn to the back of the leaflet and read the list of symptoms. Then we'll discuss them in terms of your husband."

Rosie took five minutes and did as she suggested, then shook her head. "Except for a few points, Nick doesn't seem to be showing these signs. If you'd heard the things he said last night, you would never have known he'd been a POW for six and a half years."

"Tell me."

Again Rosie found herself revealing some of the pertinent dialogue.

"Now can you understand why I'm so shaken? He's shown no anger over my engagement to Zach. In fact, he's reconciled to it. He has no confusion of identity, no loss of self-esteem. I see no signs of helplessness or confusion.

"He's very open about having disturbing dreams, but isn't preoccupied over the loss of his hand. He eats constantly. There's no diminished enjoyment of life or activities, no alienation from his parents or Cody. He has plans. He…" Rosie faltered. "A-all I can say is, his emotional health is far better than mine."

"Wait a minute. Let's back up. Tell me what you were going to say after you said, 'He has plans.'"

Rosie averted her eyes. "He wants to start divorce proceedings as soon as possible. He wants to get on with his life. He used to be a stockbroker. Now he wants to be a rancher!"

Linda sat back in her chair, tapping the pencil against the desktop. "How does that make you feel?"

"I—I know how I should feel," she muttered. "He has every right."

"We're not talking about 'shoulds' and 'rights' here. I'm asking you point-blank, what's going on inside that psyche of yours?"

"I guess I'm feeling hurt."

"And?"

"And angry."

"And?

She sucked in her breath. "And betrayed."

"Interesting. I would say that's a good place to start. Getting in touch with your own feelings. Once you understand them, then you'll know how to proceed."

"But what about Nick?"

"He's obviously a survivor. Yet, war has reminded him that he's mortal. It's forced him to consider his own 'unfinished business.' He's feeling incomplete and he wants the wholeness and peace marriage once gave him. Thus the mention of divorce—to facilitate the possibility of marrying again, of putting his life in order."

Rosie stared at Linda. "I hadn't thought of it that way."

"It appears to me he's a strong, intelligent, mature human being who has a sound grip on life and an indomitable will. But don't be deceived. He's going to suffer many of those listed symptoms. You just haven't seen them yet."

"You're right. Not enough time has passed. The trouble is, if we do divorce and he moves out, I never will see behind the facade."

"Is that important to you?"

Rosie ran unsteady fingers through her hair. "Yes. Very."

"Why?"

"Why?"

"Another question you need to answer as honestly as you can."

"I already know the answer," she retorted. "Who will help him if I don't?"

"Another woman?"

Rosie's head flew back. "Another woman doesn't know him like I do."

"Ahh…"

"He's so gallant and take-charge, you tend to forget he's lost his hand. He doesn't act like someone who's lost seven years of life!" Suddenly Rosie broke down in sobs.

"But you're engaged to another man, so you can't do what you might have done for him. That's the dilemma, right?"

"Yes," she whispered, trying to get her emotions under control.

Linda sat forward and handed her a tissue. "When he's ready, there are support groups he can join. You mentioned his parents and your son. I understand he also bonded with the other soldier imprisoned with him. Those are all terrific resources."

"I know. Especially Cody. They're extremely close already."

"That's good. Now let's talk about you and this other man. How long have you been together?"

"Two years."

"Then a great deal of energy and emotion has already been invested. As I said earlier, you need to get in touch with your true feelings toward you husband *and* your fiancé."

"How do I do that?"

"At all times be honest and open in your communication with both men. They deserve nothing less. No matter how much you think it might hurt them, don't lie about your feelings and don't hide them. That would be the worst thing you could do. In time, you'll begin to understand yourself. When that day arrives, you'll know what to do."

"That kind of honesty would take a very strong person."

"You *are* a very strong person. Don't forget that you survived the war, too!"

Rosie's head was bowed. "Thank you for that, Linda." Slowly she got to her feet. "You've given me a lot to think about."

"I hope it's helped. Remember, I'm always here. Come again soon."

"Depending on how today goes, you might hear from me tomorrow."

"Then I'll be waiting. Good luck."

By the time Rosie had gone out to her car, she'd made the decision to get in touch with Zach and find out when he was coming home. They needed to talk. Since her conversation with Linda, Rosie felt maybe she could handle it.

With Nick's folks in the house, she thought it would be better if she used a pay phone, so she drove to the nearest convenience store and called his office. Zach's secretary said he hadn't phoned in yet, but when he did, she'd give him Rosie's message.

Relieved to have taken that step, she was able to concentrate on Nick. In her mind she'd been cataloguing the things he'd need. The first order of business was to drive downtown and pick up some sweats and casual clothes for him in one of the local department stores.

"I DON'T LIKE the idea of a fake hand," Nick murmured, gazing at several varieties and colors to match a person's skin.

The technician nodded. "A lot of you vets don't. There's little dexterity. Some people want them for cosmetic reasons."

"I'd better get one for the odd occasion when I have to be out in public for any length of time. When I'm not wearing it, I'd rather keep my arm in my pocket or covered up. But I'd better get fitted with a hook to do work when I'm by myself."

A hook would increase his ability to perform many tasks, but the feel of straps around his upper body would take some getting used to. Though the experience was growing less frequent, he had moments when it felt like his hand was still there balled into a fist, driving his nails into his palm.

The doctor had told him it was called phantom sensation. The nerve impulses to the brain didn't detect the loss. That was why the thought of moving his shoulders to operate the hook seemed so odd.

"What kind of work do you do?"

"I'm thinking of buying a small ranch."

"Then you'll want this." He lifted the larger hook for Nick's inspection. "It's called a farm hook. Some people refer to it as a work hook. You can accomplish a great deal with it. For example, when you're driving a nail, you hold your hook like this to fix the nail in place—" he demonstrated "—then pound with the other hand. If you're using a shovel, you can adjust the space to accommodate the handle."

"That's the idea." Nick nodded.

"All right. We'll start you out with the regular hook to get used to it, then graduate to the farm hook. Plan on coming in here three days a week for a couple of weeks for some occupational therapy. Then you can operate both hooks without problem. Have the receptionist make you an appointment for two weeks from today."

Nick frowned. "You can't get started any sooner?"

"No. The orthopedic surgeon at Fitzsimmons who

did the surgery would tell you your arm needs to heal a little longer. It looks clean and dry, but to be safe, let's give it another fourteen days."

Nick nodded again.

The other man patted him on the shoulder. "I know you're anxious to get on with life. I would be, too. Still, you're safely back home."

"Amen," Nick said, then shook the technician's hand and left.

A few minutes later, he was once more behind the wheel of his parents' Buick.

You're home all right, Armstrong, and you're on your way to see a divorce attorney. The counselors in Germany told you to put the past behind you and resume your life. That's what you're going to do because any more time spent with Rosie—knowing she's in love with Zach—is killing you. And her!

BY THE TIME Rosie finished her shopping, she was amazed to discover it was almost four o'clock. She needed to get home and start dinner. But when she finally reached Sunnyside Avenue and turned onto her street, she slowed to a crawl, marveling at the scene before her.

Cars were lined bumper to bumper on both sides beneath the shade trees growing along the street. Their new spring foliage had been tied with hundreds of yellow ribbons. Dozens of yellow balloons had been attached to the wrought-iron stair railing leading to the front porch of her house.

Someone had erected a huge banner, which stretched across the front lawn from the driveway to the opposite boundary of her property. Rosie could read the letters all the way from the corner of Sunnyside.

Our Own Desert Storm Hero! Welcome home,
Sergeant Nick Armstrong! We love you!

Her vision blurred. It could only mean one thing: one of her neighbors must have found out about Nick from his parents and organized everyone on the block.

Rosie had always loved her friendly neighborhood, but *this*...this went beyond anything she could have imagined.

A plethora of emotions swamped her, devastating her with a brand-new anguish. As thrilled as she was about their kindness and what it would mean to Nick, a part of her was dying inside because *she* hadn't thought of it.

His own wife hadn't thought of it!

His own wife hadn't breathed the joyful news to a single soul, not even the bagger at the grocery store.

You're a fraud, Rosie. While you were trying to reach Zach, your neighbors were organizing to give your husband a hero's welcome!

What had the brochure said? Let your vet know you're proud of him for serving in the war?

She buried her face in her hands, convulsed, tears streaming down her face.

What would this do to Nick? He'd told her he was seeing a divorce attorney today. The Buick was nowhere in sight. Had he been home yet? Did he know what was here waiting for him?

When he realized all this was for him, would he think she'd been the one responsible—and then find out she'd had nothing to do with it?

Would it tear him apart as it was tearing her?

Was he ready to deal with all these people, thoughtful and generous as they were?

When she'd recovered enough to see, she moved forward and pulled into the driveway. Once out of the car with her packages, she heard the din of voices coming from the backyard.

"Martha!" she cried when she hurried around the back and saw Jeff Taylor's mom, of all people, supervising an enormous picnic barbecue. There were at least fifty or sixty people gathered, dressed in light jackets and sweaters, some of them in conversation with Nick's parents. Enough food covered the picnic tables to feed at least that many more.

"Rosie!" Martha screamed for joy and came running, her face glowing with excitement. She hugged Rosie so hard she could scarcely breathe. "Cody told Jeff the news, and he called me from school this morning. You must be the happiest woman in the world! We're all so ecstatic for you we can't stand it!

"I'm afraid once we got started, we invited practically the whole city. This party will go on until morning. The boys have kept your husband out with them, but they should be arriving any second."

Help me. Help me, Rosie's heart groaned in fresh

agony. "How can I ever thank you?" she finally managed to whisper.

"Hey, this was one party I didn't have to plan. Once people knew the reason, it organized itself. Chip LeChimenant's mother will be here within the hour to film it for Channel Three news."

Overwhelmed by the turn of events, Rosie hugged her friends and neighbors, but she was soon feeling light-headed and excused herself to take her packages inside.

She looked in the bathroom mirror, moaning at her washed-out appearance. For the next few minutes she redid her hair in its tortoiseshell clip, then washed her face and put on fresh makeup.

Searching in her closet, she found tailored gray wool slacks and a red sweater, then quickly slipped them on. Seconds before she left the bedroom, she heard the crowd break into a deafening roar with piercing whistles, car honking, shouts and clapping.

Nick had come home.

She raced through the house and out the back door. Everyone had surrounded him. They all carried American flags. Cody stood crushed at his father's side, his grin idiotic. Nick shook hands as fast as he could, answering questions, receiving continual pats on the back. Friends Rosie hadn't seen for years appeared as if out of nowhere, hugging him long and hard. Someone with a trumpet started to play, "For He's a Jolly Good Fellow," and everyone sang.

Rosie stayed, mesmerized, on the back porch step,

watching Cody and Nick make their way through the lineup of well-wishers. An old high-school buddy of his, John Seballa, whispered something in his ear. Nick's dark head reared back. He laughed that deep rich laughter, just the way he used to when he teased Rosie, driving her to fever pitch, as a prelude to making love.

A sudden ache passed through her body—an ache so intense she gasped. Almost as if Nick had heard her, his head swiveled in her direction and he met her gaze. Emotion had turned his eyes a dazzling blue, but their enigmatic expression checked her impulse to run over to him.

And do what, Rosie?

CHAPTER EIGHT

ZACH ENTERED the building that housed the Chemistry Department and stood outside the door of the room where Rosie lectured, his body wired. Four days ago Barb had given him Rosie's message—simply "I need to talk to you." He had no idea what that meant, but he'd decided to stay away a whole week so there'd be no more excuses, no chance for her to tell him she needed time to help her husband adjust to being home.

He glanced at his watch. Almost two o'clock. One more minute and her class would be over. He'd been the nice guy long enough and relished the idea of catching her off guard.

This time the element of surprise is on my side, Rosie.

At precisely two, the class broke up and the students came pouring out of the amphitheater. Through the open door he could see her standing there in her stylish green suit, explaining something on the blackboard to a male student. Zach could only remember two female professors during his undergraduate studies at UCLA. If any of them had looked like Rosie, he would've found an excuse to hang around all day.

Nick Armstrong now had the privilege of being with

Rosie all day—every day—for the rest of his life. He'd earned that right....

Zach's body stiffened. How naïve he'd been to believe that Cody was Nick's only edge.

The man is partially disabled.

His impairment would bring out Rosie's nurturing instincts as nothing else could.

Another hurdle more daunting than Cody.

Zach waited behind the door until she came out, then followed her down the hall to her office. So far she hadn't seen him, but her sober expression convinced him she was anything but happy.

Have you even thought about me, Rosie?

She paused outside her office and searched in her bag for her keys. As soon as Zach saw their glint, he approached her and took them from her hand.

She looked up in surprise.

"Zach..." Her voice shook when she realized who it was.

The urge to take her in his arms was all-consuming, but they were in a public place. He put the key in the lock and opened the door, ushering them inside. To make certain they weren't disturbed, he shut it behind them just as quickly and locked it.

"Miss me?" he demanded before crushing her in his arms. "*Lord,* Rosie. One week—it's been a lifetime—"

He cupped her face in his hands and began devouring her mouth, reveling in the taste and feel of her. He'd dreamed of this moment on the sailboat, needed this physical release as much as he needed air to breathe.

Caught up in his own desire, he didn't realize that the elusive something that had made their Caribbean trip so magical wasn't there for Rosie.

Desperate to recapture it, he instinctively turned them around in the still dark room, moving her against the door, so he could drive home his need of her. But he got the distinct impression she wasn't with him, that instead, she was *allowing* him to love her. Nothing could have cooled his blood faster.

In an abrupt move, he tore himself away and switched on the light.

Zach had been a lifeguard throughout his late teens and into college. He'd pulled numerous drowning victims from the violent California surf, hoping that it wasn't too late, that he could resuscitate them.

Rosie's face reminded him of those faces. Victims in the throes of deep shock.

Her moist green eyes frantically searched his, begging for something.

What?

Forgiveness?

Oh, Lord. She was going to tell him she had to break off their engagement.

Her eyes—they held so much pain....

He stared down at her. "You said you had something to tell me." Zach didn't recognize his own voice.

The sound coming out of her reminded him of rushing waters.

"I do." She clasped her hands to her chest. He noted the absence of any ring on her finger, but that told him nothing. "So much, I hardly know where to begin."

He raked a sun-bronzed hand through his hair. "Just say it, Rosie."

"It isn't that simple. Please—sit down."

"I can't."

"Then I will."

She sank into the chair at her desk, a rigid figure, looking like she'd crack at the slightest vibration.

His hands had formed into fists. *Somebody had to say it.* "You've decided to stay with him."

"I haven't decided to do anything," she returned in a dull voice, sending *him* into euphoric shock.

"Thank God!"

In the next instant he'd caught her up in his arms once more and rocked her the way he would a child. She began to cry.

"What is it, sweetheart?" he whispered urgently against her wet cheek. "Talk to me. You can tell me anything."

"I know. That's what makes this so hard. You're so wonderful. I'd never want to hurt you, but my life is out of c-control. I don't know where I am or what I feel. She said I had to get in touch with my feelin—"

"She?"

"The counselor at Fort Douglas."

Zach frowned. Had Rosie already gone for professional help?

"She told me that no matter how much everything hurt, I needed to be honest with you, and with Nick. Otherwise I'd never be able to take charge of my life."

"She's right," Zach said fiercely. "Terrified as I am right now, I couldn't handle it if you lied to me."

"I won't, but some of the things you hear, you're not going to like."

"You're not going to like everything I have to say, either, sweetheart." With reluctance, he released her so they could both sit down. "Your husband has been my nemesis since the first day we met. His memory had such a stranglehold on you I wondered where I found the strength to keep on persisting.

"That cruise was it, Rosie. If you hadn't reached out to me with your whole heart and soul, I would have walked away and never looked back."

"Don't you think I realized that?" she blurted. "I loved you too much to let you go."

A shudder racked his body. "But not anymore? Is that what you need to tell me?" He had to ask the question.

She stared at him with wounded eyes. "My feelings for you haven't changed. How could they?" Her words reverberated in the tiny room.

"But something else has." He kept on relentlessly, because he sensed there was more to come. "Has he made demands? Does he want six months—a year—to try to put your marriage back together?"

That's what I would have demanded, Rosie. One year to make you fall in love with me all over again. No interference!

She was quiet too long. Her eyes refused to meet his. Suddenly she reached into her purse and handed him what looked like a letter.

Had she written down what she couldn't say?

Puzzled, he opened it, noticing immediately that it was a summons of some kind. Two names appeared. Nicholas Marchant Armstrong and Rosie Gardner Armstrong. It had been served yesterday. He turned to the next page.

It was a standard complaint for divorce brought by Nicholas Armstrong, plaintiff, against Rosie Armstrong, defendant, for alienation of affection due to a seven-year absence because of uncontrollable circumstances created by war.

The plaintiff wishes that minor child, Cody, aged 13, remain in the custody of his mother.

The plaintiff asks for full and liberal visitation rights which will require some travel time for minor child, as plaintiff will be residing outside Salt Lake County, but within the State of Utah.

The plaintiff stipulates that he will pay all insurance, medical and educational costs for said child throughout the duration of his lifetime.

The plaintiff further stipulates that an inheritance fund for said child has been established and will come due on said child's thirtieth birthday.

The plaintiff asks that any funds or investments accrued prior to his leaving for war, which were used to pay for the purchase of current home, be considered as partial alimony to the defendant. Any investments still outstanding are to be continued and used at the discretion of the defendant.

The plaintiff states that until such time as circumstances change and defendant remarries, a monthly alimony payment of 2500.00 will be deposited in defendant's checking account.

The plaintiff asks for no property since all purchases were made after he was MIA and considered dead.

Zach dropped the papers on the desk. His eyes closed tightly.

Nick Armstrong was amazing. Only a man who loved his wife more than himself would be willing to do this, to put her happiness first.

The man had expected to come home to a loving wife, a wife who still waited for him. Since that hadn't happened, he was trying to get out of their lives and make this as easy as possible on everyone. Zach admired him more than any man he'd ever known.

But one look at Rosie, and Zach could see the divorce summons had torn her into little pieces. Every word played on her guilt. Nick's gesture—though meant to give Rosie her freedom—had robbed her of all inherent joy. This was the reason she couldn't respond fully to him a few minutes ago.

What woman worth her salt could walk away from a marriage so fast, from a husband as remarkable as Nick Armstrong—a decorated war hero—without suffering the tortures of the damned?

He gazed at her through veiled lashes and answered his own question. *Only a woman who had fallen out of love.*

Zach had been so sure of her until Nick appeared on the scene. Now that he was back, Zach could sense her torment. *Who could blame her?* Certainly not Zach.

But her reaction to the summons changed the situation drastically. He stood up, surprising Rosie who'd been sitting there in a stuporlike trance.

Reaching for her hands, he drew her to her feet. "All right. About this divorce. How do you feel?"

She fought to keep back the tears. "Honestly?"

He nodded.

"I think it's horrible. All of it. I still love him and the memories we've shared. He's done nothing wrong!"

"I know," Zach murmured, hating to hear the truth. "This isn't a case of right or wrong. The man is trying to do the decent honorable thing so we can get married, but I can see you're not ready for that."

"I'm not."

Zach's heart plummeted. "Does Nick know you've been served yet?"

"H-he wasn't home when the officer came to the door. After his parents left for St. George yesterday morning, he and Cody decided to go camping with a bunch of Cody's friends and their parents. It's spring vacation. They haven't come home yet."

"That's good. Rosie?"

Lord. He couldn't believe what he was about to say.

"I think you need time to see if your marriage will work again. It's the last thing I want. But on the other hand, I couldn't marry you if you weren't totally in love with me. I'm going to bow out for a while."

"What?" The horror on her face told him how much she cared. She began shaking her head, as if in a daze. "Have I hurt you so badly?"

"No…but while I was out sailing, I had a lot of time to think."

"So that's where you were!"

He nodded. "Nick deserves a fighting chance to make you fall in love with him again. I want you to give him that chance."

His words had obviously baffled her. "But why?"

"Because I don't want to win if I can only have part of you. I'm a greedy man, Rosie. I want the whole damn thing. I want your love, free and clear. No regrets. No what-ifs."

She blinked. "I want that, too."

"All right. If you're agreed, then I'm going to put Mitch in charge of the company and move to Park City for the summer where I can train for the Tour de France."

"No, Zach!" she cried, rushing headlong into his arms. "There has to be another way."

"There is no other way, Rosie, and we both know it." *All I can do now is leave our fate to destiny and hope you love me enough.* "Three months, Rosie. That gives you and Nick enough time to decide if you're going to stay married."

She looked panicked. "But I can't bear to let you go! And…and it's not fair to you."

He seized on those words she'd thrown out like a lifeline. His response, though, was calm and measured. "If you haven't noticed, I'm a big boy. I can take care of myself. I'd be happier if I could be with you, but he was there first. If he hasn't ignited that old fire by the time the summer's over, then I'll know you're all mine."

She lifted her hands to his cheeks, her eyes tender and adoring. "You're so wonderful. I love you with all my heart, Zach. How will I stand it without you?"

You took the words right out of my mouth, Rosie.

"I'm counting on your not being able to stand it. Now, before I forget all my noble intentions, let's get out of here."

"Wait." She moistened her lips nervously. "If I'm really going to go through with this, then I should give you back your ring."

A wave of pain staggered Zach. "You're right. I'll follow you home. He knows it's sitting in your jewelry box. He'll never believe you're serious if you keep it there. When it's gone, he'll call off the divorce. That's what you want him to do."

That's what I want him to do. No pressure. Then you'll have a chance to find out you're in love with me, Rosie Armstrong. And the sooner you do that, the better.

"Hold me for a minute," she begged, burrowing into him. "I'm so frightened. What if you meet someone else in the meantime?"

"Do you honestly believe that could happen?"

Oh, Rosie. You don't have a clue about the depth of my feelings.

"Mom?"

Rosie jumped as Cody walked into the foyer from the

back of the house. "I—I didn't know you were home, honey. Did you have a good time?"

"The best!"

She frantically tried to brush the tears from her eyes. Zach had barely walked out the front door. Did Cody and Nick see him in passing?

"We saw Zach getting in his car."

There's your answer, Rosie.

"How come you're crying? Did you two have a fight?"

Oh, Cody. You're so transparent. You'd give anything to hear me tell you yes.

"No. But we did reach a decision about something. Come in the bedroom and I'll tell you."

She had no idea if Cody knew of Nick's intentions to divorce her, but decided that Nick wouldn't have burdened his son that way. At least not yet.

When they reached her room, she shut the door and asked Cody to sit on the bed with her. "Today Zach and I decided to break our engagement."

His shout of joy filled the room, as she'd known it would.

"I asked him to come in the house so I could give him back his ring."

"Then you're not going to marry him?"

Her body shivered in reaction. "No. Your father has come home. I want the three of us to be a family again." *I don't know if it's possible, but I'm going to give it a try for all our sakes. Including Zach's.*

"Oh, Mom!"

For the first time in two years she could honestly say her son sounded completely happy. Those were joyous sobs shaking his body.

"I can't wait till you tell Dad."

"W-where is your father?"

"I think he's still outside talking to Jeff's dad. We had so much fun, but it would've been neater if you'd come. All the guys' moms were there."

"I'm sorry about that, honey, but I had classes and I had to prepare my end-of-term grades."

"I know."

"I'll come with you next time."

He jumped up, too excited to keep still. "Can I tell Dad?"

"If you don't mind, Cody, that's something I need to tell your father myself, when we're alone."

"Tell me what?"

Rosie wheeled around in stunned surprise. Nick had walked in on them unannounced.

If anyone had told her that a week of eating lots of good food could drastically alter a person's appearance, she wouldn't have believed it. But Nick was living proof.

His face seemed fuller. She saw a luster to his hair, which was looking a little longer. In fact, she sensed a general improvement in his overall well-being. He'd picked up some sun on their trip to the mountains, erasing the sallowness of his skin when he'd first gotten off the plane.

Cody eyed both of them intently, then gave Rosie a significant look. A private message. "I'll put my gear away."

Just like that, she was back in her son's good graces.

"What was that all about?" Nick muttered as soon as Cody had disappeared out the door.

"If you're worried that I told him about the summons, I didn't say anything. I don't want a divorce."

"Since when?"

He rarely relied on sarcasm. It stunned her.

"Nick, we have to talk."

"I'm all ears."

She hated it when his voice took on that aloof wintry tone. Clearing her throat nervously, she said, "Cody mentioned you saw Zach leaving the house."

"That's right."

"I'd like to explain why he was here."

His dark brows furrowed. "I thought I made it clear that you and Zach can do whatever you want. It doesn't matter to me."

Nick, darling. Stop being so damn noble.

Her heart hammered, and she summoned her courage to ask, "Would it matter if I told you I gave him back his ring?"

He started emptying his pockets on the dresser they now shared. "Whose idea was that? Yours or Zach's?"

She'd expected any reaction except that. Linda had told her to tell the truth, no matter how much it might hurt the other person. But *she* seemed to be the only one getting hurt!

"Zach came back from California today and I showed him the divorce complaint. We both agreed that everything's happening way too fast. We've broken our engagement."

NICK STARED AT HER in silence. Poor Rosie. Guilt was eating her alive and Zach had had no choice but to go along with her wishes.

She'd gone on talking. "This idea of divorce is too premature, Nick."

He should have been elated that she didn't want the divorce, but he knew what was motivating her response. *Guilt. Pity.* And marriage with a wife who stayed out of guilt and pity was not his idea of happiness.

Nick grabbed some clean clothes and headed for the bathroom. Over his shoulder he said, "Let me grab a quick shower and then we'll talk."

The hurt look on her face crushed him, but he needed to get away from her before he listened to her pleas and called off the divorce. No, he *had* to continue with it to preserve his sanity and hers.

It didn't matter that she and Zach had ended their engagement. That didn't change the love the two of them shared. Nick knew damn well that if she stayed with him, she'd never be able to fully concentrate on their marriage when Zach was standing in the wings, just waiting for it to fail so he could claim her.

In a few swift strides Nick reached the bathroom and adjusted the taps until the spray was the right temperature. He tried to blot the grief from his mind and enjoy the luxury of a hot shower, something he'd been deprived of for so many years.

But then, there'd been so many things he'd missed. So many people—and one above all. *Oh, Rosie! How am I ever going to let you go?*

The way he figured it, going through with the divorce was, ironically enough, the only hope their marriage had. Because unless Rosie was free to choose—which meant free to choose *Zach* if she wanted—staying together would mean all the wrong things. Be for all the wrong reasons.

A half hour later he found her in the kitchen making hamburgers for dinner. Amazing what a shower and shave could do for a man. Every day he was feeling a little more normal. A little closer to his former life. If only the part with Rosie was right...

"Where's our son?"

Rosie paused in her task of slicing purple onions and turned to glance at him. "I wanted time to talk to you first, so I told him to go play basketball for a while." Nick felt her eyes travel over him. This evening she didn't seem to mind what she saw. Most likely the shock had worn off and she was starting to accept the fact that he was minus a hand.

"Those sweats look good on you, Nick."

"They're comfortable, too. Thanks for getting them for me."

"You're welcome."

"Does Cody know you've broken up with Zach?"

"Yes."

Biding his time, Nick opened the refrigerator to get a pint of milk. "I don't think I'll ever be able to get enough of this stuff." Her eyes rounded as he drank it without stopping to breathe, then tossed the empty carton into the wastebasket.

"I realize you're starving, so I've made you nachos." She pulled them out of the oven and set them on the kitchen table.

Nick didn't need a second invitation. He straddled the back of a chair and munched to his heart's content, watching her as she put the meat in the broiler. Then she sat down opposite him, her expression anxious.

"You haven't said anything, Nick. What are you thinking?"

"What a great cook you are."

She actually flushed, a small sign of the old Rosie. "I appreciate that, but you know what I'm talking about."

He eyed her narrowly. *This is going to hurt both of us, but it has to be this way.*

"I'm going through with the divorce, Rosie."

"You can't!" The blood all but drained from her face.

He reached for another cheese nacho. "It's only a piece of paper, Rosie, but it represents freedom for both of us. A chance for all concerned to start fresh."

"A fresh start for *you,* maybe!" she cried. "But what about Cody? He'll be in agony."

"He's no stranger to it."

She shoved herself away from the table. "How can you be so callous?"

"That's your word, Rosie. I prefer realistic."

"You've grown so...cold."

He finished off the last nacho. "Sometimes those bunkers got cold in the middle of the night."

A groan escaped her lips. "I'm sorry. I shouldn't have said that. Forgive me." She rushed over to the broiler to turn the hamburger patties.

Finish it now, Armstrong. You may not have the courage later. "Since you know I'm going ahead with the divorce, do you want me to move out? All you have to do is say the word."

Her back looked as rigid as a telephone pole. "Why don't we let Cody decide? Since you're the one filing, you might as well be the one to tell him."

"He's coming through the back door right now. I guess there's no time like the present."

"No, Nick..." she pleaded with him.

Rosie, Rosie. The pain has got to stop!

Cody proceeded into the kitchen cautiously, staring at the two of them, his eyes shiny with hope. "Is it all right?"

"Of course." Nick motioned for him to sit down. "There's something I have to say, and I want you to hear it, be part of the ultimate decision."

"Sure, Dad." Cody tossed his head to get the hair out of his eyes.

Nick sat forward and grasped his son's right hand. "Cody? Have you ever had someone do you a big favor?"

"Yeah. Jeff kept my aquarium clean and fed my fish while I went down to St. George for a few days."

"Fine. That's a good example. Now, how would you have felt if you'd learned that deep down, he hadn't wanted to do it, but he felt like he *had* to?"

He hunched his shoulders. "Bad."

"Why?"

"I guess because I don't want anyone doing me any favors unless they really want to."

"Exactly. Now I'm going ask you another question. It's important. Do you think your mom *really* wanted to return Zach's ring when they only got engaged three weeks ago?"

"Nick!"

"Remember what we were just talking about," he said, ignoring Rosie's cry.

Cody bent his head. "No," came the quiet reply. "She didn't...."

Nick squeezed his hand hard, then let it go. "Thanks for your honesty, son. Perhaps now you'll understand that I don't want anyone doing any favors for me, either."

At those words, Cody's head flew back. "Does that mean you and Mom are getting a divorce?"

Nick felt the crack in his son's voice clear to his bones.

"Yes. You'll be living with your mom, but you can visit me whenever it's all right with her."

I'm doing this for all of us, Cody. Trust me, son.

He heard another muffled sound from Rosie.

Nick thought there would be tears, but Cody sat there frozen.

"Your mother and I are good friends, Cody. That hasn't changed and it never will. The point is, we both love you more than life itself. That'll never change, either.

"I don't know how long the divorce will take, but

barring any complications, the attorney estimates six weeks. Under the circumstances, I can go on living here, just as we are, until it's final, which should be around the time your school lets out.

"Or I can live in that hotel by the university until my therapy's over, and then make a permanent move."

"Where?" Rosie asked, her tone brittle. When Nick looked over, she was clinging to the counter with both hands.

Cody darted a glance at his father. "Doesn't Mom know?"

"Know what?"

"You tell her, Cody."

"Dad's going to live in Heber."

"Heber?"

"It's not exactly a fait accompli, Rosie. I told you I wanted to live in the mountains. There were a couple of properties for sale in Heber. If you recall, when we were dating, we used to drive up there a lot and talk about retiring there one day."

"I remember. It's heavenly up there," she whispered, still sounding dazed.

It *was* heavenly. But at the time, he and Rosie had been concentrating so hard on each other they scarcely knew what was going on around them.

"One of the ranches for sale seemed the perfect size and it's got a great house on it. So I've put down earnest money. The old couple will be moving out by midsummer. But Cody and I want *you* to see it before I actually buy it."

"Yeah. It's really neat, Mom. We'll be able to

waterski up there with all my friends' families. We're going to have horses and a boat."

"You really meant it about leaving Salt Lake." Her voice was quiet. Haunted.

"That's right. I knew if I didn't at least put a hold on the place, someone else would. Of course, no decision's going to be made until you've seen it and approved."

Rosie didn't say anything. Just stood there looking shocked.

"So, Cody," Nick said, picking up where they'd left off, "in the meantime, shall I stay here or go to the hotel? What would make you happier in the long run?"

His head swerved to Rosie. "What do you want, Mom?"

Rosie looked on the verge of fainting. "As your father said, it's up to you, honey."

"Then I think you should move out, Dad. Jeff says you have a right to find a new girlfriend, too. Mom? Can we eat now? I'm hungry."

Oh, Cody. Somehow I was hoping you'd give me an argument. Now I have to follow through, which means this will be my last night under the same roof with you and your mother....

CHAPTER NINE

ROSIE AWOKE from her restless sleep with a jolt. Something had disturbed her. Probably a nightmare, but she couldn't remember it. The scene in the kitchen before dinner had been enough of a nightmare to last a lifetime.

Yet Cody and his father had consumed their hamburgers with enjoyment, not missing a bite as they bantered back and forth. You would never have known anything was wrong. Afterward, they'd helped her with the dishes, then left for the gym.

Rosie couldn't stand her own company, but was strangely reluctant to call Zach. Since they'd already said their painful goodbyes, she hated the idea of calling him and starting everything all over again—when she firmly believed that Nick hadn't meant what he said.

She couldn't imagine that he'd really go through with the divorce. Of course she couldn't stop him from moving out in the next few days, but she didn't think it'd be permanent. His pride and anger had gotten in the way. When he cooled off, he'd see that Cody needed him at home.

The fact that he was waiting for her to see the property in Heber before he bought it told her that he really didn't plan to end their marriage.

There was that noise again.

Occasionally Cody talked in his sleep. It didn't surprise her that tonight was one of those times. He'd acted so brave at the table, but she knew he was heartbroken over the turn of events.

How could you do it, Nick? How could you shatter our son's dreams like that?

She tried to fall back to sleep, then shot straight up in bed as the sounds grew louder.

Without wasting another second, she climbed out of bed and hurried out of the room to see what was wrong with Cody. But when she reached the hall, she realized the sounds were coming from the front of the house.

Nick!

He must have fallen asleep with the TV on. He insisted it was the only way he could relax; he usually dropped off sometime during the wee hours. She'd tried to persuade him to at least lie down in the guest bedroom, but he always refused, saying he preferred the couch.

She shut Cody's door, then walked quickly toward the living room. But with every step the sounds became clearer. First she'd hear groans, then a voice talking at a frantic pace.

When she entered the living room and saw that the TV was off, she knew the almost inhuman noises had to be coming from Nick.

In the moonlight spilling through the windows she could see her husband crouched on the floor, wearing only his track pants, his body glistening with sweat.

To her horror his head was moving back and forth

as if he were using it as a battering ram. He kept clawing at his injured arm with his right hand.

"Got to get these shackles off. Got to get out the doors, R.T. We need transportation. Got to hijack some kind of bus, going to need some weapons, need someone who speaks Arabic. Got to get out of here, R.T. Got to find out where we are. Here they come. Don't tell them anything, R.T. Oh, God. Don't let us die. Get us out of here. Please God, Please, God. Please, God. Please, God."

Rosie stood transfixed as Nick repeated the same litany over and over again. When she couldn't stand it any longer, she threw her body down next to his and gathered him in her arms.

Even when she held him against her, he continued the rocking motion. Despite his weight loss, he was in amazingly good shape. His strength terrified her because he was in a deep sleep and had no control over his movements.

"Nick…wake up, darling! It's Rosie. Wake up!"

She took an elbow in the jaw before she managed to roll him onto his back. Now she lay on top of him, using both hands to smooth the moisture from his face and forehead. His heart was racing; his breath came in pants.

"Wake up, Nick. You're dreaming. It's Rosie. Wake up, my love. Come on."

She began shaking his shoulders.

"Don't do it, don't do it, don't do it…" he cried, trying to cover his ear with his arm, flinching repeatedly as if someone was beating him. His motions had thrown her down hard on her side, but she clung to him, wrapping her arms around his head, so that he was butting her chest.

Rosie was terrified because nothing was working, nothing was bringing him out of it. Years ago, when Cody was in the hospital dangerously ill with croup, the only thing that had calmed him was her singing. She'd sat on the side of his hospital bed and sung nonstop to him all night long.

Out of sheer instinct, she began singing to her husband.

"'Away in a manger, no crib for a bed, the little Lord Jesus lay down his sweet head. The stars in the bright sky looked down where he lay, the little Lord Jesus asleep on the hay. Asleep, asleep. Asleep, asleep. Asleep…'"

Miraculously his agitation began to subside. The screams, the mutterings, faded.

Sending up a prayer of gratitude, she sang every Christmas carol she could think of until his body relaxed and he slept in her arms.

For the rest of the night Rosie kept a vigil over her husband. She didn't dare sleep in case his nightmares returned.

Around eight, she eased away from him and staggered to her feet. Every muscle in her body felt cramped. The throbbing in her jaw was bad enough to need a painkiller.

Nick lay stretched out on his side, looking peaceful. For a few moments she studied the familiar profile, the natural male grace of his long lean body. Throughout their marriage, she'd kissed every inch of it, thrilled to every inch of it. They'd shared every thought and dream. Now, seven years later, through no fault of their own, they shared something else.

She had no name for it.

There was no name for it.

Only Cynthia Ellis knew what Rosie was feeling right now because she must be living through the same kind of experience with R.T.

Rosie reached for the down comforter and carefully covered him, then tiptoed from the room to call R.T.'s wife.

"WELL, CODY? What do you think? The black Pathfinder or the green Land Rover? They're both good for four-wheeling, and both can pull a twenty-three-foot boat."

Nick already knew his choice, but he was curious to see if his son had the same taste in cars.

"I don't know, Dad. They're both awesome."

"You're right about that. Of course, we don't have to decide today."

Cody's face fell. "But, Dad, I thought we were going to drive it off the lot."

"First we have to make a choice. Then they have to get it ready and do all the paperwork. That doesn't give me much time to get to my therapy session. As it is, I'll have to drive the rental car back to Hertz and ask them to drop me off at one of the dealerships."

"Okay. Then I say we get the Land Rover. But only if you like it."

Nick grinned and gave Cody a hug. "Like father,

like son. The Rover was my choice, too." He liked the comfort of it and the way it handled on the road. "Let's see if they can work us a fast deal."

When Cody repeated Nick's remark to the car salesman, the man said, "Since your dad's a war hero, I'll cut you another couple of thousand off the factory price. Not only that, I'll have one of the guys in the garage take your rental car back for you."

That brought a smile to Cody's face.

Nick murmured something appropriate, but he wasn't so thrilled. Not that he didn't appreciate a few breaks once in a while. But in the five weeks since he'd come home, he'd been singled out every time he appeared in public. The TV spot on him had aired on the ten-o'clock news the night of the neighborhood welcome-home party. Now it seemed he was a minor celebrity.

People meant well, but he didn't think he would ever get used to the unsolicited attention. As for children, it stung every time he saw one hiding behind a mother's skirts, staring at his bad arm. You never knew what questions or comments would suddenly pour forth from their mouths. Adults weren't much different.

"Oh, man. This is a beaut, Dad!" Cody said a half hour later, his voice rising with excitement. "I can't wait to drive it." He'd opened all the windows and turned the car radio to the K-Bear station, acting like any other teenager—enthusiastic and slightly out of control.

Nick chuckled. He could remember telling his father

the same thing when he was the same age as Cody. "If your mom approves and the sale of that ranch goes through, we'll go up to the property and I'll teach you how to drive."

"I want to live with you, Dad," he said urgently.

What else is new?

"We've been over that ground before. You belong with your mother, but the arrangement we've worked out is good, isn't it?"

"Yeah. I guess. But it seems kind of dumb. Mom and me alone in the house, and you over at the hotel."

"That was the best decision, to give your mom her privacy."

"But Zach never comes over!"

"Maybe that's because you haven't tried hard enough to make him feel welcome." The thought horrified him clear through—this other man, welcome in Rosie's house—but Nick said the words, anyway, knowing she had a right to the life and the man, she'd chosen.

"I don't care anymore."

Cody, boy. If only you could hear yourself.

"Then you need to tell your mother it's okay, so she'll start letting him come over."

Cody looked genuinely troubled. "Do you really think I'm the reason he stays away?"

Nick nodded. "Now that you know, it would be cruel not to help your mom."

Cody thought about it for a minute. "Okay. I'll talk to her when I get home. Can I come over tonight?"

"I'm afraid not, son. I'm getting together with R.T.

But tomorrow, after your class, I'll take you and Jeff up to Heber with me. We'll test this baby out."

"Cool!"

The therapy lasted until six; Cody read magazines in the waiting room while Nick worked with the therapist. It was almost six-thirty by the time they got to the house, and Nick wasn't surprised that Rosie came down the front porch steps as soon as she saw them pull into the driveway.

"Nick? Don't drive off. I have to talk to you!" she called.

Cody jumped down and ran toward her, regaling her with a blow-by-blow account of the afternoon's activities. His rapture over the new car was evident in the running commentary he kept up.

Though she appeared to be listening to their son, Nick could tell there was something vital on her mind. She started toward the Rover, determination in every step.

When she reached the driver's side, she told Cody to go inside and get washed up for dinner.

Cody waved. "See you tomorrow, Dad."

Nick waved back, then turned in Rosie's direction.

Lord, what a sight. The sunset bathed her in golden light. It was the first time since he'd come back from the war that he'd seen her hair loose like she used to wear it. The strands glistened like cornsilk and fell halfway down her slender back.

He knew what she looked like—what she *felt* like— under that navy-trimmed white suit she was wearing. He knew every singing line and curve. An ache passed through his body. It was so intense he had to stifle a groan.

"How are you, Rosie?"

Her chin lifted defiantly. "Not good."

He frowned. "What's wrong?"

Those gorgeous angry green eyes looked as if they might shoot sparks at any minute. "A warrant was just served on me for my arrest!"

The situation wasn't funny, but Nick fought not to smile. "Why?"

"Because I didn't respond to the summons."

"Why didn't you?"

"You know why, Nick Armstrong."

The blood pounded in his ears. *Oh, Rosie, sweetheart. You're sounding more and more like your old self. If only you wanted me the way I want you...*

"Because I honestly didn't think you'd go through with the divorce. Obviously I was wrong." Her voice trembled, although he knew she was doing her best to cover it up.

"All you have to do is get an attorney of your own, and you won't have anything to worry about. I'm paying the court costs, remember."

"You can be as smug as you want," she snapped. "But you won't feel the same way when I slap a countersuit against you to stop the divorce."

His heart leapt. "On what grounds?"

"Temporary insanity due to your long imprisonment."

Nick threw back his head and laughed till his ribs hurt. He couldn't help it. She was so adorable. *Dear God. How he loved her.*

"You think I won't do it?"

By now her eyes were smoldering. Her fury was something to behold.

"That would require a psychiatric evaluation."

"That's right. You have special needs and require special help."

All I need is to spend the rest of my nights in bed with you, my beloved. But...it's never going to happen.

"Dammit, Nick. Look at me when I'm talking to you!"

"I *am* looking." *I can't look anywhere else. That's my problem. That's why I need to get a divorce as soon as possible. You and Zach need it, too!*

"I'm serious. I want you to get some counseling and support. The last thing you should be thinking about is a divorce."

"I had no idea you felt this strongly on the subject. May I ask what brought it on?"

"Isn't the fact that you were a POW reason enough?" she fired back, but he had the distinct impression there was something else behind her vehemence.

"Much as I'd love to explore this more thoroughly with you, I have other plans tonight and I'm afraid I'm already late.

"Rosie," he said on a more sober note, "tomorrow I'm planning to drive Cody up to Heber after school for a few hours. If you want, we'll swing by your office and take you with us so you can see where I have hopes of living. He's been anxious for you to come, so I can make a decision about buying the place."

"I wish I could, but I have a chemistry lab on Tuesday afternoons."

"How long does it last?"

"Till five."

"We can wait until then to go. We could have dinner at the Wagon Wheel. That'll give Cody time to get his homework done. Think about it. Tomorrow he can tell me what you decide. Good night."

Her face closed up, and he couldn't tell what she was thinking. "Good night."

All the way back to the hotel, Nick reflected on the subtle changes in his wife since he'd arrived at Hill. From shock and a distanced pity to...what? Intensity, unselfishness, determination. Just now she'd seemed more like the Rosie he'd left behind. But he understood all too well that it was because she felt sorry for him and didn't want to hurt him.

I can't hang on to you knowing deep down that you're in love with Zach, Rosie. I can't!

Nick spotted R.T. in the lobby talking to one of the clerks at the reception desk. Even from this distance, he could see that his friend seemed to be putting on weight as fast as he was.

"Rutherford Topham, I presume? My, my, what civilization has wrought. Chinos and a polo shirt, no less."

R.T. turned around, a wry smile lifting the corner of his mouth. *What a wonder was a woman's love.* Nick hardly recognized the guy.

"Sergeant Armstrong, *sir.*"

Nick's ears picked up the subtle tap-tap of R.T.'s

knuckles on the counter. He was telling Nick the denim shirt and jeans looked "awesome," one of Cody's favorite words.

Chuckling, Nick tapped out a response that said, *You should see me in the sweats Rosie bought. Centerfold stuff.*

R.T. tapped, *We're attracting attention.*

It's my bad arm, Nick tapped back.

I don't think so. The clerk hasn't been able to look at anything but my glass eye since I came in. See? He's still watching.

At least you didn't have a little girl scream that there was a monster with no hand running loose in the grocery store.

I need to talk to you. Let's get out of here.

Amen. Nick gave one more emphatic tap and they headed across the foyer to the guest parking lot.

R.T. whistled as they climbed into Nick's new Land Rover.

Both of them already knew where they wanted to go. The choice had been made years ago. Five minutes later they'd pulled into Hires Drive-In on Seventh East and gave their order: two frosted root beers, two hamburgers and two cartons of french-fried onion rings.

"Where's Cynthia tonight?"

"She's staying at my aunt's till I pick her up later."

"I don't have to ask you how it's going."

R.T. blushed furiously.

"Come on, now. How long did it take her to make you her husband again?"

"That's classified...sir."

"That fast, huh?" Nick grinned.

"She wants a baby."

"Did you tell her you're going to have a whole football team, and that the first one—boy or girl—is going to be named after me?"

"Yeah. I did. She's planning on it." Suddenly he was sobbing. "I just can't believe she loves me. I mean, look at me. Old one-eye."

"Old one-eye has all the parts that count. And you've got both your hands. You know how important that is, if you follow my meaning."

R.T. sniffed hard. "One hand gets the job done, Sergeant."

Nick sucked in his breath. "I wouldn't know."

"Why the hell not? You had your chance the other night."

A tap on the car window announced that their meal had arrived. Nick paid the waitress, then distributed the food.

"What are you talking about?" he demanded when they were alone again.

"You mean, *who.* Rosie's been down to our place a couple of times already."

Nick almost dropped his mug in surprise.

"How come you're divorcing her, Sarge?"

"She can't marry Zach Wilde if I don't do the honorable thing."

"She's not engaged anymore."

"A mere technicality, Watson."

"I'm not so sure. Perhaps you ought to know that a

couple of weeks back, while you were putting on one of your more colorful productions of the late, late show, as Cyn calls them, your wife wrestled you to the ground and held on to you for dear life until morning."

R.T.'s words hit him like a boulder dropping from a mountain. His appetite ceased to exist. "I don't believe you."

"Did you ever ask her about that big purple bruise on her jaw?"

His body went rigid. "She said she ran into a cupboard door."

"Well, for what it's worth, that cupboard did enough blabbing to provide a carbon copy of one of *my* nights. Just thought you'd like to be informed."

"She held me all night?"

How could that have happened and you didn't know about it, Armstrong?

"I guess she sang to you, too. That's when you calmed down. Cyn's going to try it on me next time. The point I'm attempting to make is, what's she doing holding you when she's got a perfectly good fiancé ready to take her off your hands?"

"Hand, R.T., hand."

"You know what I mean, Sarge."

Is that why you're fighting me on the divorce, Rosie? Because the mother in you has bonded with the terrified child in me?

"Did it ever occur to you she might've wanted an excuse to hold you?"

"No."

Rosie had always felt sorry if an ant got crushed. He could just imagine how sorry she'd feel after witnessing his madman performance.

"I know what you're thinking, Sarge, but it isn't that way. For one thing, Cyn said that Rosie was so happy to finally connect with you she practically went to pieces for a while. According to my wife, Rosie said some stuff that kind of puts a different slant on things."

"I don't want to hear it."

"Well, you're going to," R.T. persisted doggedly. "Rosie told Cyn that she'd been cheated out of seven years with you, and now she's jealous of me because I know things about you that *she* doesn't know. When you had that bad night, she felt like she was right there in that cell with you, sharing it. She said it made her feel close to you again, like she used to feel before the war when she knew things about you nobody else did. She said—and this is a quote—'It was like I was given a little present, one I'll treasure forever.'"

She said that?

Nick couldn't talk, couldn't think.

"Sure as hell doesn't sound like pity to me. Sure as hell doesn't sound like Zach Wilde could've squeezed his way in between you two." After a long pause, R.T. muttered, "She said something else, but I guess you don't want to hear that, either."

"Go ahead," Nick half grunted.

"Is that an order, *sir?*"

"What do you think?"

"Just checking. Well, according to Cyn, Rosie's terrified you're going to divorce her and share those seven lost years with some blond bimbo who's only out for your body and won't connect with you on any other level."

Nick's mouth quirked, despite his pain.

"She has one more secret fear."

"Go on."

"Just checking to see if you're still with me. What Cyn says is that Rosie's afraid you'll find the bimbo's, uh, performance better than hers. Apparently she's nervous about being able to make all the right moves after seven years of abstinence. She's afraid you're dying to experiment now, and Zach has given you the excuse you've been looking for."

Quiet reigned.

"Could she be right, Sarge? Have you been holding out on me all this time?"

More quiet.

"I wasn't supposed to tell you all that. It was top secret. Classified. You never heard it from me."

"I never heard it from you," Nick repeated.

R.T. turned his head and stared at him. "What's eating you?"

"She's been in love with another man for two years."

"Correction. She's been *seeing* another man for two years and couldn't commit to him until the eleventh hour. And we know why, don't we, Sarge? Because she was in love with another man for seven years before that."

Nick gritted his teeth. "She's in love with Zach now!"

"You were there first, Sarge. She still loves you, yet you're practically throwing her at him."

"Because Zach's the man she wants to marry."

"Maybe. Maybe not. All I know is, you're not giving this thing half a chance. If I thought for one minute that Cyn was hanging on to me out of pity, I'd be long gone, so I can understand your reasoning. But I'll tell you, what Cyn heard coming out of Rosie's mouth the other night—that wasn't pity or anything close to it."

Nick groaned. "You think I don't want to believe you?"

"I think maybe you ought to visit a shrink at the Veterans' Hospital."

"Rosie told me the same thing earlier today."

"Maybe you ought to take her advice."

"Maybe. But it won't solve a damn thing if in the end she'd still rather be Mrs. Zach Wilde."

"Excuse me, sir, but you don't sound like the same man who kept me alive all those years and wouldn't let me give up!"

"That man died the morning we flew into Hill, R.T."

"CODY?"

It was a couple of hours since Nick had dropped Cody off. They'd finished supper, and Cody had settled down to his homework at the kitchen table.

"Yeah, Mom?"

Rosie rushed through the kitchen and grabbed her purse. "While you finish your math, I've got to run to the drugstore."

"If you're meeting Zach there, why don't you just tell him to come over to our house, instead?"

Rosie came to a complete standstill and turned around. She'd never imagined the day she'd hear something like that from Cody.

"What makes you think I'm meeting Zach?"

"Well, aren't you?"

Rosie expelled a deep sigh. "No. But I was going to phone him."

"Then phone him from here."

"Cody, I know you don't like him. I've tried not to bring him around, because the last thing I've wanted to do is upset you."

"I know. I've been a jerk."

She blinked. "Does your father have something to do with this complete turnaround?"

His guilty face spoke volumes. "Yeah. But Dad's right. I've been really mean to you. I'm sorry, Mom. I love you." Crying, he got up from the table to hug her.

She wrapped her arms around him and held him tight. "I love you, too, honey."

"If you want to marry Zach, it's okay. I'll be nice to him. I promise. Now that Dad's home, it doesn't matter anymore. Like Dad said, you couldn't help loving another man. He says it's natural for you to want to get married. He said that you and he were really happy once, more than other people, and that's why you want to try it again."

We were happy, Cody. Happier than you could possibly comprehend.

"What else did he say?" she prodded quietly, shaken by everything she was hearing.

"While we were waiting for him to start his therapy, he said that you're not getting any younger and you probably want to have a baby with Zach right away 'cause that's what real joy is all about. And I'll be its brother and baby-sit and teach it things—you know, stuff like that."

Nick...

"Dad asked me about the saxophone in my closet. I told him Zach was a really good musician, that he'd bought it for me and had tried to teach me to play it. Dad got really mad when he found out I wouldn't take Zach up on those lessons. He says he would've given anything to be blessed with musical talent and thinks I'm lucky to have someone like Zach to teach me."

Rosie eased herself away from Cody so he couldn't tell how badly she was shaking.

He wiped his eyes on his arm. "Maybe if Zach's not too mad at me, he'll start teaching me after you get married. What do you think?"

I don't know what I think, Cody. I don't know anything anymore.

"Oh, honey, I love and admire you more than ever for telling me all these things! And as long as you've been this honest with me, I'm going to be honest back.

"I haven't seen Zach for a while and I need to talk to him. If he's home, I'm driving over to his condo. You have the phone number. If I'm going to be late, I'll call you. All right?"

He nodded. "If you're worried, Dad can always come over."

"Not tonight, I'm afraid. I think he had a— I think he had other plans."

"Yeah. He and R.T. are hanging out."

Nick's with R.T., not another woman. It shouldn't matter to you one way or the other, Rosie Armstrong, but somehow it does.

"They need time together," she murmured.

"I know. Dad's crazy about R.T. They talk on the phone every night now."

Rosie had imagined as much. "R.T. feels very close to your father."

"R.T. and Cyn want to move up to Heber, too. He's thinking of buying that other property for sale, the one next to ours, so he and Dad can ranch together."

"I—I didn't know that." She reached blindly for the back-door handle.

"I just found that out when Dad was driving me home. They're even talking about writing a book about their experience. Cyn does word processing, and she'll help them get the book ready to send to a publishing company. Dad said that while they were in prison they kind of wrote it in their minds. They're even thinking of going around the country someday to talk to other vets who've been disabled, to try to help them. Isn't that neat?"

"It is, Cody, and it sounds just like your father. He's a fantastic human being."

"Yeah. I just wish that you and he—" Cody stopped midsentence. "Oh, forget it," he mumbled before running out of the kitchen.

CHAPTER TEN

"ZACH?"

"*Rosie!* It's lucky you caught me before I left for Park City. I've been hoping against hope to hear from you. I know I told you I'd keep strictly away, but now that I hear your voice, I can't take this separation any longer. I'm coming to get you, wherever you are."

"I'm downstairs in the foyer of your condo."

She heard his gasp. "You wouldn't tease me…"

"No, Zach. I'm here. I need to talk to you."

"Whenever you get that tone in your voice, I know it's serious. I'll give you the code to the inner door so you can come up."

"I'll be right there," she assured him.

Zach was waiting for her the second the elevator doors opened to the fourth-floor foyer. He was in his blue sweats—he must have just come back from cycling. It reminded her of the first time she'd met him. He'd looked like a Norse god then, too.

"Come here," he murmured huskily, pulling her across the hall to his apartment. He shoved the door closed, then picked her up in his arms and carried her to the couch.

When she was nestled in his lap, he covered her mouth with smothering force. Rosie let go of a long sigh and kissed him back, deeply, fully. She needed to blot out the world, to experience the rapture she'd felt in his arms during their cruise, when she'd begged him to ask her one more time to marry him.

"I don't care why you're here or what you have to say. All I know at this moment is that I want you," he whispered, raining kisses on her face, her hair. "I want you so much, it's agony. Come to bed with me tonight. I can't wait any longer."

"In six weeks, maybe less, my divorce will be final," she murmured against his lips. "We can fly to Las Vegas and be married, then honeymoon anywhere you say for as long as you want. How's that sound?"

His body stilled, then he gently removed her from his lap and stood up, raking a hand through his dark blond hair. "I thought the divorce was called off."

She averted her eyes, stirring restlessly. "I thought Nick would call it off when I told him I wanted to try and make our marriage work. But he said he didn't want me to do him any favors."

"When did this conversation take place?"

Oh, Rosie. You're going to hurt him again.

"The night I gave you back the ring. He moved to a hotel after that."

Zach's face went ashen. "And it took you this long to tell me?"

His voice grated, bringing her to her feet.

She wrung her hands unconsciously. "Zach… I

thought he was bluffing. I couldn't believe he really meant to go ahead with the divorce, that he'd disappoint Cody like that. So I waited before saying anything to you. Surely you can understand."

He stood there unmoving, totally unapproachable. She'd never seen Zach like this. It frightened her.

"Tell me what he did that's suddenly convinced you he means business."

"I didn't respond to the first summons. This morning I was served a second. Apparently I owe a fine to the court. Nick is dead serious about this, so I had to retain an attorney today. Mr. Reynolds informed me that because of the unusual nature of the grounds, the divorce should go through quickly."

"So nothing's been resolved."

"Of course it has," she protested. "We can go ahead and make our wedding plans."

"What about the three-month waiting period we agreed on?"

"Nick changed all that when he chose to divorce me!" No matter how hard she tried, she couldn't disguise the tremor in her voice.

Something about his remote demeanor made her heart sink. "Zach, why are you being like this?"

He lifted his head, staring at her as if he didn't know her. "Why do I get the feeling this all sounds too easy?"

"Maybe because I've made you wait such a long time, you're looking for complications where there aren't any. Would it help if I told you that Cody gave me his permission to marry you? He told me tonight..."

Zach's lips thinned to an angry white line. "Then we have your husband to thank for that miraculous change of heart."

"Don't be this way, Zach," she pleaded. "Of course Nick has a huge influence on Cody's behavior these days."

"So if I were to move in with you before the wedding, Cody wouldn't mind?"

Her eyes closed tightly. Zach wanted the ultimate proof that she loved him. If she put him off again after all they'd been through…

"Does this mean you won't move to Park City, after all?"

Zach gave a deep agonizing groan. "Sweetheart? Do you honestly think I'd go anywhere if I thought we could be together from tonight on?"

Her mouth went dry. "Y-you want to move in with me tonight?"

"Well…" His body relaxed and she saw the ghost of a smile soften his stern expression. "Not everything in the condo. How about just me for starters? To give Cody a chance to get used to having me around the house. Every day we'll move a little more of my stuff over, so he hardly notices."

"I—I hope you understand that I haven't changed my mind about making love before marriage."

His mouth quirked. "If anyone knows about that, *I* do. But there's no law that says we can't hold each other all night long, is there?"

A picture of Nick thrashing about in her arms flashed into her mind, haunting her with its clarity and poignancy. That spot on her jaw was still tender, but a little makeup had concealed the worst of the bruise.

"*Rosie*. I asked you a question."

Her head came up sharply. "I know. Of course we can hold each other at night. I was just thinking I should go home before you do—to prepare Cody."

He studied her through shuttered lids. "That's probably the best idea. I need to get a few things together and lock up here. But before I do anything else, there's something I want to give you."

He pulled the engagement ring from his pocket. "Hold up your left hand, sweetheart. I'm putting this back on your finger where it belongs."

She stared at the exquisite two-carat, princess-cut diamond. She simply couldn't hurt him again. If she showed any hesitation, any at all, Nick would notice it immediately. He'd—

No. Not Nick. Zach!

"Until the divorce is final, I can't legally wear your ring," she began in a low voice. "But if you want to give it to me when we get home, I'll wear it on a chain around my neck."

A satisfied gleam entered his eyes. He repocketed the ring and reached for her again. "Tonight, Rosie, you've made me the happiest man alive."

THE NEXT AFTERNOON, Nick was just getting ready to leave his hotel room and drive over to the house to get Cody when he heard his son knocking on the door, calling out to him in an urgent voice.

He crossed the room in a few swift strides and let him in, then gave him a bear hug. "Where's Jeff?"

"He had to go cut his grandma's lawn."

"So how come you didn't wait for me at home?"

"Because there's been a change in plans."

His spirits plummeted. Rosie had probably decided not to go with them.

"That's okay. Your mom can join us another time."

"She and Zach are going to meet us at the Wagon Wheel around six."

Zach?

Nick gazed at his son. "You must have done a great job of patching things up with your mom where Zach is concerned."

"Yeah. Everything's fine. He even slept over last night."

Nick felt as if a grenade had just blown up his gut.

"Excuse me a minute, Cody. I think I left my wallet in the other room. Why don't you go out and wait for me in the car? It's not locked."

"Okay, Dad."

Nick raced to the bathroom in time to lose his lunch. R.T. had warned him about precipitating events too quickly.

"Dad?" Cody murmured cautiously, opening the bathroom door a crack.

"I thought I told you to go outside."

"You looked sick. I didn't want to leave you. It's 'cause of what I said, huh? About Zach. 'Cause you love mom."

His son was too astute for his own good. "Don't worry about it." He put the cap back on the toothpaste and left the bathroom, his arm around Cody. "Thanks for always being there for me, bud. I love you."

"Love you, too, Dad."

Nick suddenly needed to get away. On impulse he asked, "How would you like to sleep under the stars tonight?"

"Could we?"

"I don't see why not. The people selling the ranch told me I can have the run of the place. There's a beautiful meadow over by the stream. We can put our sleeping bags there. First thing in the morning, I'll get you back down in time for school."

"That'll be awesome. But, Dad, you don't have a sleeping bag, and mine's kind of wimpy."

"On the way out of town we'll stop at a sporting-goods store and pick up a couple. In fact, we'll buy a bunch of camping things while we're at it."

"Oh, man, I need a lot of stuff. Can we get one of those flashlight lanterns?"

"Sure," Nick replied, eager to grant his son his slightest wish. Especially after what he'd learned tonight. It was going to be just the two of them....

Forty-five minutes later, they were loading gear into the Rover. "Wow! Dad, I think we bought out the whole store."

"Looks that way, doesn't it? When you camp with me, you do it right. Let's head over to the grocery store and load the cooler. Then we'll take off for the canyon."

With Cody discussing the instructions for their new

Coleman lantern and stove, time passed quickly, and they arrived at the Wagon Wheel before Rosie.

"Heck. Mom's not here yet."

"While we're waiting, let's sit on the grass over there and I'll show you how to play cards. We'll start with twenty-one."

"Mom doesn't like card games."

"I suspect your mom doesn't want you to know how good she used to be at twenty-one and five-card stud. Of course, she could never beat me, but she came close a couple of times."

"Mom?"

"Your mom was one exciting woman, Cody."

He'd loved their midnight poker games after the baby was down for the night. She'd lose her concentration and he'd wipe her out of all her money. Then she'd have to divvy up whatever she was wearing. And then…

On a sharp intake of breath, Nick pulled the pack of cards he'd bought out of his shirt pocket. After placing one of the lantern boxes between them for a table, he started shuffling.

"Cool, Dad. How'd you learn to do that with one hand?"

"Have you ever heard the expression 'Necessity is the mother of invention'?"

"Yeah." They grinned at each other.

"All right. I'm going to deal each of us a card facedown, and one faceup. You want both cards to add up to twenty-one, or as close to it as possible, but you don't want to go over. Take a peek at your bottom card and decide if you want another card, or if you want to stay as is. If you want a card, say, 'Hit me.'"

Cody had a quick mind. It didn't take him long to catch on and start trying to outsmart his old man. They must have played at least fifteen hands before a shadow fell over them. It was Rosie. He'd know her perfume anywhere.

"What are you two doing?" Her voice sounded half-amused, half-exasperated.

He turned his head, taking in the gold-and-blue vision that blinded him to everything else. "Nothing you and I haven't done on innumerable occasions. Of course the stakes were a little different then," Nick added before he could catch himself.

A becoming flush filled her cheeks. *She remembers.*

Cody was still figuring his numbers and could hardly stop long enough to greet his mother.

"D-do you want to eat first?" She seemed to have trouble meeting his gaze.

Rosie, sweetheart…you're acting just like you did when we first met. All breathless and nervous. Why?

"It's getting darker. Maybe you'd better follow me and Cody to the property while we can still see."

She nodded jerkily, then walked back to the Passat parked three cars down. Nick couldn't stop staring at her. That was when he unexpectedly met Zach Wilde's cool gray eyes. The other man had been watching him, sizing him up.

Nick nodded in acknowledgment. Zach reciprocated.

Because of blindfolds and the darkness of the underground bunkers, he never saw his enemy in Iraq.

Coming face-to-face with the enemy in Heber, Utah—as benign a setting as anywhere in the world—was a whole new experience.

"We'll continue our game before bed, Cody," he announced, then turned on the ignition.

"Okay, but let's hurry. This is a lot more fun than video games."

"Now you're showing some real maturity."

Five minutes later they'd left the small town and were driving along a country lane toward the snow-capped mountains to the west. Reaching elevations of eleven thousand feet, they towered majestically over the Swiss-like landscape of the lower hillsides.

"Ah, Cody, this is the life. Everything in this valley is so green and fresh. Smell that air."

His son made a face. "Yeah. Manure. Someone's been fertilizing."

Nick threw back his head and laughed.

Every now and then he glanced at the rearview mirror. Zach maintained several car lengths' distance.

"We're here!"

"We are."

Pulling to the side of the road, he turned off the engine and jumped out of the Rover. He had decided to wear the black T-shirt and Levi's jacket Rosie had picked out for him the other day to let her know he appreciated her doing some shopping for him.

Not pausing in his stride, he headed for the Passat and walked right up to the driver's side as Zach levered himself from the car. Cody had joined Rosie, who stood nearby, looking anxious.

Nick could tell at a glance that he and Zach were the same height. This close, he was forced to admit Rosie had found herself a good-looking man.

"Hello, Zach. I've wanted to meet you for some time. From all I've heard, you've been wonderful to Cody. I appreciate everything you've done for him." He extended his right hand.

Zach gave it a firm shake. "Nick. It's an honor to meet you. Congratulations on surviving an ordeal few men will ever have to go through. Welcome home."

He nodded. "It's good to be home." His gaze switched to Rosie. "If you'll look to the west over here—" he gestured "—that Swiss-style chalet and barn, all the property going to the foothills, is going to be my ranch in a month or so, but only if you like it and approve of the whole idea."

Her voice sounded faraway when she said, "It's beautiful, Nick. There isn't anything not to like. How about you, Cody?"

"I love it up here, Mom, and it's not that far from home."

"No, you're right. Of course I approve."

"I'm glad." Nick managed to find the words, then once again addressed Zach. "The property due south, with the ranchstyle house is still for sale. My friend, R.T., and his wife, would like to move up here, too. We plan to ranch the land together, and I think we can make a go of it."

"I don't doubt it," Zach replied. "I've lived near the ocean most of my life and it's a part of me, but I have to admit it's beautiful up here. If I'd been in prison as long as you, I'd head for the mountains, too. Being in the outdoors makes all the difference."

"Cody told me you're quite the cyclist, which means you're outdoors a lot."

"I'm not the nine-to-five office type, either."

Nick nodded, then looked around at the pink-frosted peaks. "I dreamed about retiring to this place long before I went to war. If I do live here, Cody will be spending a lot of time with me.

"As I told Rosie, since you're going to be the other man in my son's life, I want us to be able to communicate so that we all get along and do what's best for him."

"I couldn't agree more."

The man's sincere. I can't fault your choice, Rosie.

"You'll be joining us for dinner at the Wagon Wheel, Nick?"

"Thanks, but no. Maybe another time."

"Yeah," Cody piped up. "Dad and I decided to camp out tonight."

Rosie seemed astounded. "Where?"

"Here, on the property."

"But, Cody, you have school in the morning."

"It's all right, Rosie," Nick intervened. "I'll have him down in time. Tonight we're going to count stars and tell Big Foot stories."

"Do you have anything to eat?" she blurted, her

troubled gaze passing from Cody to Nick. *Worried about me, sweetheart? Won't the mother in you let go?*

"We've got everything, Mom. T-bone steaks, hash browns, alligator jaws."

"Alligator jaws? Those pastries with the whipped cream inside? I didn't think anyone made them anymore. Nick, those were your very favorite snacks after school. I can remember the filling getting all over your—" She stopped abruptly.

Another memory, Rosie. We share so many it's going to be hard not to be haunted by them.

"Are you going to be warm enough?" She recovered in time to ask a question on a completely different subject.

"We bought all new gear," Cody said. "Do you want to see it?"

"I think Zach and your mom are anxious to go back to town for dinner. As for us, bud, we've got a camp to set up before we get lost in our own cow pasture."

Cody seemed to find the remark funny and laughed. Rosie's expression remained unaccountably sober.

"Are you all right about this, Rosie? If you'd prefer that I take Cody home, I will."

"N-no," she stammered. "It's fine." Her gaze fused with his. "Just take good care of yourselves."

Are you worried about my having another nightmare? Afraid Cody will see it?

"Cody and I will watch over each other," he reassured her. "Zach, it was nice meeting you."

"My pleasure." They shook hands.

"Let's go, son. See you two later." He nodded to Rosie, then turned and headed for the Rover.

Cody followed suit and jumped into the car. Nick started the engine and drove past the chalet, forcing himself not to look through the rearview mirror.

Don't think about them. Just don't think.

He gave two brief honks to let the Olsons know they were there. The houselights blinked twice in response.

"Hey, is that the secret code you worked out with them?"

"That's right."

"I want to learn Morse code."

"I'll give you a couple of lessons tonight, and you can practice."

"This is so awesome. I wish Mom—" He stopped himself, embarrassed.

"So do I, son. But I'm afraid it's going to be just you and me from here on out."

ROSIE GOT BACK in the Passat, trying not to stare at the Land Rover driving off through the meadow.

"I've hated his guts since the day you first told me you had a husband named Nick who died in the war. When you phoned me and said he was coming home, I prayed his transport plane would crash. Now I wish to God I'd never met him."

She shivered at the vehemence in his tone. "I'm sorry, Zach."

"Rosie, let's go back to Salt Lake for dinner."

"I—I was just going to suggest it."

"Why don't we pick up some Chinese and a video? We'll spend a relaxing, low-key evening, since we've got the house to ourselves."

"That sounds lovely."

He reached for her hand. She clung to his, even when he had to shift gears, and tried hard not to think about anything. What she really wanted was to attain that glorious state of oblivion where there was no hurt, no pain, no guilt. Just *nothing*.

"Hey, sleepyhead. We're home."

"So fast?" Rosie lifted her head to look around. "I can't believe I passed out on you like that."

"I can. You've been under a lot of stress."

He leaned over to caress her hair. "You go on in and I'll run over to Charlie Chow's. Any movie preferences?"

"Something happy."

He came around to her side of the car and helped her out. "I'll see what I can come up with." After giving her a swift hard kiss on the mouth, he left.

Rosie hurried into the house and locked the door, relieved that he hadn't insisted she go with him. This was one time she couldn't burden Zach. Her emotions were in such a chaotic state that she couldn't explain them to herself, let alone to him.

Why wasn't she jumping up and down with excitement at finding herself truly alone with Zach—her husband-to-be? It didn't make sense. They'd been given a whole night of privacy, to talk without interruption, to hold each other, to make definite plans for the future.

Shaking her head as if to ward off the guilt, she

made her way to the bathroom to freshen up and replace the clothes she'd worn to work with her quilted robe and slippers.

As she walked toward the living room, it struck her as odd that the house felt so empty. Heavens, she'd been alone many times. Cody often slept over with friends or spent a few nights in St. George with his grandparents.

Why did the emptiness seem different tonight?

You know why, Rosie. Because you're feeling lonely. Because Cody's not in any of his usual places. He's in paradise. He's with Nick.

She could see them now, the lanterns lit, fierce looks of concentration on their faces as they tried to beat each other at poker and outdo each other with scary stories. When the lights went out, they'd place their sleeping bags side by side, then climb in and gaze up at the heavens.

They'd philosophize a little, chat about nonessentials. Eventually Cody would ask questions about the war. How did Nick keep himself alive in prison? What did he think about? What frightened him? What did it feel like not to have a hand anymore?

Nick would answer some of Cody's questions with a watered-down version of his experiences, then change the subject to something more on Cody's level, like friends, sports, girls. They'd talk about all kinds of things, all kinds of people—except one. Cody's mother, Nick's wife.

A sharp pain pierced Rosie's heart. She cried out in the oppressive stillness of her empty home.

Face it, Rosie. You wish you were there with them. You feel left out.

Terrified at the direction of her thoughts, she rushed over to the couch and began rearranging the pillows. She tried not to think about Nick using it as a bed. She fought the memory of his hunched body, fallen to the floor as he relived his imprisonment.

When the divorce was final, what lucky woman would have the privilege of holding him at night, of sharing his future? Who else knew how to scratch his back in just the right way, rub the ache out of his legs when the muscles tightened up?

Who else knew he was his most amorous at four o'clock in the morning? Who else knew how ticklish he was behind his knees? That if you kissed him there, he was putty in your hands? Your slave for the night?

What woman would be the recipient of that secret smile of his that said, *I've got you where I want you. There's no one to save you. You're all mine. Come here, little girl. You know when your number is up.*

The memories of Nick chasing her around their old apartment making ridiculous hooting sounds like a gorilla were so real she found herself giggling out of fear and excitement.

"Sweetheart?"

"Nick!" she screamed laughingly in automatic response, whirling around.

Too late she realized her error. Zach had stopped dead in his tracks, the bag of food in one hand, a video in the other.

Like an automaton, he put the things on the coffee table, then straightened, his expression grim.

"Do you want to tell me what that was all about?"

Remember. To get in touch with your feelings, you have to be honest. Always tell the truth, no matter how much it hurts.

She gazed into his eyes without flinching. "I was reliving a memory of life with Nick before he went to war. I didn't mean for it to happen. I'm sorry if it hurt you. I love you, Zach. I think you know that."

The muscles twitched along the side of his jaw. "Has this been happening a lot?"

"No," she answered with conviction because it was true. "In fact tonight is truly the first time I've entertained any intimate thoughts of him."

"*How* intimate?" he fired back.

She couldn't sustain his glance and looked away. "Intimate," she whispered.

She could tell he was struggling for breath. "I swore I wasn't going to ask you this question—"

"I haven't slept with him!" She cut him off before he could say another word.

"But you want to."

At all times be honest, no matter how much you think it might hurt. In time you'll begin to understand yourself. When that day arrives, you'll know what to do.

"I—I don't honestly know."

"*Rosie!*"

"Zach," she cried, "make love to me tonight. It's long past time for us to create our own intimate memories. That's what's wrong here. All this time I've asked you to wait. I've asked too much of you, of myself. I made a mistake!" She took a deep, shuddering breath. "Forgive me. I've loved you so long. Let me show you how much."

"You think I don't want that?" His voice shook.

"I know you do. Come on, darling." She lifted her hand, willing him to take it.

"If I make love to you tonight, Rosie, there's no going back."

"No going back."

"Be sure, my love."

I'm going through with the divorce, Rosie. It's only a piece of paper, but it represents freedom for both of us. A chance for all concerned to start fresh.

"I'm sure."

Finally he took her hand and she led him through the house to the guest room, where he'd taken some of his clothes and personal articles.

When they entered, she grasped his other hand and held on to both as she looked up at him. "I'd take you to my room. But that's the bed Nick and I slept in."

His features tautened. "Nick won't be in this one," he vowed fiercely.

Relinquishing her hands, he unclasped the chain around her neck. Within seconds, the ring was back on her finger.

"The first thing I want to do, Mrs. Wilde-about-you," he murmured with a half smile playing around his mouth, "is take a shower with you. Since the day we met, I've had this fantasy of shampooing your hair and rubbing soap into your skin and…"

The world tilted as he lifted her in his arms. With his

mouth fastened to hers, he carried her out of the bedroom to the bathroom across the hall.

"Yoo-hoo, Rosie!" a familiar voice called from the front foyer. "It's Grandpa and Grandma. Are you here? Rosie? Cody?"

CHAPTER ELEVEN

"JUST A MINUTE!"

Rosie was absolutely horrified. "Darling…" Her eyes darted to Zach's.

"Go!" he whispered against her lips. "I'll be in the kitchen."

She fairly leapt out of his arms and tore off her robe on the way to her room. Once there, she pulled on jeans and a sweatshirt. Then she ran through the house to greet her in-laws, totally out of breath. "I didn't know you were coming!" She gave both of them a hug.

Janet patted her hair in the hall mirror. "We called and left a message."

Rosie urged them into the living room, where they sat down. "Zach and I just got back from Heber. Nick and Cody wanted to show me where he plans to live."

Her in-laws would have seen Zach's car in the driveway, so she didn't dare lie about it.

Might as well take the bull by the horns.

When nothing was forthcoming, she continued, "Cody and Nick are camping out on the property tonight. They'll be back early because Cody has to go to school in the morning. Zach and I were just about ready to eat some Chinese food. I think he bought enough to feed an army." She walked to the doorway and called to him.

"Zach, bring plates and cutlery for four, will you?"

"What's that ring on your finger, Rosie?" Janet demanded.

Oh, no!

"Rosie and I are officially engaged, Mrs. Armstrong." The announcement came from Zach, who entered the living room loaded down with dishes and containers of food. "We're going to be married as soon as the divorce is final."

Nick's father sat there attempting to pacify his wife. He kept clearing his throat.

"We heard you'd become engaged on the cruise, but we thought of course you'd call it off now that Nicky's back home." Janet's voice had grown cold and stiff.

Rosie's hands shook as she dished the food onto four plates. "I returned Zach's ring and told Nick I'd like to try to make our marriage work again. But he said no, Mom. He's filed for divorce. I received the complaint yesterday. He wants to get on with his life.

"In a few weeks he'll own a ranch in Heber. He's doing everything possible to carve out a new future."

Janet's eyes glittered a hostile blue. "He's only doing this because you think you're in love with Zach. It isn't what he *wants* to do. I can assure you of that!"

This time Nick's mother was too angry for tears. She turned her venom on Zach. "How does it feel to move into another man's house and steal another man's wife, Mr. Wilde?"

Rosie shook her head at Zach to indicate that he shouldn't respond. This confrontation had been coming for some time. With Cody out of the house, tonight was as good a time as any to set Nick's parents straight.

"Mom, I know you're hurting terribly. I know you are too, Dad. But we can't change what's happened. We've all got to move forward. Nick's doing better than any of us. This evening he and Zach met and shook hands. They're both behaving like civilized human beings because they know what it means to Cody."

Now that she'd started, she couldn't stop. "I wish this decision didn't have to cause you and Dad so much pain. You know how much I love you, how grateful I am for everything you've done for me over the years. I want your love and friendship to continue forever. But the fact remains that Nick has made his choice."

"And you can't even wait until the divorce is final to put that man's ring back on?" Janet lashed out.

"I'm in love with Rosie, Mrs. Armstrong," Zach inserted in a calm tone. "She's in love with me. We've known each other two years, and we're ready to have a life together."

"What kind of life can it be when *she*—Nicky's wife—took an oath before God to love him through the good times and bad, in sickness and health, to comfort and keep him until…until *death…*?"

Zach's lips had thinned, a ready sign that he was barely containing his rage. Rosie was feeling really frightened and tried to hold him back, but it was like trying to single-handedly change the course of a rushing river.

"Your son was presumed dead for more than six years, Mrs. Armstrong. Did you expect your daughter-in-law to stay in mourning for the rest of her life? Do those vows reach beyond the grave?" he asked furiously.

Janet got to her feet. "There was no grave, Mr. Wilde. My son is very much alive. He fought for his country. Did you? I don't see any hands or eyes missing on you." She drove the point home.

Rosie flinched, sick to her stomach. "Mom...don't say another word!"

But Janet was too far gone to listen. "He spent six and a half years in a prison underground where they tortured him, beat him up repeatedly, day in and day out. They put a gun to his head every morning, threatening to kill his wife and child if he didn't talk. Every time they pulled the trigger, he didn't know if he'd be dead or not." She broke down sobbing hysterically.

"They did *that?*" Rosie weaved and would have fallen if Zach hadn't been there to hold her. *I can't bear it. I can't bear it.* She clapped a hand over her mouth, trying to stifle her pain.

"They did that and more. But they didn't destroy him. We all know who did that, don't we, Mr. Wilde? I've heard of kicking a man while he's down, but I never dreamed you could stoop that low."

Rosie couldn't look at Zach. "Stop it!" she shouted, half sobbing. "Zach doesn't deserve any of this. If you're going to start placing blame, then blame me." She pounded her chest. "I'm the one who didn't believe Nick was still alive. I'm the one who let Zach think he had a chance. It's not his fault! I want you to apologize to him. If you don't, you're not welcome in this house anymore."

"Rosie..." Zach whispered with compassion.

"I mean it, Mom."

When he could see that his wife wasn't about to speak, George got tiredly to his feet. "We'll go, Rosie. Janet and I will stay over at the University Plaza Hotel tonight. Then we can meet up with Nick tomorrow."

"Dad?" She swung around. "Surely you don't blame Zach for this."

He stood there and shook his head. Tears ran down his pale cheeks. "No. War is an evil thing. It's the handiwork of the devil."

Rosie watched them leave. Even when the front door closed, she stayed frozen to the spot.

Zach didn't say a word. He simply picked her up in his arms and carried her to the couch. She burrowed her face in his neck and sobbed.

"WERE YOUR BUNKERS ever bombed, Dad?"

Nick took a deep breath and turned on his side to face his son. He'd thought the time would come when he'd want to talk about the past, but thoughts of Rosie alone with Zach were tearing him apart.

"Several times, near the beginning of our captivity."

"What did it feel like?"

"Well...I can remember one night. I knew it was

night because they'd just transferred us from one bunker to another. It was cold. No sun. Even blindfolded, you knew it had to be night. Anyway, they'd just shoved us inside when the air-raid sirens went off. Suddenly I heard the front end of a low-altitude fighter coming in.

"It's easy to determine when a fighter's pointed at you. There's this very distinct sound, kind of a crackling noise, then there's the concussion of the bunker.

"I can't describe it very well, but you kind of feel like you're floating in air while the bunker's being hit. It's an unbelievably strange feeling. The bunker vibrates and there's this popping in your ears, but it's more than a pop. You wonder if you're dead or alive. And then you hear the second fighter, so you know you're not dead yet and you wait for a third then a fourth.

"Since most formations fly in fours, that wait for the fourth one seems extra-long. By now the whole bunker's in chaos. Everyone's shouting and yelling. The Iraqi guards scream at each other, at us.

"That one time I kept thinking if R.T. and I could run out the doors, we'd get transportation by hijacking a local bus, and we'd steal some weapons and find somebody who spoke English.

"But then the fighters stopped coming and we were shoved in a cell, and any chance for escape was gone."

"Whoa! Dad!" Cody audibly gulped back sobs.

"Whoa is right."

"I don't see how you lived through all that." After his tears were spent, he said, "Dad…"

Here it comes. "Yes?"

"I wish Mom were here."

"So do I," Nick said softly.

"I wish Zach would die."

"Don't ever say that again, Cody!"

"I'm sorry."

Nick put his arm around his son and hugged him close. "Even if he was dead, your mother would still love him. Death wouldn't change a thing. You kept loving me, right?"

"Yeah."

"Go to sleep, son. We've got to be up early in the morning. Listen—just in case I have a nightmare, I'm going to move my bag a couple of yards away from yours. Sometimes I fling around. I'd never hurt you, but if you try to touch me, I might hit you thinking I'm trying to protect myself from one of the guards. Do you understand what I'm saying?"

"Yeah."

Nick was tempted to tell Cody about his mother's bruise, but thought the better of it for fear Cody might read more into that night than was there. *Hell*. Nick sighed. If only he'd been aware of Rosie's arms around him….

"Are you scared, bud? If so, you can sleep in the car."

"I'm kind of nervous. But I figure if you survived all that torture, I ought to be able to survive one of your bad dreams."

"Like father, like son, eh? You know what? Your mother not only raised a wonderful boy, she raised an honest one. You're terrific, Cody."

"You're the best!"

"Tell me that in the morning and I'll believe you."

"I love you, Dad."

"Love you, too. Good night."

Fortunately for Cody, Nick couldn't sleep, not when his thoughts were filled with visions of Rosie in Zach's arms.

As soon as Nick knew his son had fallen off, he got out of his bag and walked around for hours, making plans for his ranch, thinking about the innovations he and R.T. could make. Together they would be successful. He was determined about that.

Whatever the future held, he wanted to build something solid for his son. Right now he couldn't imagine marrying again, having more children. He supposed it was possible. One day he'd try dating, but he wasn't going to hold his breath that anything would come of it.

Thanks to his father, who'd watched over an investment of Nick's no one else knew about, he had enough income to keep him going until he made the ranch profitable.

As early as his senior year in high school, Nick's business teacher had taught the students how to make money through rollovers on stock options. It was risky, but if you knew how to play it right, your success could be impressive. Nick had applied the theory and begun seeing results.

That led to his working for a brokerage, which in turn led to his making some good money, which he kept putting into investments. With the army paying for his education, he didn't have to touch them. He had no doubt that in today's market, he could make a lot of money in very little time if he wanted to.

However, all those years in prison had taught him that other things were more important. Family topped the list. Helping those less fortunate came a close second. The next time he went for his therapy, he wanted to talk to the sixteen-year-old foot amputee who was also getting fitted for a prosthesis and having a hard go of it.

By the time the sun's rays were sending pink and gold shafts slanting across the valley, Nick realized he should begin making breakfast. Cody's school would be starting in a little over an hour. They'd have to hustle to arrive on time.

It was no news that Cody wasn't a morning person, especially after their late night. He ate with his eyes closed and had no idea what he was doing when he helped Nick load the Rover. The minute they were off, he fell asleep and was out for the count during the forty-minute drive down the canyon to his school.

Nick pulled the car up in front and had to practically shove his son out the door. Cody muttered something incoherent but managed to give his dad a hug before he disappeared into the building with the other kids. Nick watched the scene with pure pleasure. *This was the stuff of life, what he'd missed out on. Never again.*

Eager to clean up, Nick headed to the hotel. The temptation to drive by Rosie's and see if the Passat was there was overpowering. But Nick figured that, if he was reduced to spying on the enemy, he'd lost more than his hand in this war.

The minute he entered his hotel room, he saw the light flashing on the phone. Someone was trying to reach him. He wanted the message to be from Rosie, but it was probably R.T. To his surprise, the desk informed him that his parents were staying at the hotel.

Though pleased that they'd driven up from St. George to see him, he wondered why they hadn't slept at Rosie's. When he called their room, his father answered. Apparently his mother was still asleep, but George would be over in a few minutes. He had something serious to discuss with Nick.

The somber tone of his voice didn't bode well. Nick felt a sense of dread as he showered and dressed. His worries that something was wrong were borne out when his father appeared at the door looking pale and drawn. Nick had the distinct impression Rosie was involved in some way.

Nick drew his father into the room, then ushered him to the small dining table, where they could sit down.

"Nicky—" George leaned forward with his hands on his knees "—I hardly know where to begin. It's about your mother…"

Nick was sitting back in the other chair, his long legs extended in front of him, ankles crossed. "I'm aware that Mom hasn't been herself. She probably needs some counseling, Dad."

His father nodded his head sadly. "If you'd seen her in action last night, you wouldn't have recognized her."

"This has to do with Rosie, doesn't it?"

"Yes. Your mom hurt her deeply. Maybe irrevocably."

A jolt like a current of electricity passed through Nick. "Tell me what happened."

Listening to his father relate the incident of the previous night, Nick felt as if his insides had exploded. He couldn't sit still any longer. The thing he'd been dreading had happened. He'd lost Rosie, finally and completely, and now his family was reacting.

"I couldn't get your mom to apologize. I'm hoping you can influence her. She refuses to face reality. When we heard you were MIA, we couldn't believe it. We *wouldn't* believe it. We never gave up hope. Your mom was the strongest of us all, and I love her for it.

"But Rosie and Zach are another matter. They're planning to be married, and that's a fact your mom simply has to face or I don't know what'll happen. Janet's unreachable right now…."

Face it, Armstrong. The world has blown up in your face. Now you're going to have to put up the bravest front of your life.

"Tell you what, Dad. After my therapy today, we'll take off for Yellowstone for a while. Just the three of us. Since I got home, Cody and I have been pretty much inseparable. I think he'll be able to handle my being gone for a week or so.

"Mom needs to understand that I'm going to make it without Rosie. Maybe by the time our vacation's over, she'll believe it."

Even if I don't.

"Thank you, son. You don't know how good that sounds. We've wanted to be able to spend time with you. This will be the best therapy Janet could have."

"I agree. So it's settled. Why don't you go on back to your room and tell Mom what's up? I'm going to take care of some last-minute business concerning the sale of the ranch—I want to make sure everything goes through while I'm gone. So, let's plan to leave here about two."

His father stood up. "Ah, Nicky." He hugged him hard. "It's so wonderful to have you back home."

"I feel the same way, Dad. It's what I longed for, too. All that time."

"...HAVE ONE S ORBITAL. The P orbitals have a more specific orientation of charge distribution. One of you asked about the hourglass distribution. This refers to the P orbital. For any one P orbital, the region of high-charge distribution is oriented with respect to an atom passing through the nucleus.

"This phase correctly implies the orientation as far as an axis is concerned, but it incorrectly implies that the electrons are confined to a specific volume.

"For a given principal quantum number of two or higher, there may be a maximum of three orbitals."

A movement out of the corner of her eye made Rosie pause in her lecture. She saw a tall dark male figure enter the auditorium and take a seat near the back.

Nick!

Her body started to tremble. *He knows what happened last night.*

Since his return from the war, he'd never made an appearance in her classroom. He'd never shown a modicum of interest. She could think of only one reason he was here.... Class would be over in a few minutes. She dreaded being alone with him, but his presence ensured that she had no other choice.

Clearing her throat, she tried to remember where she'd left off. "There may be a maximum of three P orbitals, P_x, P_y and P_z, oriented at right angles to each other along the x-axis, the y-axis and the z-axis, with the nucleus and constricted portions of the hourglasses at the origin."

Taking an unsteady breath because she couldn't withstand Nick's scrutiny another second, she announced that class was dismissed. Immediately the students began filing out of the hall.

Needing some way of channeling her nervous energy, she wiped off the equations she'd written on the portable blackboard.

"While I was sitting there—" his deep familiar voice said, "I had to keep telling myself that the impressive and attractive Dr. Armstrong was once Rosie Gardner, the fun-loving, carefree girl who used to skip math and physics classes with me to go for a ride in my old Jeep. You've come a long way, baby."

Despite her fear about the outcome of this confrontation, his words brought a smile to her lips. She hesitated turning around to face him. She felt a reluctance to mar a shared memory that represented a time of pure bliss for her. In those days she would have done anything to be with Nick.

"All you had to do was flash that sunny smile and I thought I'd died and gone to heaven."

At least she turned to meet his gaze. "Nick Armstrong was the big man on campus. Captain of the football team and financial wizard all rolled into one. Every guy's friend. Every girl's secret fantasy. All *you* had to do was beckon me with those famous Armstrong eyes and I forgot who I was and what I was doing."

Nick's smile devastated her. It came to her then that he was starting to look more and more like the Nick she remembered. An older version, of course, but in all honesty, better-looking. She'd married a boy.

Now he was a man. An amazing man who'd come back from the dead a true hero. He was bigger than life. Bigger than death...

"We had our time in the sun, didn't we, sweetheart?"

She averted her eyes. It pained her to hear him say that. His use of the past tense had the effect of dashing every dream.

What dream, Rosie? You're marrying Zach. It's all settled.

"H-how was your camp-out with Cody?"

"Honestly?"

Her heart skipped a beat and her head came up abruptly. "What happened?"

"I think it's more a case of what didn't happen."

She shook her head. "I don't understand."

"Cody missed you. In his words, you're a totally awesome mom."

Don't tell me that, Nick. The things you say clutch at my heart. Every time we talk, I bleed a little more.

"I missed him, too. I always miss him when he's gone. The house feels so empty."

"Until my mother showed up and a bomb exploded."

She looked away. "I imagined that was the reason you came to see me. I love your mom as if she were my own, but…"

"You were right to demand an apology from her. I'm sorry she caused you so much grief. Mom's got a problem right now. Dad and I both agree she needs professional help. The trick is to get her to see a psychiatrist. That's why I'm going away with them for a while."

Going away? Her heart started to pound out of control. "Where? For how long?"

"You know how much the folks love Yellowstone. We'll be gone for a week or ten days."

That would sound like an eternity to Cody. Unless…

"Did you want to take Cody with you?"

"Much as I'd love to, it wouldn't be a good idea. I need to spend some time alone with my parents. Maybe it's what Mother needs."

"Are you going today?"

He nodded his dark head. Rosie could see that his hair was getting longer and starting to curl around his neck. When he was asleep, she used to love playing with those curls until she roused him enough to kiss her. That was all it took to get his total attention. Those kisses would set off a conflagration that brought both of them rapture for the rest of the night and gave Rosie a thrilling reason to greet the day.

"One of the reasons I came here was to ask your advice on how to tell him. Dad wants us to leave around two. It's twelve-fifteen now. Do you think it would be better if I just left and you told Cody after he gets home from school?"

"No!" she cried. She felt an immediate sense of panic because she walked a shaky line with Cody these days. "I think you should go over to his school and get him out of class. Explain to him that your mom isn't very well and you're going to spend a week or so with her.

"Even knowing that, Cody's going to have a hard time. Maybe you can reassure him that you'll phone him at night so he won't feel abandoned."

"I'll do that. I was also thinking it might be a good idea if you came with me to see Cody. When's your next lecture?"

"I'm through for today."

"Then let's talk to him together. If we present a united front, he'll be more accepting."

You always did put me first. You're always thinking of me, always smoothing my path with Cody. How do I thank you? Any other man might have tried to create a wedge. Not you, Nick Armstrong. Maybe it's time I returned the favor and thought of you.

"I agree. I'll come with you," she murmured. "Let me grab my purse from the office."

As they walked through the auditorium, a memory

came back so strongly she found herself expressing it
to him. "Do you know that the first time I ever taught
a chemistry class in here I wondered if you could see
me from the other side."

"Of the grave?" he quipped, clasping her elbow as
they went out the door.

She smiled. "Yes."

"Frankly, my dear, I don't give a damn about the
other side. I much prefer seeing you in the flesh."

"Why, Rhett, how you do turn a girl's head," Rosie
couldn't resist responding in an exaggerated Southern
accent before breaking into laughter.

She loved his old imitation of Clark Gable in *Gone
with the Wind*. Sometimes when he used to call her
from the brokerage, he'd ask for Scarlett. It had been a
silly private joke between them and was as amusing to
her now as it was then.

As she let herself into the office to retrieve her purse,
Nick flashed her an answering smile that made her heart
turn over, exactly the way it had when they'd first met
during a school-sponsored carnival.

There'd been a pie-throwing contest—the football
team got to throw pies at the pep-club girls. All the
girls' faces were covered in whipped cream. Everyone
looked like the characters in her favorite childhood sto-
rybook, *Snipp, Snapp and Snurr,* about the little boys
who fell into a gingerbread vat.

When it was Rosie's turn, there was Nick, towering,
virile and holding a pie in his hands. She'd started to
scream—and that was when he'd laughed. Then he'd

thrown the pie at her. Through it all, his white smile and brilliant blue eyes became the focus of her world. She'd never been the same again.

"Rosie?" Nick's voice brought her back to the present. "Zach's out in the hall."

"Oh, dear. I forgot we were going to have lunch together. Stay here for a minute and I'll talk to him."

Nick put a detaining hand on her arm. "Don't break your lunch date. I'll go to the school without you."

The touch of his hand on her arm was electric. Stunned, she pulled away from him. "No. Seeing Cody is much more important. Why don't you go out to the car? I'll join you in a minute."

He nodded and left her office. She gave him a minute's head start, then locked her door and went in search of Zach.

She didn't have to look for long. An arm slid around her shoulders and for a moment she was crushed tightly against Zach's lean body. They began walking toward the entrance of the building.

"What was Nick doing here?"

Without stopping for breath, Rosie explained what had happened. "I'm so sorry, darling. Do you mind?"

"Not at all. In fact, I don't envy you your job. Cody's just been reunited with his father. If this isn't handled right, it could set him off again."

"Thank you for being so understanding, Zach." They'd reached the outside steps. "I'll see you at six." Nick's Land Rover was in her line of vision.

How many times had she seen his Jeep in front of the

high school with him in it, waiting for her? Again her heart gave a curious kick.

"Maybe earlier." Zach swooped down to brush her mouth with his before loping off in the opposite direction.

Though the kiss was an automatic gesture with him, she wished he hadn't done it, on the off chance that Nick had seen it.

Rosie felt a strange lingering guilt as she made her way toward the Rover. Never in their lives had either Rosie or Nick tried purposely to make the other jealous. Theirs hadn't been that kind of relationship.

It felt like a betrayal of the great trust they'd shared to know that Nick might have seen her being kissed by another man. Then she chastised herself for criticizing Zach. They were engaged. What could be more natural? Everything was out in the open, understood.

Still, when she got into the Rover and they drove off, the disquieting premonition that Nick had been witness to that small intimacy hurt her.

Because you know it hurt him, Rosie.

CHAPTER TWELVE

"I'LL RUN IN and get him out of class."

Before Rosie could respond, Nick had leapt out of the Rover. She watched him sprint across the concrete and up the stairs with that familiar male grace of his.

A tense disturbing silence had prevailed during their five-minute drive from the university to Cody's school. She lamented the loss of the rapport they'd shared for those brief moments in the building where she taught.

While she waited, she glanced around the car's interior, noting the gear that had been stashed in the back. Despite her absence last night, she had no doubt Cody had been in a state of ecstasy. Part of Nick's charm lay in his ability to make every moment count, to turn even a routine activity into an event.

There'd never been a man as exciting to her as Nick. He made things happen, lit his own fires.

"Hey, Mom?" Cody jumped into the back seat of the car as his father came around the front. "Dad says we're all going to have lunch together."

Her eyes read the message in Nick's as he slid behind the wheel. "We thought it would be fun, honey."

"This is so cool."

Cody's face glowed. Obviously he approved of this simple outing, just the three of them.

"Tell me about your camp-out," she asked as they drove off. Had Nick had a nightmare? Would Cody mention it? How many secrets did they share that she'd never know about?

"Dad told me what it was like when his bunker got bombed. I told my class about it during Channel One. Mrs. Clegg thinks it would be neat to have an assembly at school so you and R.T. could come and talk to everybody, Dad. Do you think you could? Do you think R.T. would do it?"

Nick didn't bat an eyelash. "Of course. You just tell us the day and we'll be there. In fact, I'll promise to do that favor for you if you'll do one for me."

Rosie could feel it coming.

"Sure, Dad."

"Your grandma got upset at your mom last night and really hurt her feelings."

Cody blinked. "Grandma did?"

"That's right. It's because I'm her son and because of what happened to me. You know how she cries all the time and just keeps wanting to hold me. Stuff like that."

"Yeah. I know."

Rosie closed her eyes. *Nick's a master father, a master psychologist.*

"*Well,* she wants me all to herself for a little while. Your grandfather told me that when I was born, she had to count my fingers and toes to make sure they were all there. Now that I've lost a hand, I guess she wants to find out if anything else is missing. Of course, nothing is. But do you know what I mean?"

"Yeah."

"The thing is, your mom's all upset, too, and now she wants *her* son to herself for a little while. Fair is fair."

Cody sat forward and put his arms around Rosie's neck. "I'm sorry, Mom."

"It's okay, Cody. I'll get over it—especially if you're with me and we can do some fun things together."

"You mean just the two of us? No one else?"

Rosie had to make a split-second decision. *Forgive me, Zach.* "No one else, honey."

"Great!"

"So how about us working out a deal, son? You take care of your mom for a week and I'll take care of mine."

"It's a deal."

"Where do you suppose your grandma would rather go than anyplace else in the whole world?"

"Yellowstone Lake."

"You think if I took her up there and we did a little fishing, it would calm her down?"

"Yeah. She and Grandpa love to fish."

"Suppose I call you every night, and we all get on the phone and tell you who caught the biggest fish."

Cody giggled. "Grandpa always gets the biggest."

"No matter what, right?"

"Right!" Cody laughed.

"So, how about you and Jeff flying up to West Yellowstone a week from Saturday morning? I'll meet you two guys at the airport and we'll go horseback riding

on Ferron's Dude Ranch. Then we'll drive back after a
couple of days. Is that all right with you, Rosie?"

Rosie couldn't talk.

*They'd spent part of their honeymoon at Ferron's in
a tiny cabin hidden away in the forest. It was a time of
such love, such ecstasy, Rosie could hardly breathe, remembering it.*

"It sounds wonderful." Her voice quavered a little.

"Why don't you come, too, Mom?"

"You know why she can't, Cody," his father intervened.

"Yeah. I know. I was just asking. Where are we going
to have lunch?"

"Hires."

"They have good onion rings."

"I know. I dreamed about them for seven years."

"This morning in English, Jeff and I made a list of
the things we'd miss if we were in prison for seven
years. Mr. Magleby caught us, but when he found out
what we were doing, he made it a class project. Do you
want to see it?"

Nick's deep rich laughter was so contagious Rosie
started giggling, too. Then laughing—she laughed until
her sides ached. She couldn't recall enjoying a moment
this much…in seven years. Before Nick's reserve unit
was called up for Desert Storm.

*Be honest, Rosie. You haven't known this kind of
happiness for so long you've forgotten until just now
what it feels like.*

Their lunch turned out to be a lighthearted affair,
with Cody doing ninety-nine percent of the talking,

never noticing his parents' silence. Rosie smiled and laughed frequently, but hardly spoke, savoring the feeling of closeness and contentment. But it was a bittersweet emotion, tinged with regret.

Later Nick dropped her off at the university and took Cody back to school. Rosie went to her office and prepared for the next day's lecture, then drove to Zach's office in North Salt Lake. At four o'clock she entered the parking area; he'd indicated he might leave work early and she wanted to surprise him. To her chagrin, his Passat wasn't there. His secretary, Barbara, said he'd already left for the day.

Frustrated, she called Zach's condo from the office, but got his answering machine. There was nothing to do but leave a message that she was coming out to his place and asking that he wait for her there. Then she thanked Barbara, and returned to her car.

Last night, or rather early this morning—when Rosie had finally stirred from Zach's comforting arms, where she'd sobbed half the night—she'd gotten up from the couch to make coffee. They'd talked everything over and had decided that Zach's moving in would only add fuel to the fire. So, until their wedding, they would live apart as they'd been doing for two years.

Secretly Rosie had been relieved by that decision; she'd only agreed to his living with her before their marriage as a way of proving her love to him. Circumstances—set in motion by the arrival of Nick's parents—prevented her from following through on that decision.

Neither of them had counted on Janet's vitriol. And though they hadn't discussed it, Zach knew Rosie had been devastated by the revelations concerning Nick's torture in prison. It was an ugly moment. Rosie sensed that Zach had been affected by it, as well.

It was better to forget the incident and simply maintain the status quo.

With one difference.

They were now making plans for their wedding. Zach wanted to build a home for them farther south and east in the valley. But he acknowledged that uprooting Cody would be the wrong thing to do.

They both hoped that by the time her son graduated from high school, they could build their dream house together, and Cody would play an active part in that project.

As soon as exam week at the university was over, Zach wanted Rosie to fly to California with him for a round of family parties and wedding showers. When the divorce was final, they would be married in Newport in Zach's family church. Afterward, there would be a reception at the Newport Beach Club and another one in Salt Lake at the Colonial House on the Avenues.

Rosie had picked the Avenues area of Salt Lake because it wasn't linked to any memories of Nick or their life together. She needed to start her new life without shadows. Without regrets.

She reached Zach's condo and once again saw that his Passat was missing. Letting out a sigh, she turned around and headed home.

No doubt she'd hear from him before dinnertime. Twenty minutes later, when she got home, she listened to her messages and heard Zach's voice.

"Sweetheart? After I left the office, Mitch called me on the mobile unit. There's a problem I have to see about. I hope it's all right if we give dinner a miss. I'll call you later tonight. I love you."

Rosie was sorry she'd have to put off talking to Zach about Cody. On the other hand, there was no time like the present to prove to her son that she wanted to spend some quality time with him alone. He loved her homemade pizza. She'd fix that and have it ready by the time he walked through the door.

Though Cody had taken the news about Nick's going away better than she could have hoped, he would start missing him once dinner was over. That was when he and his dad went to the gym—their special time together. Maybe she could distract Cody by playing poker with him. He'd find out his mother wasn't in her dotage yet!

She'd never played poker with anyone but Nick, which was an experience too personal to talk about to anyone else. Somehow he beat her every time and exacted payment in ways that still had the power to make her blush.

I've learned a lot since my days of being a blushing bride, Nick Armstrong. Just once, I'd love to have the opportunity to beat the pants off you. Literally. Just once I'd love to make you blush!

"Mom?"

"Hi, honey."

"I'm home. Has Dad left yet?"

"I think he has. Why?"

"I stopped at Jeff's on the way home. His mom said he could go to West Yellowstone with me. I just wanted Dad to know."

"He'll be calling you tonight. You can tell him then."

"I can't wait!"

It was going to be a long ten days.

ZACH SHOULDERED his way through the throngs of people at the L.A. airport, anxious to meet his brother, who was picking him up in front of the terminal.

"Richard!" he shouted when he saw the blue Oldsmobile. He sprinted over to the car. "I owe you for this, especially when you had to battle five-o'clock traffic."

"Hey, bro, it isn't like I don't want to see you or anything, but it would be nice to get a little more notice. Do you mind if I ask what in the heck is going on with you?"

Zach couldn't answer him. Since the scene in Rosie's living room last night, his world had exploded in his face. He had a sickness in his gut that wasn't about to go away.

"The last time you flew down here, you didn't tell anybody. Today at lunch my secretary informs me that I'm to pick you up at six o'clock, but no one else is supposed to know. The folks would come unglued if they found out you were in town again and didn't phone them. As it is, I had to make up some story to Bev about working late tonight."

"Like I said, I owe you. Big time."

Richard sighed. "Where do you want to go?"

"Anywhere, but not too far from the airport. I have to get back to Salt Lake tonight."

"How about we just pull off at the first exit and sit at a Stop sign?"

"Fine."

"Whoa. You *are* in bad shape." As they wound in and out of traffic leaving the terminal, Richard kept looking over at him. "Did you and Rosie have a fight?"

"No. Last night we got engaged for the second time." *Last night showed him a whole new meaning of the word "terror."*

"*Second* time?"

"It's a long story."

"Spill it!"

"Hell, Richard. Her husband didn't die in the war. After seven years as a POW, he's back home in Salt Lake."

"What?"

Richard pulled off the road and braked in front of an elementary school.

"I saw a clip about that on the news a while back! But I never would've associated him with Rosie. Zach—look me in the eye and tell me you're putting me on."

Zach turned his head and faced his brother.

"*Oh, Lord*—you're *not!*" He reached across the seat to give him a brotherly hug. "No wonder you couldn't just tell me this on the phone."

Zach raked a hand through his hair. "I think I'm going to lose her, Richard. If that happ—"

"Shut up, Zach. Just start talking to me!"

"She loved me, Richard. She really did. We were making it. On that cruise she finally agreed to marry me. The first night out at sea, the band was playing requests. Suddenly the lead singer asked if there was a Zachery Wilde in the room. Naturally I wondered what Rosie was up to.

"When I stood up, he announced that the next song was dedicated to me. Then he called Rosie to the microphone. She whispered something in his ear, and he said into the mike, 'She's expecting a marriage proposal when the song is over. Are you ready, Zach?' They played Eric Clapton's 'Wonderful Tonight.'" The words of that song would be forever impressed in Zach's memory.

"Before she'd even sat down, I had that ring on her finger. At the end of the cruise, I drove her and Cody to her door, knowing that the rest of my life was going to be pure happiness because Rosie and I were getting married in June.

"Six hours later I got a phone call. Her husband, Sergeant Nick Armstrong, had been freed from captivity and was on his way home to Hill Air Force Base. Rosie had to go. She'd call me later."

Richard groaned, then suddenly leaned across the seat to grasp Zach's shoulder. "Tell me the rest. Don't stop until I've heard every damn thing that's eating you alive!"

Zach heard the love in his brother's voice. Richard had been at his side when Zach's former fiancée died in the hospital. There wasn't another human being who understood him the way Richard did. Zach had repressed his feelings for so long it served as a catharsis to be able to confide in his brother.

Once he'd begun, he didn't stop until he'd told him every detail and had admitted his deepest fear. "I have the gut feeling Rosie's falling in love with her husband all over again."

"But that's crazy, Zach! Last night she agreed to wear your ring. You made specific wedding plans."

"I know. I know," Zach said. "But you didn't hear what I heard in Rosie's voice when her mother-in-law started in about the tortures Nick had been subjected to. What I heard came straight from Rosie's soul. It sounded like love."

"Does that really surprise you? He was her husband all those years. But they're getting a divorce and she loves *you,* wants a life with you now."

"I know Rosie loves me. But you didn't see what I saw today at the university."

"Okay. What did you see?"

"She was talking to Nick. They didn't know I was standing there watching. Have you ever been near a couple who are so involved with each other they have no awareness of anything else around them?"

"Zach, you're paranoid. Not without good reason, but I honestly think you're looking for trouble where there isn't any."

"No. I know what I saw. This was different. There was a...light shining in Rosie's eyes. I never saw anything like it. She even *acted* different. I could hardly believe it was her."

"What you saw is the way Rosie responds to the man she married. If he saw you and Rosie together, he'd say the same thing—that she doesn't seem like the same Rosie to him—because you bring out certain things in her that he doesn't.

"Those two had a particular chemistry together. They made a child. You and she have another kind of chemistry. You'll create your own child one day."

His brother had a lot of wisdom. "What you're saying makes perfect sense. But I've got this awful feeling that one day after we're married, Rosie will wake up and wish she was with Nick. He's never going to go away! They share a son. Cody will be around as a constant reminder of their marriage. For the past two years I've done everything but stand on my head trying to erase his shadow. Now he's back—in the flesh!"

"Zach, thousands of couples are in second marriages and they work beautifully. Once you and Rosie are living together as husband and wife, you'll forge bonds so strong nothing will threaten your love."

"Those thousands of women weren't married to Nick Armstrong first."

"Aside from the fact that he was a victim of war, which turned him into a hero, why is he such a threat to you? I don't get it."

Zach looked over at his brother. "The truth?"

He nodded. "Is there any other way?"

Zach squeezed his arm. "Her husband reminds me of a man I pretty well idolize."

"In other words, if you didn't hate Nick Armstrong's guts, you and he would probably be friends."

"He's got many of *your* qualities, Richard."

Richard eyed him soulfully for a minute, then patted his shoulder. "I appreciate those kind words, bro. But if what you say is true, you've got something even more remarkable going for you. Despite the fact that her husband's a paragon—" he gave a self-deprecating grin "she's picked *you* for her husband."

"Maybe. Then again, the fact that Nick filed for divorce may have made me the winner through default, and you're looking at Rosie's consolation prize. I don't doubt she'd go through with our wedding. With her noble little heart, she wouldn't dream of hurting me again. She'd be a real trooper and try not to let on. But something deep inside tells me Nick would always be in bed with us. I couldn't handle that." His voice was harsh with pain.

Richard had no ready comeback. His expression grew solemn. "Zach, if you're really that unsure of Rosie's feelings, if your gut's telling you something's wrong, then you need to have it out with her. I mean a knock-down, drag-out, bottom-line session. No holds barred. You know what I'm saying?"

Zach nodded.

Oh yes, Richard. I know exactly what you're saying. Rosie might have had a legitimate excuse to go off with

Nick and Cody today. But something tells me she wanted *to be with them.*

He sucked in his breath. "That's why I came down here to see you, Richard. Before I left Salt Lake, I'd half made up my mind to confront her—to get inside her heart and soul, even if I had to fight my way past every defense. I just needed to hear you confirm it."

WHEN ROSIE HEARD the front doorbell ring at eleven o'clock, she knew it had to be Zach. Cody had gone to bed an hour ago, but he wasn't asleep. Nick hadn't phoned yet. Something must have detained him. The waiting was killing both of them, for different reasons.

Zach hadn't called, either. All evening she'd been expecting word from him, yet she'd been dreading that conversation because she'd made a promise to Cody. Spending all her free time with her son meant she wouldn't be seeing anyone else. Including Zach. *Especially* Zach. She could just imagine his reaction.

It wasn't fair to him. Nothing had ever been fair to him. They'd just gotten engaged for the second time. Now she'd have to ask for his understanding about not seeing him in the evenings until Cody flew to West Yellowstone to be with his father. Even a man as marvelous as Zach had his limits. She knew this would be pushing them, but Cody had to be her first priority. Keeping her son emotionally stable with Nick away translated as cruelty to Zach, a no-win situation. Rosie honestly didn't know how much more stress she could take. As for Zach…

With a mixture of reluctance and trepidation, she walked to the door and called out, asking who it was.

"It's Zach."

Something was wrong. He didn't say, "It's me, sweetheart. I've missed you."

She opened the door, expecting him to reach for her the way he always did. It threw her when he remained in place, almost aloof. "I'd almost given up on you tonight. Come in, darling."

After closing the door, she headed for the living room, waiting for his arms to slide around her waist and pull her against him. To her surprise, he came to a standstill just inside the entry to the room, his hands on his hips.

"Has something serious happened at work? Is there trouble?" She was starting to feel anxious.

"No."

The one-syllable answer filled her with a new form of dread. "So you got everything straightened out with Mitch?"

"I lied to you, Rosie. I needed some time to think, so I made up an excuse for not having dinner with you."

She shook her head sadly. "Why did you have to lie to me? Why didn't you just tell me you wanted to be alone? I would've understood."

"I know you would've. But I didn't want to alarm you, not when you're dealing with so much here at home."

"Zach, I realize everything is precarious right now." Her voice trembled slightly, despite herself. "In fact, there's another favor I have to ask of you, and I'm afraid to ask it. But I know we'll eventually get past all this, because we love each other."

"What favor?" he demanded, his features taut.

"Nick left for Yellowstone today with his parents. He'll be gone ten days and he's worried about Cody's reaction. That's why he came to see me at the university, to decide how best to tell Cody."

She moistened her lips nervously when she realized Zach wasn't going to help her out. "Nick told Cody his grandmother needed her son, just as I needed Cody. So they made a deal. Nick would spend time with his mother. Cody would spend time with me."

"And nobody else." Zach filled in the blanks. "So I'm to get lost for ten days while you fulfill your part of the bargain."

"Don't put it that way, Zach. He was only thinking of Cody. It worked. There were no hysterics."

"But there will be if I step foot in this house before the ten days are up. Under the circumstances, I'm surprised you bothered to let me in." By now his face was completely drained of color. "It looks to me as if from now on I'd better check with Nick before I make plans with my future wife."

He was out of the room and the front door so fast she had to run to catch up with him. She'd just managed to slide into the passenger seat as he got behind the wheel and started the ignition.

"Get out of the car, Rosie."

"No! Not until we talk."

"I'm off-limits, remember?"

"I know it sounds horrible. It's just that Cody's been a different boy since Nick came home. If everything can stay on an even keel until Nick returns from vacation with his folks, you and I won't have to worry about Cody as much anymore."

"Until the next time," he ground out.

"What do you mean?"

Zach's hands tightened on the steering wheel. "There will always be a next time where Cody's concerned, Rosie. You're his mother. For the duration of our lives, you will always put him first. And he will always resent me. He'll pit us against each other to test your love for him. He'll try to make you choose between us. I'm not saying that to be cruel. I'm saying it because it's true.

"Today you made a promise to him. I realize you have to keep it. In fact, you're breaking it by being out here in the car with me."

"Zach, I need to talk to you, darling. Please, will you take time off tomorrow to be with me while Cody's at school? As soon as he walks out the door, I'll drive over to your condo." She paused, then added, "I can always go to the University later to work on my grading."

Zach hesitated for a moment, then nodded. "I'll expect you at nine."

She waited for him to take her in his arms. "A-aren't you even going to kiss me good-night?"

"No. If I start kissing you, I won't be able to stop. Go in the house. Now!"

With tears blinding her, she got out of the car and

raced up the lawn to the front porch. She heard a screech of tires as Zach drove away. The sound had a kind of desperate finality about it.

She had expected way too much of Zach. He was the one who felt fragile right now. She had to do something, quickly. Tomorrow they'd talk, and she'd try to reassure him... But while she stood there in a quandary, the phone rang. She dashed over and picked up the receiver.

Nick.

"Hello?"

"Rosie?" came the deep voice. Her heart began to race. "I'm sorry it's so late."

To hear Nick over the phone sounding so natural and familiar made it feel as though they'd never suffered a seven-year separation.

"Are you all right?" she asked anxiously.

"I'm fine." There was a pause. "If you're worrying that this is something war-related, then stop."

"Thank heaven! When I think what you've lived through... I wish I had a magic pill I could give you to make it all go away. I can't—"

"Rosie—"

She was so choked up she could hardly talk. "I can't get the things your mom told me out of my mind. Oh, Nick... Nick... When you flew off on that plane, I suffered a thousand fears, but the reality is so much worse. I wish there were something..."

By now she was sobbing.

"It's over, Rosie," he murmured. "The only problem facing me now is a broken thermostat on Dad's car."

She sniffed. "You didn't take yours?"

"No. Dad had the Buick all packed, and he wanted to drive. You know how much he loves that car."

"I do know." She managed a quiet laugh. "You probably could have fixed it if you'd had a replacement."

"True. Instead, I had to flag down a motorist with a cellular phone. Remind me to get one when I return."

"Dad has one."

"He left it in St. George."

"Every time they come up here, they forget something."

"It's kind of touching to know they've stayed true to form."

But I didn't. I didn't.

"Rosie, I didn't say that to upset you."

He could read her thoughts. He always could. "I know you didn't. Oh, Nick… I've always loved you. So much. I never wanted to hurt you. I'm so sorry for what you've had to endure and so proud of you at the same time. I'm…I'm in awe of you, Nick. It's such a helpless feeling to know what happened to you, and not be able to do one thing about it."

Another silence.

"You can do something for me now."

"What's that? Anything."

"Get on with the rest of your life and be happy. Don't look back."

Another paroxysm of tears threatened. "Where do you find the strength to say that to me?"

"In prison I discovered many things. That God lives,

that life is fleeting and precious. I plan to make the most of the time I have left. That's what you need to do, too, sweetheart."

But you're going to do it without me. I won't be there. I can't bear it.

"Mom? Is that Dad?" Cody came bounding up to her. When he saw her wet face, his crumpled, too. "What's wrong? Has something happened to Dad?" He started to cry.

"Just a minute, Nick," she said in a gravelly tone. "Here's Cody."

CHAPTER THIRTEEN

THE BLARING SOUND of the test pattern on the TV brought Rosie awake. Six in the morning. She sat up on the couch with a tension headache and cramps in her stomach. *Today she had to face Zach.*

When she hadn't been able to get to sleep last night, she lay on the couch to watch TV, hoping it would relax her, get her mind off things. Cody had wandered in to say good-night again, his peace of mind restored after talking to Nick for half an hour.

Once he'd left the room, she turned on the classics channel to watch a movie. It was *Random Harvest*. She hadn't seen it since she was a girl. Rosie had been too young then to really understand the story of the man who'd lost his memory and the wife who loved him so much she stayed in his life as a stranger rather than let him go.

Rosie knew she should have turned it off. Instead, she felt a compulsion to watch it. The ending, in particular, tortured her—the husband got his memory back and the wife got her husband back, while Rosie's story...

She honestly didn't know how her story was going to end. In the movie, the hero's amnesia made things simpler, more straightforward. There was nothing remotely simple or straightforward about Rosie's life.

After staggering to her feet, she left the living room, bleary-eyed, in search of Cody. He needed to get up and take a bath. She needed one, too. Long and hot.

"Cody?" She opened the door to his room. "Time to wake up, honey. I'll start your tub."

"I'm sick, Mom. I can't go to school."

Her eyes closed tightly. No, this just couldn't be happening. Not this morning. Not to Zach. Not again.

Taking a determined breath, she marched into his room and over to his bed. He didn't look sick. But after reading the brochure Linda Beams had given her, she realized that Cody had his own ways of dealing with grief and confusion. Psychosomatic illness was just one of the manifestations.

He'd caught her in tears last night. No doubt that had created new monsters, new fears, in his mind. She had to put them to rest, whatever they were.

She sank onto the side of the bed and smoothed the hair out of his eyes. "Where do you feel sick, honey?"

"I don't know. I just don't feel good. Do you have to go to work today?"

"Yes," she lied. "For a little while. If you want, I'll ask Mrs. Larson across the street to look in on you while I'm gone."

"I'm not a baby, Mom. I don't need a sitter. I just wish Dad was here."

"I know. But since he isn't, we'll make the best of it. Do you just want to stay in bed?"

"I think I'll get up."

"You can watch TV in the living room or play video games when I go."

"Okay. How long are you going to be gone?"

"Two hours," she improvised.

He climbed out of bed and followed her into her bedroom. "Why were you crying last night?"

I knew it.

"I was just talking to your dad about the war."

"He loves you, Mom."

"I know. I love him, too."

"But I mean he *really* loves you."

She couldn't endure another minute of this. "Honey…I have to get ready."

He waited outside the bathroom door. "Mom?" he called.

She turned on the shower, preparing to step inside. But she couldn't ignore him completely. "What is it, honey?"

"I know you love Zach, but do you *really* love him?"

Oh, Cody, my darling boy. You've asked the question I've been skirting all night. This morning I believe I know the answer.

"Let me finish my shower and then we'll talk."

"Okay," he said in a grumpy tone. She heard him stomp off down the hall.

She purposely took a long time to wash and blow-dry her hair, hoping he'd be engrossed in something once she was dressed and ready to drive to Zach's.

No such luck. He was waiting for her when she went

to the kitchen to find some painkiller for her headache. The huge bowl of cereal he'd poured testified to the state of his physical health.

"You know I'm running late? I've got things to do at the office before I teach class." She bent to give him a kiss on the cheek. "We'll talk when I get home. I'll call you in a little while and see how you're doing. And don't forget—you can always phone Mrs. Larson."

"Okay. But hurry!"

"I will."

Zach would be shocked to see her on his doorstep at eight, but there was no help for it. She waved to Cody as she backed the car down the drive. *Two hours.* That was all she had to give Zach. But she might not need that long when he heard what she had to tell him.

SOMEONE WAS TRYING to get him on the phone. Whoever it was had rung three separate times in succession. Zach rolled over and glanced at his clock through bloodshot eyes. Five to eight. He rolled back onto his stomach.

There was only one person he wanted to talk to, and she wouldn't be here until nine.

The ringing started again. *Damn the phone.*

He put the pillow over his head, but nothing deadened the sound. The person on the other end wasn't about to give up.

Muttering a curse, he reached blindly for the receiver. "Yes?"

"Hello? Is this Zach?"

Zach tried sitting a little straighter. "Rosie?"

"It didn't sound like you. I'm down in the lobby. Can I come up?"

"What do you think? Hell, Rosie, I'm sorry. I wasn't expecting you for another hour. I'm a mess."

"I'm afraid there was an unavoidable change in plans. Cody didn't want to go to school this morning. I've left him at home alone."

He shook his head to clear it. "You know the code. I'll leave the door open."

He levered himself from the bed with difficulty. Last night he'd had a few too many at the Alpine Club. This morning he was paying the price.

Throwing on his robe, he hurried through to the front door. When he'd unfastened the bolt and opened it a crack, he took off for the bathroom. A quick shower and shave would help restore him. By the time he'd dressed in a clean T-shirt and jeans, he felt he could face Rosie without totally revolting her.

Normally Zach didn't drink much. But he'd wanted everything about yesterday and last night to be obliterated from his consciousness. Unfortunately the memories were back this morning, and his heart felt so heavy he knew he couldn't go on like this any longer.

Rosie wasn't a drinker, either, but judging by her haggard appearance, she looked as if she needed something a lot stronger than coffee to sustain her.

With painful clarity it came to him then that they weren't the same two people who'd danced the night away on the cruise.

Gone were the carefree lovers. Gone were the whispers in the night about a honeymoon.

Gone was all talk of the baby they were going to make together. All gone.

When she didn't rush into his arms, he called her name.

One tear, then another, coursed down her pale cheeks. Her shoulders started to shake. "Zach?"

With that one word, a groan escaped his throat. He shook his head, sensing a burst of adrenaline that was making him feel like a crazy man.

He took several deep breaths, attempting to hold on to his sanity. "Rosie..." he began.

"Yes?"

She was facing him as bravely as she would a firing squad. His adorable Rosie, noble to the bitter end.

"Can you look me in the eye and tell me you want to live the rest of your life with me?"

The energy radiating between them could have lit up a small city.

"You know how much I adore you, Zach. You know it," she whispered fiercely.

"That's not the answer." He folded his arms to keep from touching her. "I'll ask it again a different way....

"Knowing that your husband's alive, that you'll be seeing him coming and going in Cody's life, that you'll be talking to him from time to time, consulting him on occasion, being at functions where he'll be, standing with him in Cody's wedding-reception line one day, seeing him at the hospital when Cody's wife has a baby, or two or three... Knowing all that...

"Do you, Rosie Armstrong, take me, Zach Wilde, to be your lawfully wedded husband, do you promise to cling only to me, to want only me, to dream only of me, to have children with me, to forsake all others— to put Nick Armstrong completely away—until death do us part?"

I know what your answer is, Rosie. But I have to hear you say it.

"Take your time. This day had to come. This question had to be asked. I'm asking it now."

"I know," she whispered. "That's why I'm here."

The quiet grew more ominous. His mouth had gone dry. "I'll ask it a third way. Will it tear you apart when Nick marries another woman and starts a new life in Heber?"

She buried her face in her hands.

"Will it tear you apart to think of him on a honeymoon with another woman? Making love to her as only you can imagine? Giving her a baby like the one he gave you?"

A knock-down, drag-out, bottom-line session. No holds barred.

"Will it tear you apart that he comes home to *her* every night, instead of to you? Will it tear you apart that he's living out the future with someone else when it should have been *your* future?"

After an eternity she lifted a ravaged face. "It's already tearing me apart that I've hurt you so deeply."

"Say it, Rosie," Zach demanded. "Get it over with. Say, *'I'm in love with Nick.'*"

He heard the sob. Then, "I'm in love with Nick."

Zach reeled. "Thank you."

Unable to hold back any longer, he reached for her and caught her in his arms, crushing her to him. "Rosie, Rosie...I'm dying now, but if I'd heard those words after we were married... I don't even want to think about it."

"If Nick hadn't come back..."

"I know. We would have had a fantastic life together."

She raised her head and grasped his face between her palms. "We would have. You're the most wonderful man, Zach. I'll always love you."

"And I'll always love you, my darling Rosie. But Nick's so deep in your heart, so deep and tight, there's no room for anyone else. That's the kind of love I want, Rosie. So deep and tight it's forever."

I'm telling you these lies because you want to hear them.

"I pray to God you find it."

I won't. I've had my quota of lost loves.

"It's time to take back my ring," he said.

A new pain shattered him when she thrust a hand in her purse and handed the ring to him. She'd come over early to give it to him....

"I'd let you keep it, but Nick's as possessive a man as I am. You don't want a major fight on your hands before you've settled down to loving each other again."

That won a smile from Rosie, whose drenched green eyes lit up at the very thought of her husband.

Nick's seven-year nightmare is over. Mine's just beginning.

"What will you do, Zach?"

"Mitch is going to be put in charge of the company here. I'm moving back to California."

Another lie, but it'll make you happier to think of me there....

She squeezed him hard. "I'm so thankful you have family. I know they'll help you."

No one will be helping me. I'm going to finish what I set out to do when I came to Utah and got sidetracked by you, Rosie. After that, it doesn't matter.

"I'm going to miss you," she said with an ache in her voice.

"Maybe until Nick gets back from Yellowstone."

The tears were starting again. "If there'd been any way to know that he was still alive... You've spent two years of your life on me... It isn't fair, Zach—"

"Shh. I don't regret one single second of what we had together. I'll treasure it all my life." He kissed her forehead. "Now, go home to Cody. His happiness is going to make all of this worth it."

With their arms around each other he propelled her to the door. She looked up at him, searching his eyes. "Zach, how can I leave you like this?"

He put a finger to her lips. "Make it easy for me and go."

The second she was out the door, he dashed to the kitchen and phoned his brother. His nephew answered. Luckily Richard hadn't gone to work yet.

"Go get your dad out of the shower for me, Richie."

"Okay, Uncle Zach. Just a sec."

Come on...

"Hey, Zach?"

"I confronted her, Richard. No holds barred. Now I'm a free man."

"*Zach...* I'm flying to Salt Lake. I'll be there as soon as I can."

"I may not be here."

"Just stay put till I get there."

"I thought I could handle it."

"You'll handle it."

"You want to make a bet?"

"Zach? We've both been through a lot together. We'll get through this, too. For the love of God, hang tight till I get there."

"HI, CODY. I'm home! How're you feeling?"

"Not good." He wandered into the kitchen still dressed in the sweats he liked to use for pajamas. They matched Nick's. "You've been crying again, huh?"

She nodded. "Yes. I've been crying hard." *Forgive me, Zach, darling. Please, God, let him find happiness again soon. Please—*

"Over Dad?"

She set her purse on the counter. "Over a lot of things. Come here." She held out her arms and they hugged. "I think you and I could use a little cheering up about now. Are you too sick to drive down to Orem with me?"

"You mean to see R.T.? Heck, no!"

"Of course to see R.T. Who else do we know in Orem?"

"How soon can we go?"

"As soon as you get dressed."

"Does he know we're coming?" he called minutes later from the other part of the house.

"Yes. I just phoned him. Cynthia's at work and he'd love the company."

"He's the coolest guy."

"He is."

When Rosie had told R.T. she needed a friend to talk to, he didn't ask any questions. He just told her to come and stay as long as she wanted.

Forty-five minutes later, R.T. had Cody ensconced in their study, teaching him the fundamentals of a new computer game. With his quick mind, Cody didn't take long to catch on. Soon he was too engrossed to talk to either of them.

She and R.T. shared a secret smile and left her son entertained while they made their way to the living room of the small home.

R.T. gave her a long thorough appraisal. "You're so sad. It makes me feel guilty."

"For you to say something like that tells me you and Cynthia must be getting along terrifically."

His shy smile touched her heart. "To be honest I'm so happy it scares me. Only one thing could make me happier."

"What's that? The news that she's pregnant?"

"Well, that, too, of course." He grinned, then sobered. "To see you at peace."

Rosie sat foward on the chair. "R.T., this morning Zach and I said goodbye to each other forever. He took back his ring. It's over."

R.T. had been sitting with his head bowed, but at her words he looked up quickly, astonishment written on his face. "Are you putting me on?"

"No. That's why I look this terrible. Zach's a wonderful man and I'm hurting for him. He's in a lot of pain."

"Ah, Rosie…" R.T. lunged for her from the couch. She had no idea his hug could be so powerful. "I know you loved him, but there's no one like the sarge. No one."

She hugged him harder because they were both crying. "You're right, R.T. Nick's one of a kind. I've always been in love with him. I always will be.

"If he'd never come home, Zach and I would have had a marvelous marriage. But Nick *did* come back, and I want to live with him again. Forever."

R.T. just hung on to her, weeping. Pretty soon that got Rosie's tears going again.

"How come you guys are always crying?"

R.T. let go of her and turned to Cody. "We're just happy."

Cody scratched his head. "Mom? You're both acting kind of weird."

"I know. Why don't you sit down, honey? I've got something important to tell you."

Immediately alert to the inflection in her voice, he perched himself on the arm of the couch, his expression anxious.

"The thing is, I have a problem only the two of you can help me solve. That's because your father loves you and R.T. more than anyone in the world."

"What's wrong?" By now Cody was starting to look ill.

"Cody? Do you remember the question you asked me early this morning and I told you we'd talk later?"

"Yeah?"

"Well, now I'm ready to answer you."

"You are?" He sounded scared.

"Zach and I have said goodbye to each other because I *really* love your father."

It took a moment for her message to get through. When it did, even she wasn't prepared for her son's ear-piercing whoop. Cody practically levitated from the couch and knocked her over in his eagerness to show his joy.

"How come you're always jumping around and yelling, Cody?" R.T. baited him. That brought an hysterical giggle from Cody.

"Have you told Dad yet?"

"No," Rosie replied. "That's what I need to talk to the two of you about. I thought if we put our heads together, we could come up with a plan. Right now he's in the process of divorcing me."

"One phone call to your attorney telling him you and Nick are back together again ought to fix that in a big hurry."

She clasped her hands together. "Therein lies my dilemma, R.T. Nick might not want me back. He'll think I'm doing it out of pity."

R.T. didn't deny it.

"Hey, you guys?" Cody said. "I've got an idea. You know that religious ad on TV about the family that kidnaps their dad because he doesn't spend enough time with them?"

Rosie nodded while R.T. looked blank.

"Well, we could kidnap Dad and you guys could get married again or something. Dad would go for that big time!"

R.T. jumped to his feet. "You know something, Cody? I think you're on to a great idea. I've been thinking about doing something special for Cyn, to let her know how happy she makes me. I even had this idea we'd get married again."

"A double ceremony?" Rosie interjected.

"A *surprise* double-wedding ceremony," R.T. muttered. "One the sarge won't know about until it happens. I'll get him to the church on the pretext of coming to my wedding. Then we'll have the pastor say something like, 'We're all gathered here to witness the marriage of R.T. and Cyn, and Nick and Rosie. Will the two couples step forward?"

"He won't be able to say no, will he?" she cried. "Not when everyone's there watching and waiting? Not if he loves me."

R.T. shook his head. "He won't say no. Trust me on this one, Rosie."

"I want to trust you. I want to believe it. The thing is, I hate going behind Nick's back. Maybe I shouldn't."

R.T. looked her in the eye. "Has the sarge told you he's still in love with you?"

Rosie took a deep breath. "He told me he was in love with the Rosie he left behind."

A smile lit up R.T.'s face. "Then you've got nothing to worry about. Go ahead and plan to your heart's content."

"You think so?" she almost squealed.

"I know so," he pronounced firmly.

"Dad told me he wished you were with us on the campout, Mom."

"Really?"

"He didn't sleep all night. He just walked around and around. Oh, Mom, you're going to make him so happy! When's all this going to happen, anyway? Jeez, why did Dad have to go to Yellowstone in the first place?" he grumbled.

Now Rosie was on her feet as another idea came to mind, an idea so exciting she could hardly stand it. "There's this little Chapel of the Pines in West Yellowstone. Your father and I commented on how quaint it was when we were up there on our honeymoon."

"And his parents are already up there with him..." R.T. had immediately picked up on her train of thought.

"That gives us about one week to get everything ready." If she called old Mr. Ferron and arranged for that little cabin in the forest...

"Can Jeff still come?"

"Of course, darling. Grandma and Grandpa will be happy to take care of you. The four of you can have fun on the dude ranch while R.T. and his wife and your father and I enjoy a short honeymoon."

In fact, Janet and George are going to be so happy they'll become the people they used to be—before Nick went missing in action.

"Cody, when your dad calls tonight, you've got to act perfectly natural and not give anything away. Remember how smart he is. Nothing ever gets by him."

"Don't worry, Mom. This is one time I'll outsmart him. You can count on me."

"Sure we can." R.T. tousled Cody's hair. "When your dad calls me tonight, I'll start setting him up."

Rosie's gaze swerved to his. "Has he been calling you a lot?"

He gave her a serious look. "We talk every day. Did I ever tell you about this funny thing that happened on the way to the minefield?" Rosie smiled through the tears. "We can't seem to break the habit."

"Don't ever break it!" she murmured fervently. Her love for R.T. was growing deeper and deeper.

"So that means we have to wait a whole week?" Obviously Cody couldn't comprehend keeping a secret that long.

"Honey, I've got a lot of preparation to do so I can go up to West Yellowstone early and get everything ready. I'll take the car."

"Jeff's mom will let me stay with them until we fly up with R.T. I'll tell Dad he has to call me over at Jeff's. If he asks to talk to you, I'll tell him you're out with Zach."

At the mention of Zach, she felt another stab of pain. "I think it'll work. I'll show up at the airport in the car and tell Nick that it was a last-minute decision on my part to drive up and see R.T. and Cyn get married."

Cody beamed. "Yeah, and I'll say that I'm going to be the guy who gives the ring during the ceremony."

My rings! "That's right, Cody. You can carry them."

"Do we have to get dressed up and stuff?"

R.T. answered him. "No. Up until the last second, while he's sitting in that pew watching the pastor, we have to fool your dad." A huge smile broke out on his face. A face that was fuller and looked more handsome every day. "The sarge isn't going to know what hit him!"

"R.T.—" CYN CAME running into the study where he was working "—it's Nick on the phone," she whispered. "Can I sit here and listen?"

He pulled his wife onto his lap and kissed her hard. "If you can keep from squealing with excitement, I'll let you. You think you can do that?"

"I promise I'll be good. I want this to work as much as you do," she murmured with tears of happiness in her voice.

"Okay. Here goes."

He picked up the receiver and sat back on the couch with Cyn still curled in his lap. "Hey, Sarge? What's up?"

"I've got Mom busy thinking about how to help me redecorate the chalet in Heber. While she was poring over some *Better Homes and Gardens* this evening, ten German brown trout sprang for my fly before it even touched the water."

"Oh, come on."

"I swear it. Dad's caught and thrown back at least a dozen fish that were fifteen inches long. He's waiting for a trophy."

"Sounds like quite the life! I haven't been fishing in years."

There was a pause. "To be honest, I'd rather be doing what you're doing. It's been a hell of a long time. You know what I mean?"

Just you wait, Sarge. Just you wait.

"Yeah, I know. Just remember, all good things come to those who wait."

"I believe that. But seven years?"

R.T. chuckled, then gave his wife a kiss. "Speaking of that particular subject, I was thinking of getting married."

Silence.

"Run that by me again?"

"You know, Cyn and I taking our vows over. Maybe going on a little honeymoon." Her hand entwined with his and she kissed it.

"Sounds great. You two ought to be up here, instead of me." R.T. could hear the despair hidden under Nick's light tone.

"Are there any churches in the park?"

"I don't know about that, but there are several in West Yellowstone."

R.T. squeezed her hand tighter. "Maybe I'll check it out. When did you say you were going to be there?"

"Barring anything else happening to the Buick, we should arrive there next Saturday morning in time to meet Cody's plane from Salt Lake."

"Maybe Cyn and I could fly up with him."

After a pause, "If you did that, you'd make me a very happy man."

R.T. sobered. The sarge was in pain. *It was bad.*

"You'd make me even happier if you'd agree to be my best man."

"I wouldn't let you get married without me."

"If I had known you way back when, I would have asked you to be my best man the first time."

"Yeah, well, you know what they say. It's better the second time around. At least it's going to be for you."

You're going to believe it, too, Sarge. And that day can't come soon enough.

"Well, I'm thinking seriously of looking into it. As your son always says, it would be kind of *cool* to go on a second honeymoon and then carry my wife over the threshold of our new home in Heber."

"You've got that right." Nick's voice sounded like it had come from a great distance. "I say go for it, R.T. Make every second count from here on out."

That's exactly what we're all going to do, Sarge. Just hang on seven more days.

"I guess I'd better sign off. I still have to talk to Cody."

"Right, Sarge. Over and out till tomorrow."

"Till tomorrow."

CHAPTER FOURTEEN

FRIDAY EVENING Nick packed all their fishing gear and suitcases in the trunk. It was only an hour to West Yellowstone from Old Faithful, but he wanted to be sure they were on the road in plenty of time to get to town before the plane arrived.

Much as he adored his parents, he missed Cody and R.T. like crazy. As for Rosie, she was never home at night anymore. In fact, for the past three nights he'd had to phone Cody over at Jeff's house. The pain of not hearing her voice, of not discussing their son, was getting to be more than he could stand.

Thoughts of her and Zach alone together, planning their life, were ripping him to shreds. Her name never came up in his conversations with Cody, who'd apparently accepted the situation without question.

The sooner he moved to Heber, the better. The sooner he met another woman, the better. Actually he'd met a couple of extremely attractive women who worked at the lodge. They'd be willing, *if* he'd given them as much as a smile. But he couldn't even consider it. Neither of them had green eyes and golden hair. Neither of them had a smile like sunshine.

At least for tonight, he had R.T.'s wedding to think about. It was kind of exciting to imagine them renewing their vows. When he thought of those empty years in the bunkers…

Don't dwell on the past, Armstrong. Don't look back.

R.T. and Cynthia deserved a special present. Nick couldn't think of anything better than getting checked in at the dude ranch as fast as possible so he could arrange for that little cabin in the forest. It was the perfect place for their second honeymoon. Maybe they'd find the same joy there that he and Rosie had fourteen years ago.

Since he hadn't brought a suit and tie with him, he thought he'd buy a Western suit and some cowboy boots for the occasion. Maybe he'd get a matching one for Cody, do R.T. proud.

Speaking of Cody, it was time for their nightly phone call.

It's Friday night. Rosie and Zach have the weekend ahead of them and no Cody.

Feeling sick, Nick headed for the lodge on a run. Sometimes he just wanted to take off and keep running until he'd left every crucifying thought behind.

He reached his room out of breath, but it wasn't from exertion. Rosie'd had a stranglehold on his heart since the first time he'd seen her, when she'd cried in terror because he was going to throw a pie in her face.

After he'd hit his target, all he could see was a bewitching smile and jewel-toned green eyes pleading with him to be kind, not to rub the cream in her face. He'd started toward her with another pie, then stopped, unable to move while his heart performed maneuvers he'd never before experienced. That was when it happened. That was when he fell in love with Rosie Gardner.

What if he never got over her?

The terrifying thought drove him to the phone. He needed distraction. He needed his son. It was ten. Their arranged time.

"Hi, Dad." Cody picked up on the first ring.

"It sounds like you're as excited as I am about tomorrow."

"You can say that again. Jeff's folks said he could stay up there as long as we wanted."

"That's great. I was hoping we could do a little fishing, as well as riding."

"Mr. Taylor bought us some new flies to try."

"I'll let you in on a secret, Cody. The fish are biting just about anything that moves."

"Awesome! I can't wait!"

"How's your mom?" *I swore I wasn't going to ask, but I have to know.*

"She's okay."

"You're not giving her any more trouble about Zach?"

"No, Dad. I promised you I'd be good."

Nothing else was forthcoming. *What did you expect, Armstrong?*

"Dad? You'll be sure to meet us? Ten-thirty exactly."

"Yup. I'll be there."

"How's Grandma?"

"Better."

Mother will be fine until the next time she sees Rosie with Zach. Then the tears and recriminations will start all over again.

"I can't wait to see you," Cody said.

"Ditto, son. Until tomorrow."

"Bye, Dad."

THE LANTERN had been lit. Rosie looked around the little cabin on Ferron's Dude Ranch, just outside Yellowstone Park. She felt slightly feverish. Luckily the indoor and outdoor snapshots of their honeymoon trip had helped her recreate that halcyon time, down to the clothes they'd worn, the snacks they'd eaten.

She'd brought Cody's portable tape player. In order to provide the music they'd listened to, she'd asked Jeff's older brother, Mike, to tape songs from the early to mid-eighties.

The only thing left was to arrange her hair as she'd worn it at the church on their wedding day.

Her eyes darted to her wedding dress, hanging on a peg. She'd had it cleaned, along with the veil. She couldn't wait to wear it again to meet her husband.

There'd been one change in plans since that meeting at R.T.'s a week ago. Rosie would stay out of sight until the wedding.

After she'd discussed everything with the pastor, who was delighted to be a part of this unusual ceremony, it was decided that he would give a small speech first.

Nick would already be up in front at R.T.'s side, as

his best man. When the wedding march began, Cynthia would proceed down the aisle, followed by Rosie.

Seeing all of it in her mind, Rosie extinguished the lantern. She slid under the covers of the bed where she'd known rapture with her husband thirteen years ago. Where she would know rapture with him again tomorrow night.

Tomorrow.

There would be two brides, two grooms, one ceremony, two happily married couples.

Please, God. Make it come true.

THE YELLOWSTONE AIRPORT, three miles from the park entrance, was seething with activity. From the observation window inside the lounge Nick could see another plane coming in.

Nick felt again the sensation he'd experienced as he and R.T. approached Hill. The tightness in his gut threatened to cut off his breathing. *This isn't like last time, Armstrong.*

He watched the plane touch down. There was precious cargo inside. He expelled a sigh of relief as he saw it swing around and come toward them.

"Oh, I can't wait to see my grandson!" Nick's mother exclaimed, leading the way to the door where the passengers would be arriving.

Nick followed with his father at his side, fighting disappointment that the little forest cottage had been taken by another honeymoon couple. But Mr. Ferron had said there was a kind of honeymoon suite at the main ranch house, which he was sure R.T. would like, so Nick reserved it. A bottle of champagne on ice and two glasses stood ready.

"Look at your mom, Nicky. She's happier than I've seen her in a long while. Thanks for taking time to be with us."

"You don't have to thank me for something I wanted to do, Dad. I love you both." He gave his father's shoulder a squeeze, then turned to watch the incoming passengers.

As soon as Cody and Jeff burst through the door there was mayhem. R.T. and Cynthia were right behind them. For the next few minutes, everybody hugged everybody. The reunion with loved ones warmed Nick's heart. Only one person was missing, one person who could have turned the occasion to the greatest joy.

Like those seven years in prison, you've got to put Rosie away, Armstrong. You've got to do it, or you won't survive the rest of your life.

They all agreed to head to the dude ranch to get settled in their rooms, then enjoy a prewedding brunch.

Though he realized this would only be a reenactment of the real thing, Nick couldn't shrug off the feeling that everyone was caught up in the kind of nervous excitement that preceded a real wedding.

R.T. was higher than a kite, and Cynthia walked around with stars in her eyes. But the biggest change seemed to have fallen over Cody. Nick had never seen his son so jubilant, almost euphoric. He knew Cody was excited to see him again, but there was something else. Nick couldn't put his finger on it.

In a way it worried him. Had Rosie's love for Zach caused their son to shut off his feelings for his mother? Had her absence at night hurt him too much?

Nick could only praise Rosie's mothering instincts. But Zach was a different matter altogether. Possibly Cody was overcompensating to deal with what he viewed as his mother's defection from the family. Nick thought about this on the drive to the lodge; he was still thinking about it as they prepared for the wedding. Maybe he and Cody should go in for some group counseling after the trip. The army urged vets and their families to participate. Nick hadn't given it much credence until he'd seen Cody's behavior today.

Naturally he was thrilled that his boy seemed so happy. But Cody was overdoing it, and that troubled him a lot.

"Hey, Dad! We match!"

"We sure do." They both stood in front of the mirror in Nick's room. The brown Western-cut suits didn't look half-bad. Nick was back up to 160 pounds. Twenty-five or thirty more pounds to go, but he wasn't complaining. The natural-toned cowboy boots would be great around the ranch.

"Whoa, Dad! That Stetson looks cool on you."

Using his good hand, Nick dipped the brim down level with his eyes, then stared at Cody in the glass. *"Make my day."*

Jeff and Cody shrieked with laughter.

Then it was time to go to the church.

ROSIE HAD ARRIVED at the little Chapel of the Pines two hours before the ceremony to get all the ribbons and flowers arranged. She'd left her car parked behind the forest cabin. One of Mr. Ferron's employees had driven her to the church.

The rings lay inside three tiny pockets on a white satin-and-velvet pillow left on the front pew. Cody's job was to carry the ring pillow and distribute the carnation boutonnieres to all the men and give the gardenia corsage to Nick's mother.

When everything looked as perfect as she could make it, Rosie hurried to one of the little anterooms off the foyer used as changing rooms for bridal parties.

The box of bridal bouquets had been placed on a chair. Fashioned of white roses, baby's breath and fern fronds, they looked exquisite.

Almost sick with excitement, she removed her T-shirt and jeans, then began to put on her wedding dress.

"Most married women can't fit into the gown they wore at their wedding. Yours fits like a dream," Cynthia murmured as she let herself into the room, carrying her wedding finery over her arm.

"Cynthia! You're here!" They hugged. "I'm so relieved. That means everyone's arrived safely. H-how's Nick?"

Cynthia started to change out of her clothes. She eyed Rosie solemnly. "He's putting on a great show for everyone, especially the boys, but Rosie—the man's heart is broken. There's only one thing he wants, and that's to be married to you. R.T. and I agree we would never have forced him to go through with this today if we hadn't known you were going to make his greatest dream come true by the end of the ceremony. It would have been too cruel otherwise."

"I know." Rosie's voice shook. "Sometimes I wonder if I've done the right thing."

Cynthia smiled her sweet smile. "If you could see the way you look, you'd know this is the *perfect* plan. Believe me."

"It's got to be. Here, Cynthia. Let me help with all those buttons. This dress fits you beautifully. You must be exactly the same size you were the day you got married."

"Hopefully, eight months from now I won't be able to step into it, let alone pull it all the way up."

"*Cynthia!* Does R.T. know?"

"No, that's going to be my wedding present to him."

When she'd finished doing up her dress, Cynthia started on Rosie's. "It won't be noticeable, but I can tell you're a little thinner than you were thirteen years ago."

"If all goes well, I'll be in your condition soon. I want our children to grow up together."

"I think I'm too happy, Rosie."

"I think I am, too."

They both looked in the mirror to arrange their veils.

"Cynthia, our dresses are amazingly alike." They wore full-length, off-white silk with lace trim. Both dresses had long sleeves with a scooped neck and empire waists. The biggest difference lay in their veils. Cynthia's was shorter and fashioned of nylon tulle.

Rosie's matched the lace cutouts on her dress and cascaded to her shoulders.

She turned to Cynthia with tears in her eyes. "We're the two most fortunate women around. Our men came home."

They clasped hands and said a little prayer to remember the men who didn't.

NICK REMOVED his Stetson and entered the chapel, marveling at the beautiful decorations. The scent of flowers produced a flashback of his own wedding. He shook his mind to clear it of the memory and proceeded down the aisle.

Cody darted his father a brilliant smile and was right there to pin a red carnation on his lapel. Once again Nick had the distinct impression that something was wrong with his son.

The pastor came in, followed by the organist, breaking Nick's train of thought. Soon all the introductions were made, and the pastor showed Nick and R.T. where to stand.

Cody was positioned on the other side of the altar. Nick watched his mother give Cody a kiss and hand him the ring pillow. Then she took her place in the first pew with his father and Jeff.

Nick could feel R.T. shifting his weight. "How come you're so nervous? You've done this before."

"How come *you're* nervous?" he fired back. "I heard you doing Morse code through lunch. You're still doing it. *Got to get out of here. Got to get out of here.*"

"I don't know. It doesn't mean anything. It's just a habit."

"Yeah, sure. You're nervous, all right." R.T. grinned. "Maybe it's that new getup you're wearing."

"You don't approve? I bought it in your honor."

"Hey, I approve, Sarge. You look like a hero out of a Western. I hardly recognized you."

"And you look like the smitten bridegroom if ever there was one, all decked out in that fancy suit and white shirt."

"Do you think Cyn will notice?"

"Nope. She's too crazy about you to bother with the details."

Nick loved to tease R.T. about Cynthia because he could always get his buddy to blush.

The pastor began to speak. "Let us first say a prayer."

Nick had been prepared to hear the wedding march. Quickly he bowed his head and closed his eyes.

"We thank you, oh, God, for your bounteous blessings. Two of your servants, Nicholas Armstrong and Rutherford Topham Ellis, are home with family and loved ones after their seven-year exile in a foreign land."

Nick's head jerked back and he stared at the pastor. Slowly his gaze passed over everyone. All heads were bowed except his. He lowered his head again, but his eyes remained open.

"They've served you and their country honorably, and now they wish to repledge their love and devotion to their wives in front of you and these witnesses. Amen."

"Amen," the congregation returned. Immediately the organ broke into the wedding march.

Wives...

"Steady, Sarge," R.T. whispered. "Don't pass out on me."

"What's going on, R.T.? Tell me, dammit!" he whispered back fiercely.

His palms were clammy and the room felt too hot.

"Just keep your eyes focused on the back of the church, and all your questions will be answered."

At R.T.'s injunction, Nick swung his head around. He saw Cynthia start down the aisle. Her sweet face glowed as she kept her eyes on R.T. Then he saw another bride emerge from the foyer of the chapel. The lacy veil looked familiar.

Out of nowhere he heard his mother cry out in shock. His father looked like he was going to faint.

She drew closer.

Dear God. Rosie?

His heart was racing. "I think I'm sick, R.T." he said in a low aside. "I'm starting to hallucinate. Get me out of here."

"Steady. What do you think you see?"

"It's Rosie! She's wearing the dress she wore at our wedding. I'm telling you, R.T. I'm losing it."

"No, you're not, Sarge. I see her, too. It's no hallucination. But I admit Rosie *looks* as heavenly as a vision."

Nick's whole body began to tremble. *"What the devil...?"*

"You're a smart man, Sarge. You figure it out."

"Rutherford," the pastor said, "if you'll make room for your bride here and clasp hands. And, Nicholas, if you'll do the same and clasp hands with your bride, we'll begin the ceremony."

Like a heat-seeking missile, Rosie's eyes locked on Nick's. The light that had been missing in them at Hill blazed green fire now. She reached boldly for his right hand and squeezed so hard he felt pain. He welcomed it, though, because it proved he wasn't experiencing some kind of weird flashback.

Nick could hear the pastor talking to R.T. and Cynthia, but he wasn't cognizant of anything except the flesh-and-blood woman at his side, pulsating with life, looking at him as if he was her whole world and everything in it.

"For as long as we both shall live." She mouthed the words to him.

Those were the words they'd had inscribed on their wedding bands.

"Rosie Gardner Armstrong, inasmuch as you're already joined in the bonds of holy matrimony to your husband, Nicholas, do you renew your vows before God and these witnesses to love, cherish and honor him, through sickness, through health, clinging only to him and forsaking all others, until death do you part?"

Nick watched breathlessly as Rosie turned, her whole heart reaching out to him.

"I, Rosie Gardner Armstrong, consider it the greatest privilege to renew before God, before our son, Cody, before our dearest parents and friends, my vows to my beloved—" her voice shook "—my beloved husband, Nick, whom I've always loved and adored.

"I ask his forgiveness for any pain I have unintentionally caused, but I vow that from this moment on, I will do everything in my power to bring him nothing but joy all the days of our lives." She paused. "I come to him having forsaken all others."

Is it true, sweetheart? Zach really has no more claim on your heart? Rosie? Do you know how much I want to believe you?

"I come to him prepared to be all the things I was to him in the past, prepared to be even more in the future. Dearest friend, dearest lover, dearest wife, dearest mother of his children."

"Nicholas Armstrong?" the pastor addressed him.

Nick felt as if he were in a dream.

"You've heard your wife's solemn troth. Since you are already husband to Rosie Gardner Armstrong, do you wish to renew your marriage vows before God, family and friends?"

Rosie's body started to shake like a leaf. Fear had robbed her cheeks of color.

Why are you frightened, Rosie? Don't you know this is what I've longed for? Prayed for?

I'm the one who's afraid.

Clearing his throat, he began, "I, Nicholas Armstrong, in front of God, my family and friends, wish to renew my vows to my beloved wife, Rosie, the mother of my son, Cody, the light of my life whose love has sustained me through thirteen years of marriage, whose love kept me alive through a dark and perilous time."

He felt her body go limp with relief, and he braced her with his hand and arm, holding her close.

"I forgive her for any pain she might have unwittingly caused and ask that she forgive me for any pain I might have inflicted on her. I am the most blessed of men to have the love of such a woman, and swear to do everything in my power to show her what she means to me. I swear I will respect her, watch over her, honor her, keep her in sickness, in health, until death do us part."

Nick heard her cry his name.

Ah, Rosie...can this really be happening to us?

"You may now exchange rings as symbols of your love. First, Mr. and Mrs. Ellis, and then Mr. and Mrs. Armstrong."

Nick couldn't take his eyes off Rosie.

She's going to live with me again. She's going to be my wife!

"Dad! Take the rings," Cody whispered.

Cody. *He'd known all along.* There was nothing wrong with his son. *Joy* had transformed him.

Suitably chastened, Nick flashed the boy a conspiratorial smile, which he returned, then felt in the little pocket for the rings he'd put on Rosie's finger thirteen years earlier.

Rosie lifted her left hand and helped him slide the rings home with his good hand.

To his surprise, she reached in another little pocket and brought out a ring that looked exactly like the one he'd lost when they'd run into that land mine.

"As long as we both shall live." She read aloud the

inscribed words before taking his right hand and pushing it onto his third finger.

"Sweetheart..." His voice caught in his throat.

Suddenly Rosie threw her arms around his neck and pulled his head down, kissing him exactly the way she'd kissed him before he'd gone off to the war.

They might be in a church, but her hunger, her passion, broke all the rules and he felt himself going under. No one had ever loved him the way she had. No one ever could. His Rosie was back where she belonged, burrowing into his arms, into his heart. Her mouth set him on fire.

The war was finally over.

"Hey, Sarge—" Nick felt a nudge in his ribs "—maybe you better take it easy. Another minute of that and this holy house is going to go up in holy smoke."

Rosie must have heard R.T., because she tore her lips from Nick's and hid her face in his shoulder, still clinging to him as if she feared someone would drag him back onto that plane.

Holding her against him with his left arm, Nick fought for the presence of mind to extend his right hand to the pastor. That seemed to signal the cessation of formalities. In the next instant Cody had launched himself at them, laughing and crying at once, jumping up and down. Jeff was right there with him.

Nick saw his mother out of the periphery. She had collapsed in his father's arms. He knew she was overcome with joy. He and his father made eye contact. His father was weeping. They smiled at each other with an understanding that surpassed words.

Behind his back he could hear R.T. sobbing uncontrollably in Cynthia's arms.

With Rosie still molded to his body, not saying a word, he lowered his head to R.T. "Haven't you done enough of that already?"

"I can't help it, Sarge. Cyn just told me I'm going to be a father in January."

Nick knew life didn't get much better than this.

"And you called me up because you were afraid to make love to your wife on your first night home…" He quietly baited him with relish.

"Ah, Sarge!"

He felt Rosie stir. She finally lifted her head, a beguiling smile on her face. "The getaway car for the four of us is outside the chapel."

Without taking his eyes off her, he said, "Did you hear that, R.T.?"

"I'm ready when you are, *sir.*"

"Are you ready, sweetheart?"

In answer she pressed her mouth to his. That was all Nick needed before picking her up in his arms and carrying her down the aisle. He didn't have to look back and wonder what R.T. was doing.

Everyone had preceded them outside. Cody and Jeff held the doors open while George took pictures.

Rosie's car stood parked a few yards away. At least he thought it was her car, but it was covered with shaving cream. Just like his old Jeep that his friends had gotten hold of thirteen years ago. There were cans and streamers tied to it, writing all over it.

JUST MARRIED! WAY TO GO, 57. NAUGHTY NICK'S GOING TO CALL ALL THE PLAYS TONIGHT. HAVE FUN! HAVE A ROSIE OLD TIME.

"You remembered!"

Again he felt a sense of wonder that his darling Rosie hadn't forgotten a single detail about that night of nights.

Still holding her in his arms, he walked around the front of the car to the passenger side. There was more writing.

REDHEADS HAVE MORE FUN. THERE'S SIN, AND THEN THERE'S CYN. TONIGHT RUTHERFORD TOPHAM WON'T KNOW THE DIFFERENCE. MORSE CODE'S A LOT OF FUN WHEN YOU DO IT RIGHT!

Nick burst out laughing and shot an amused glance at his buddy. R.T. was helping his wife into the back seat of the Nissan. His face had gone beet red.

"Oh, Rosie. You did it this time. R.T.'s a wreck," he whispered against her delectable neck.

"I love him, Nick. He's so much fun to tease."

I love him, too. I love you for loving him.

He set her down on the seat and helped fit her gown inside. "Where are you taking us, my adorable wife?" He couldn't resist kissing her again.

"*Sarge,* come on. Let's get out of here!"

Her eyes held his. "I'll give you one guess."

I'm sorry, Mr. Armstrong, but our little forest cottage has already been booked by a honeymoon couple.

Nick felt a swelling in his throat and couldn't talk. Struggling for breath, he straightened, then shut the door.

As he walked back around to get in the driver's seat, he realized they had an audience and rushed over to embrace his parents.

"Nicky, Nicky," his mother murmured. "I'm so happy for you. Tell Rosie I'm sorry."

"I will, Mom. Now, all of you have a wonderful time. I'll see you back in Salt Lake."

"Be happy, son," his father said hoarsely.

"Dad," Cody said as they hugged one more time, "she *really* loves you."

Nick clung to his son. "I think I kind of figured that out, Cody. Be a help to your grandparents. We'll see you soon."

"Thanks for coming, Jeff." He tousled the affable teen's blond head before getting back in the car.

Afraid to look at Rosie for fear he'd lose all sense of time and propriety, he turned on the ignition and headed toward the dude ranch at full speed.

"Go easy on the sarge, Rosie. He almost passed out on me in there. Maybe you ought to have someone at the clinic look him over."

Nick grinned. "No one's looking me over but my wife!" Now Rosie was blushing.

"Do you have our room number extension, Rosie?" R.T. asked.

"Yes." Her voice sounded more like a squeak.

"That's good. When the sarge gets to the part where he doesn't know what to do, call me."

"Dammit, R.T.!"

Cynthia started to laugh.

"You made him blush, R.T." Rosie screamed in delight. *"Finally!"*

Unable to resist, he flicked his wife a probing glance. "What do you mean, *finally?*"

"You know exactly what I mean, Nicholas Armstrong."

He did. *Midnight poker.*

"I'm warning you now, you're in for a *big* surprise."

He shook his head. "You'll never win, sweetheart. Don't even think it."

CHAPTER FIFTEEN

ROSIE HARDLY NOTICED the jack pines along the road that wound through the forest, taking them farther and farther away from the main cluster of cabins. She was so absorbed in her thoughts that she didn't even notice the darkness around them. The late-afternoon sun could scarcely penetrate the green canopy.

Nick had escorted R.T. and Cynthia to their honeymoon suite in the main lodge. Now she and Nick were finally alone.

Last night Rosie had felt slightly feverish. Now she knew she was running a temperature. She'd reached her emotional saturation point while waiting for Nick to respond during the ceremony.

He might not have. Not because he didn't love her, but because she wasn't sure he'd accept that she'd come back to him out of love, not pity. And because he might not believe that she and Zach were through.

The fact that he'd made his vows to her—with no warning, no explanation, and in front of everyone— meant he was going on pure faith. Rosie was humbled by that faith and planned to take away every lingering doubt he hadn't allowed her or anyone to see.

They needed to talk. She would insist that they talk before she made love to her husband. He'd gone all quiet since coming back to the car.

If God would grant her just one more wish, the intricate preparations she'd made would prove her love to Nick, show that she was wholly his, forever. *Tonight had to set the seal on their marriage.*

As soon as Nick had parked behind the cabin, she turned in her seat so her back was to him.

"Darling? Would you undo me? I need to go inside first and prepare a couple of things. Then I'll signal you."

Still no words. She felt his fingers on her back, releasing each button down the long row. He'd become incredibly adept at managing with one hand.

When he'd finished his task, she felt his hot palm against her skin with a sense of wonder. His hand followed the curve of her spine, then slid compulsively to her waist and around to her hip, as if he couldn't help himself.

She never wanted him to stop. But the time wasn't yet. *Soon, darling, soon. I promise you it will be worth the wait.*

Forcing herself to get out of the car, she disappeared into the cabin and quickly changed out of her dress and veil into the outfit she'd resurrected from the past.

The jeans were new, but they looked exactly like the ones she'd worn here on their honeymoon. More important, she still had Nick's old T-shirt, the one she'd had on when they'd arrived at this cabin the first night.

Reaching for her brush, she caught her hair back in a ponytail. She'd been practicing so she could do it just right. A few drops of bath oil behind her ears and on her wrists, and she was ready.

The only difference was in the outfit Nick had been wearing that night. The original clothes lay in a brown sack at the foot of the quilted double bed. She knew they'd be a little loose on him now, but she'd added a belt, so it wouldn't matter.

She picked it up and went to the door. Opening it enough to set the bag on the ground, she called to Nick and told him to change outside.

"What are you planning in there? A costume party?"

She smiled. "Don't be embarrassed. The chipmunks will never tell. When you're ready, knock."

"It's a good thing R.T. can't see me now. He'd never let me live it down."

She pressed a hand over her pounding heart. "In a minute you're going to forget R.T. and everything else."

"Is that a promise?"

That voice—the old Nick.

"What the hell?"

She had to stifle her excitement.

"Where did this old shirt come from?"

"Don't ask questions. Just put it on."

"Already she's ordering me around."

"And you love it!"

There was a slight pause. "I love it."

She waited, anticipating the next outburst.

"My Dodgers baseball cap!" Another silence. "Rosie…"

She bit her lip. "Are you ready to come in?"

When there was no answer, she turned on the tape player and started dancing in place to their song.

The sounds of Toto's "Rosanna" resounded in the cool air as the door flew open.

On the night she'd come home from a long miserable vacation with her grandparents—miserable because she was dying to be with Nick—he had played that song on his Jeep's tape deck and had sung along, a little off-key.

When the song was over, he'd leaned across the gearshift and placed his hands on her shoulders. His dark handsome face was within centimeters of hers and he whispered, "You're my Rosanna. You know that, don't you? You know we're in love. Tell me you're in love with me. Tell me now."

She'd stared into the flame-blue eyes, her heart skipping crazily. "I'm in love with you," she'd answered him honestly. It had been no less true all those years ago than it was now.

"That's all I needed to hear. We're getting married," came his fevered response.

Rosie could believe it was that same handsome young man who entered the cabin now and shoved the door closed with his boot. He wore the baseball cap backward, as he had the first time they'd come home.

His chest rose and fell. "You still look eighteen and too beautiful to be real."

"I'm real, Nick. Come here and find out." She held her arms wide.

The smile he'd always reserved for her transformed

him. Rosie's senses ignited as he moved toward her and drew her into his arms. He pulled her close against him and they slow-danced to the music, delighting in the feel of each other. She heard his voice, still a little off-key. But he made a few changes in the words. He said "Rosie" in place of "Rosanna." And he changed one line to, "It's been a long time since I went away."

Then he was kissing her. She was kissing him. All the things they hadn't been able to say over the past month they were saying now. They clung together, talking, remembering, laughing, kissing, through a dozen songs.

She could *feel* them healing. It expanded and lifted her to a fullness of ecstasy. Caught up in the same intensity of feeling, he finally raised his head, revealing the eager tremulous face of joy.

In an awestruck voice he whispered, "I have my Rosie back."

"You always had me, darling. Don't you see? Until six weeks ago, I couldn't make a commitment to Zach—because of you." Her eyes clouded over.

"If I'd truly been in love with Zach, I would have—*should* have—married him two years ago. Obviously what I felt for him was never enough. Deep down, a part of me wasn't ready. I was too much in love with you, even when I thought you were dead. Even then, I couldn't—"

"Rosie, you don't have to explain."

"Yes, Nick, I do. When Zach took Cody and me on that cruise, I noticed that most of the other tourists were older couples. I envied them because they had someone to share their lives. It made me think about Cody, that he was growing older and would be gone sooner than I could imagine.

"That's when I broke down and asked Zach to propose to me again. I loved him very much, and inside I wanted a reason to go on living. I didn't want to grow old alone."

Nick's eyes softened. "I would have wanted that for you, Rosie."

She ran her hands lovingly up and down his cheeks. "I know that. Then I got the phone call from your parents telling me you were alive and coming home. Nick…I went into shock!"

He lowered his head and pressed his forehead against hers. "I won't presume to understand how you felt, but there's no doubt that kind of news would have turned your world inside out."

She nodded. "It did. And do you know why? Because it threw me into a morass of confusion and guilt and torn loyalties.

"Last week, my head cleared of that confusion. I realized that no matter what you and I had once meant to each other, if I had truly been in love with Zach— the way I'd been with you—I would have gone up to Hill wearing his ring. It would have killed me to hurt you that way, but I would have done it because I was so certain of my feelings.

"Obviously I *wasn't* certain. That's how I *know* that what Zach and I shared wasn't the profound love I'd had with you."

"We have something extraordinary," he said, his voice husky.

She nodded. "It was an illuminating moment for both of us when Zach asked me if I was going to wear his ring to meet you."

Nick's eyes searched hers intently. "What did you say?"

"I told him I'd put his ring in my jewelry box with yours. Consciously I didn't realize that, in saying this, I'd taken a giant step away from Zach. I'm afraid he recognized what was happening to us long before I did.

"From the time you and I drove down from Hill, things started to degenerate between Zach and me. The more I tried to make it work, the more it didn't work.

"I have no doubt we would've been very happy together, if nothing else had changed. But the second I knew you were alive, the part of me that was your wife wouldn't let me give myself emotionally to Zach.

"I found myself wondering what you were doing, what you were feeling. I was so jealous of the time Cody spent with you. I was jealous of your relationship with R.T. I felt left out at every turn.

"Those weren't the feelings I should have had when I was planning to marry another man! Nick, when you told me you were going to divorce me so you could start fresh—with someone new—I almost died.

"Zach knew I was in agony. Last week I went over to tell him that I couldn't go through with the marriage. He'd come to the same conclusion. I hated hurting him, but it felt so good to finally say the truth out loud—that I was in love with you. That I wanted to stay married to you."

Nick frowned. "Where is he now?"

"He's moved back to California."

"The man must be in hell."

"I know he is. But as he said to me the last time we were together, he would rather hear those words about my loving you *now* than after we were married. I'm counting on that wisdom to help him recover."

Nick's eyes narrowed and his right hand tightened on her arm. "You'd be impossible to replace."

"Your bias is showing, darling. He'll find a woman who loves and needs him desperately. I'm sure of it. In the meantime, he has an amazing family, and all the support he needs from his brother, Richard. Zach's a strong man. I know that in time he'll end up as happy as I am."

She pressed a hungry kiss to Nick's lips, needing him as much as she needed water, air, sunlight.

He rocked her back and forth. "Now that I have you in my arms, I can feel compassion for him. But when I first found myself kissing a stranger, the pain was worse than everything I went through in all those seven years."

"Nick—"

"Shh. It hurt too much, Rosie. I couldn't stand it. And the other thing is…I wanted you to be happy. So I had to file for divorce. There wasn't any other way."

"I'm so thankful you did!" she cried. "It straightened out my confusion in a big hurry. The thought of you belonging to anyone else… I couldn't let it happen. You were *my* Nick. No one but me was going to hold you during one of your nightmares!"

He ran his finger along her jaw. "R.T. told me about that night. I'm grateful you didn't end up with anything more than a bruise."

Tears gathered in her eyes. "I'm glad it happened. That night I felt like I was a part of you."

A pained look crossed his face. "It could happen tonight."

"Not if I have anything to say about it." She smiled provocatively.

That little comment took the pained look away in a hurry. "Is that right?"

"That's right." She slid her hand into his and drew him over to the bed. "Now, you sit down here. And I'm going to sit here."

"You're too far away from me, sweetheart."

"It's the perfect distance to play poker."

He gave a devilish chuckle. Then grabbed a Snickers bar from the nightstand and tore off the wrapping with his teeth.

Taking a bite, he grinned. "You trying to sweeten me up on the same stuff you fed me the last time we were in this room?" His intent look reminded her he was a fierce competitor. "As I recall, you lost every game. In fact you lost a lot more than that." His piratical half smile sent delicious shivers across her skin.

She sat cross-legged on the bed and pulled out a pack of playing cards. "I learned a few tricks while you were gone."

"Who from?"

"I bought a book."

He reached out and covered one of her hands with his. "You shouldn't believe everything you read."

"You're scared, Armstrong. Admit it."

"You've got that one wrong, sweetheart." He offered her a bite of the candy bar. "Win or lose, I win."

She fluttered her lashes at him. "We'll see about that. You need a handicap so we'll start with twenty-one. Here's hoping your little brush-up session with our son did the job. Winner decides the penalty. I'll deal."

At this point, Nick stretched full-length on his left side, his smile almost wolfish. She felt breathless with anticipation. "Ready when you are," he murmured silkily.

She dealt two cards facedown, then two more faceup. She had an ace. They both checked their cards.

"Hit me."

She gave him a card.

"Hit me again."

With a deadpan face he said, "I'll stay."

"So will I."

"All right, Rosie, baby. Let's see what you've got."

She turned the card over. "A jack. Now let's see yours."

He eyed her suspiciously, then turned everything over.

"Hmm. Nineteen. You lose, Armstrong. Give me your hat."

"You have to come and get it."

"That's not part of the rules."

"What's the matter? Are you scared?"

She felt a quiver of excitement. "No."

"Then come here."

Rosie leaned over the cards to take it from his head.

"Oh!" The next thing she knew, she was flat on her back and he'd rolled on top of her. He pinned both her arms with his injured one.

"The problem with you, sweetheart, is that you never did know when your number was up."

"No, Nick!" She screamed and giggled at the same time because he was feeling in her pockets with his right hand—and taking certain liberties as he did so.

Suddenly he pulled out a bunch of cards. "My, my, my. What have we here? All aces and jacks." He tossed them over his shoulder. "I wonder if there's any more where *they* came from."

A further exploration turned into something else as their mouths fused in passion and Rosie found herself clinging blindly to her husband.

A SERIES OF ODD TAPPING sounds outside the cabin brought Rosie out of a sound sleep. As she started to stretch, she felt the heavy weight of Nick's arm and leg thrown across her body, his right hand tangled in her hair.

Their lovemaking had been so feverish and intense, their desire for each other so insatiable, they couldn't have fallen asleep before six or seven in the morning. Nick had gotten up during the night to close the wooden shutters. There was no way to tell what time it was. She would have to remove his hand from her hair if she wanted to take a look at his watch.

The tapping started again, a little louder. This time

Nick stirred. Just feeling him take a breath ignited her desire for him all over again. She kissed her way to his mouth.

He groaned in satisfaction, returning her kiss with shocking ardor for one still groggy with sleep. To her joy he shifted his weight and began to make love to her in earnest. The tapping continued, even more loudly than before.

"I think we have a woodpecker outside our door," she whispered against his lips.

Nick raised himself up on one elbow to listen. "That's no woodpecker, sweetheart. That's R.T."

Intrigued, Rosie asked, "What's he saying?"

His body shook with silent laughter. "He says it's two o'clock in the afternoon, and he and Cyn are getting worried."

"You're kidding! Two?"

He nuzzled her neck. She could feel the rasp of his beard. "After our all-nighter, are you really surprised?"

Heat swept up her body. "What else is he saying?"

"He's afraid we've both suffered cardiac arrest from too much excitement. He wants permission to enter." Nick kissed her in a very sensitive spot. "Sometimes he worries about me. Do you mind?"

"No, of course not. I know exactly how he feels."

For that she was given another passionate kiss. "Put on the robe I gave you."

"I didn't bring it—or a nightgown."

"Did I ever tell you you're every husband's fantasy?"

"Yes. Last night. You told me over and over again."

"No nightmares?"

"Not one."

"Tell you what. You snuggle down in the covers and I'll get the door."

"Okay."

She heard a few grunts and groans as Nick felt his way around in the dark. Suddenly the room filled with dazzling light, outlining his lean physique, which had started gaining mass and muscle. But even thin and haggard, he'd been a beautiful man to Rosie; he always would be.

She watched him pull on jeans and T-shirt. He darted her a quick glance. "Ready?"

She nodded.

He opened the door. "Come on in, R.T."

"Is it all right?"

"Is it all right, Rosie?"

"R.T., you're welcome anytime."

He entered the cabin hesitantly. "I'm sorry to disturb you. Cyn and I were wondering…if you don't have anything else to do, you might like to come horseback riding with us."

Rosie decided to say nothing and let her husband answer for them.

"We have something else to do, R.T. Trust me."

"That's what I figured. I was just checking."

"Go on and find your wife. I'm sure she wants you to herself for a while. We'll see you at the lodge for dinner."

His face lit up. "Thanks, Sarge. See you later."

Nick shut the door.

"It's time for a shower, Scarlett." He tossed the covers aside with his good hand.

Rosie didn't move a muscle. She bestowed a bewitching smile on him, instead. In her phony Southern accent she drawled, "I declare, Rhett Butler, you are no gentleman, sir. Why, I just go pink all over when I think what you were doing to me all nigh—"

"*Hey, Mom? Dad?* R.T. says you're up. Can I come in?"

"Quick, darling. Hand me the comforter."

Nick let out an expletive and threw the quilt over her.

She heard the door creak open.

"Hi!"

"Hi, bud. Where's Jeff?"

"He's over at the corral."

Rosie sat a little straighter in the bed, the covers up to her chin. "Hi, honey! How are you?"

Cody finished hugging his father and ran to the side of the bed to hug her.

"Hey, Mom? How come you're still in bed? Are you sick?"

Over Cody's shoulder she eyed her husband, who was smiling with unholy delight. *The wretch isn't going to help me out of this one.*

"I feel fine. Your dad and I are just taking it easy, but I love you for caring."

If anything, Nick's smile had broadened.

"Are you and Dad…well, you know, are you happy and everything?"

She swallowed hard, realizing how important this

was to their son. "We're divinely happy, Cody. Aren't we, darling?" she said to Nick who'd come to sit on the bed next to her.

He pulled Cody onto his lap and gave him a hug. "We didn't know we could be this happy."

"I didn't know I could be this happy, either," Cody confessed. "Are we all going to live on the ranch then?"

"Yes."

"What about Mom's job?"

"She's going to commute from Heber to Salt Lake when she starts teaching again in the fall. That way she can drive you down to school every day so you won't have to be separated from your friends."

"That's great, Dad! I want—"

"Yoo-hoo! Knock, knock!"

Rosie heard Nick's frustrated sigh of resignation, then felt his hand slide around her waist and give it a squeeze.

"Hi, Mom and Dad. Come on in and join the crowd."

"We just wanted to know how the lovebirds were doing today."

"They're doing great, Grandma," Cody answered. "Mom's just relaxing."

"That's good, dear. You need it, Rosie."

George chuckled, then winked at Nick, who'd started laughing. Rosie joined him.

"What's so funny, Dad?"

"I thought they taught you everything there was to know on Channel One."

"I'm going to go ask R.T. He'll tell me."

"You do that, son."

"Come on, Cody," his grandfather urged. "Let's leave your poor mom and dad alone. Come on, Janet. Give them some privacy."

Nick closed the door behind them.

"It's almost three o'clock." Janet's voice carried all too easily. "I mean, there is such a thing as…"

Rosie held out her arms to her husband. When he was back in bed with her, she nestled close to his heart. "There's a lot of love in this family."

"Amen."

"I love you, Nick Armstrong. More than you'll ever know."

He gave her another possessive kiss. "Most men get one shot at life. I was given two, and both times I ended up with you. That's my blessing and my joy."

"Oh, Nick…"

* * * * *

Fall in Love with...

MEN
in UNIFORM

MUBPA10

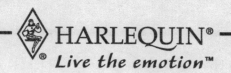

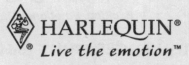

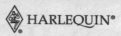

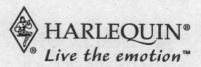

HARLEQUIN®
INTRIGUE®

BREATHTAKING ROMANTIC SUSPENSE

Shared dangers and passions lead to electrifying
romance and heart-stopping suspense!

Every month, you'll meet six new heroes
who are guaranteed to make your spine tingle
and your pulse pound. With them you'll enter
into the exciting world of Harlequin Intrigue—
where your life is on the line
and so is your heart!

THAT'S INTRIGUE—
ROMANTIC SUSPENSE
AT ITS BEST!

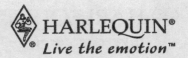

HARLEQUIN®
Live the emotion™

HARLEQUIN®

Super Romance®

...there's more to the story!

Superromance.
A *big* satisfying read about unforgettable
characters. Each month we offer *six* very different
stories that range from family drama to adventure
and mystery, from highly emotional stories to
romantic comedies—and much more! Stories
about people you'll believe in and care about.
Stories too compelling to put down....

Our authors are among today's *best* romance
writers. You'll find familiar names and talented
newcomers. Many of them are award winners—
and you'll see why!

If you want the biggest and best
in romance fiction, you'll get it
from Superromance!

Exciting, Emotional, Unexpected...

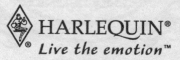

HARLEQUIN®
Live the emotion™

Harlequin® Historical
Historical Romantic Adventure!

*Imagine a time of chivalrous
knights and unconventional ladies,
roguish rakes and impetuous
heiresses, rugged cowboys
and spirited frontierswomen—
these rich and vivid tales will
capture your imagination!*

*Harlequin Historical . . .
they're too good to miss!*